# Ripple Effect

A novel by

KI STEPHENS

Cover Design: Ki Stephens
Editor: Sandra Dee, One Love Editing

This book is intended for an 18+ audience.
For content warnings, please visit www.kistephens.com.

*For those looking for a light in the darkness.*

We won't forget, we can play in the waves of the ripple effect.

SCOTT HELMAN

# Playlist

| | | |
|---|---|---|
| BEIGE (UNBURDENED) \| YOKE LORE | ♥ | 3:16 |
| RUN \| HARRISON STORM | ♥ | 3:17 |
| WITH YOU \| GARRETT KATO | ♥ | 2:51 |
| BELIEVER \| SYML | ♥ | 4:23 |
| FEELS LIKE \| GRACIE ABRAMS | ♥ | 2:32 |
| THE SUNSHINE \| MANCHESTER ORCHESTRA | ♥ | 1:57 |
| DAYLIGHT \| TAYLOR SWIFT | ♥ | 4:53 |
| SHUT UP \| GREYSON CHANCE | ♥ | 2:50 |
| FRIENDS \| EMMIT FENN | ♥ | 3:07 |
| STRAWBERRY WINE \| NOAH KAHAN | ♥ | 4:46 |
| BEDROCK \| WILD RIVERS | ♥ | 3:30 |
| OLDER THAN I AM \| LENNON STELLA | ♥ | 3:02 |
| BANKS \| NEEDTOBREATHE | ♥ | 4:00 |
| SUN AND MOON \| ANEES | ♥ | 2:32 |
| EXPLAIN YOU \| JP SAXE | ♥ | 3:18 |
| LIKE THAT \| JP SAXE | ♥ | 2:54 |
| EVERYWHERE, EVERYTHING \| NOAH KAHAN | ♥ | 4:18 |
| YELLOW - LIPLESS REMIX \| EMMIT FENN, LIPLESS | ♥ | 4:05 |
| RIPPLE EFFECT \| SCOTT HELMAN | ♥ | 3:22 |
| I AM NOT WHO I WAS \| CHANCE PEÑA | ♥ | 2:25 |
| BROKEN (ACOUSTIC) \| JONAH KAGEN | ♥ | 2:58 |

# Chapter One

ELIO

"Fuck yeah, baby, just like that," groans the man on the screen in front of me.

His face is obscured, the angle focused on the play of muscles across his back, the gleam of sweat highlighting the definition. A sleeve of black linework tattoos decorates his left arm, the inked skin moving rhythmically with each thrust.

The husky timbre of his voice fills my cramped apartment, each calculated moan designed to entice, to promise, to seduce. Another deep, heavy groan rings out.

I pause the video, my eyes tracing over the digital version of myself. Everett Rain, as my subscribers know me. I recognize the same detached script, but every performance is new, and the game is always different.

A character created out of necessity. An alter ego living in the virtual world of AfterDark, a popular site for sex workers to post their content.

My fingers slowly move across the trackpad, slicing through the footage with clinical precision. It's a methodical process, trimming and discarding the unwanted parts. The missteps, the stumbles, the all-too-human moments.

The final product needs to be flawless. Passionate yet distant, intimate yet anonymous. The perfect fucking fantasy for my subscribers.

It's well past three o'clock in the morning here. My brain's buzzing from hours of editing, each cut leaving a hollow echo in the silent room. The glow of the laptop screen is harsh against my tired eyes, transforming my familiar space into a landscape of long, distorted shadows.

The muffled snores of my dog, Bentley, an aging golden retriever, are a soft lullaby beside me. I glance at him, sprawled across his faded dog bed, his chest rising and falling in a steady rhythm, and a pang of affection hits me.

Over the past year, Bentley's become my silent companion, an unwitting participant in the chaos of my life.

He entered my world unexpectedly, a curveball thrown by my older sister. With a newly moved-in, allergic partner and a cramped apartment, she wasn't able to care for him. And my older brother, Luca, already swamped with commitments, couldn't take him in, either.

So, I did what I always do. I adapted. And now, Bentley's wedged himself so deeply into my day-to-day life. He's become more than just my little sidekick; he's now my most loyal friend here at Coastal U.

"Alright, boy, time for a break," I murmur, pushing away from the laptop. His tail thumps gently against the rug, the sound dragging me out of the digital world and back into reality.

I retrieve my keys from the hook in the kitchen, Bentley's ears perking up at the jingle. "Beach?" His response is immediate—a bark of agreement and a rush toward the door.

We take the familiar path to my Jeep, Bentley's excited barks echoing in the stillness of the early morning. He jumps into the passenger seat, his tail wagging nonstop as I slide in behind the wheel.

Thankfully, Amber Isle sits just on the outskirts of town, a short drive from my apartment. It's a little haven I've grown up beside all my life.

We pull into the lot and slowly trot our way to the shoreline, past the Boyer Inlet Pier, the place where my brother used to work when he was a student here. His old boss, Pawel, has long since retired, leaving the pier to be manned by a newer, younger version of himself. But even still, it's too early in the morning for anyone else to be on the beachfront.

As we pass by, Bentley tugs on his leash, guiding us close enough to the water to touch, and I bend down to unlatch his collar. He stays close, and we're alone, so it's the perfect space and time for him to explore.

While he wanders, I stare into the open water, breathing low and deep. It's as if each new wave carries away a piece of the tension knotted between my shoulders. The chill of the ocean air is a harsh wake-up call, shaking off the remnants of Everett and grounding me back into being myself, if only for a little while.

After a few minutes, Bentley trots back to my side, his movements slower than they used to be but his spirit as lively as ever. He carefully ambles ahead of me once more, sniffing and exploring, and I let my mind wander along with him.

Another academic year looms ahead—my final one in the electrical engineering program. It's a bittersweet feeling knowing I'm a year behind the rest of my peers, but at least I've made it this far. There was a point in my life where I was positive that it wouldn't happen. That it couldn't happen.

A point where I didn't know if I would make it to the next day, let alone the end of a four-year bachelor's program.

And I know I'm up for grueling hours of studying, constant pressure, and the unending juggle of my double life. But for once, I'm optimistic, even though I'll have to do it all alone now.

Kaia, my closest friend since childhood, isn't here anymore to reassure me. She's off to graduate school hours away at Dayton. Don't get me wrong, I'm proud as hell of all she's accomplished despite the fact that I miss her. We still keep in touch, our texts and calls bridging the physical distance, but it's different now.

She has a life partner, a boyfriend whose career as a professional athlete leaves her constantly booked and busy. She has no issues making time for me amidst her studying and dating life, but I'd rather not be a burden to the few people I care about.

And then, there are concerns about splitting my time with my job. The late-night filming sessions, the constant worry of my two worlds colliding, the gnawing loneliness that comes from selling intimacy while yearning for it myself.

A bitter laugh escapes me because fretting about all this is so fucking pointless. I don't have any other choice. Not now. Not when my identity, my livelihood, my entire fucking being is wrapped up in my sex work.

But life goes on despite it all, the rising sun setting off a new day. A day that begins with Elio and Bentley on the beach but will end with Everett fucking some virtual stranger on a screen.

A life split in two.

I nudge a piece of driftwood with my foot, the waves greedily snatching it up and carrying it away. How simple it would be to tag along with it, aimlessly floating along the waves, carried by the whims of the ocean.

No fucking deadlines, no expectations.

Bentley breaks away from his inspection of a particularly interesting seashell, bounding toward me. His tail wags in excitement, and I can't help but crack a tiny half-smile, crouching down to ruffle his thick, golden fur.

As he stares at me with his bright eyes, I heave a tired sigh. I have to remember that I'm not just putting in the work for myself. I'm doing it for Bentley, for Kaia, for my family, and even for Everett, that little piece of myself I've carved out and set on a platter for public consumption.

Somehow, the walk back to my car feels shorter, the countless deadlines already pricking at the edges of my consciousness. I glance down at my furry companion, his tongue lolling out in a pant, tail wagging with contentment.

Out in the distance, a lone surfer takes advantage of the pre-dawn stillness, riding the waves under the faint light of the morning sun. It may be early, but life around us is already buzzing, shaking off the last remnants of night.

"Let's head home, buddy," I mutter, stopping to scratch behind his ear.

Once we're home, I unlock the door to my apartment and let my dog take the lead, waiting as he shuffles toward his bed. I follow him in, closing the door behind me. And now, after a much-needed break, the sight of my work laptop feels a little less daunting.

Everett might rule the night, but when the sun is out—the world outside waking up to a fresh day—it's Elio's turn.

THE REST of my Monday is a dizzying rush of lectures, seminars, and half-baked assignments. Professors speak, my pen moves, but my mind is elsewhere. When the sun sets and campus is mostly emptied out, I trudge back home, exhaustion clinging to me like a second skin.

I head into my apartment, and Bentley trots over, tail wagging as he nudges against my legs. As much as I'd like to spend time with him, I have another role to play first. So, I give him a quick pat and a promise of a longer cuddle later. Then, I retreat down the hall, the sound of his whining tugging at my heartstrings.

In the emptiness of my bedroom, I quickly work to become my other half. It's a simple change of clothes, a shift in demeanor, and a switch from the physical world to the digital. But even as I strip, trading in my normal attire for an outfit that my subscribers prefer, I can't help but acknowledge the divide.

The person in the mirror looks like me, but the cool detachment in his eyes is far from the man I'd like to be.

My setup for filming is simple. A single camera, carefully adjusted for the perfect angle, a laptop for streaming, and a reliable internet connection, the lifeline to my audience.

I log in to AfterDark, my eyes scanning the familiar interface. That's when I spot a live one-on-one request—a rare but expected occurrence—from a user called SapphireDream. The name is random, impersonal, just how I like it.

Anonymity is the norm here, and over time, I've learned to detach myself like it's second nature.

The Accept button glares at me, a reminder of what I'm about to do. The role I need to play, the script I need to follow, the performance I always promise to deliver.

I take a steadying breath and enter the conversation. The screen bursts into life, and SapphireDream's chat window opens up on one side, her icon some random pin-up girl from Pinterest.

"Hi, Everett," she types, and I can't help but snort a laugh at the contrast between her timid greeting and her chosen profile picture.

"Hello, Sapphire," I say, my voice steady, betraying none of the thoughts racing through my mind.

The conversation starts off innocently enough. Small talk

and questions float back and forth, Sapphire's shyness apparent in her short replies. But this is where Everett excels. He's the smooth-talking, charming person she needs him to be, guiding her into comfortable banter and conversation, instilling trust and an easy connection.

As the minutes turn into an hour, I peel off my shirt, leaving my torso bare. She asks me questions, her words growing bolder, while I respond with practiced ease. There's a method to all of this—being someone else—and it's one I've perfected over the years.

"I want to see you. All of you," she types, so I unbutton my jeans, my fingers working slowly, deliberately. My movements are calculated, a skill honed from countless nights of playing into the façade.

I slide out of my pants, leaving myself in just my boxers. All the while, Sapphire's words continue to dictate my movements. She's the puppeteer, and I suppose I'm her willing puppet.

As the intensity of our conversation kicks up, that familiar dissociation sets in, a necessary self-preservation tactic. I might be naked under the harsh gaze of the webcam, but there's a larger part of me that remains veiled, protected.

Jerking myself off becomes just another act, another service Everett provides. There's no lust, no longing, just the mechanical movements of my hand, dictated by the desires of a faceless person living in my screen.

She asks me to touch myself, and I do. It's another job, another performance for my counterpart to nail.

When the session ends, her parting message promises a return, a compliment for Everett, another satisfied customer. I breathe out, the tension uncoiling from my muscles as I log off.

Drained and heavy with the aftermath, I tug my clothing back into place, the cold fabric clinging to my sweaty skin. I close the laptop, severing the final connection to Everett's world for the night.

Back in the realm of reality, I'm Elio again. I'm just a student, a dog owner, a brother, and a part-time friend. A person trying to make it through another day relatively unscathed.

Bentley's soft whine echoes outside my door, and I stand, stretching the stiffness from my body. It's late, and as much as I want to collapse onto my bed and escape into sleep, I have one more promise to keep.

With a final look at my switched-off laptop, I open my bedroom door, stepping out into the living room. Bentley's ears perk up, his tail wagging as he springs to his feet, ready for some long-promised attention.

I absentmindedly run my fingers through his fur, and the anxious buzz finally goes quiet, the divide between my two selves blurs until I'm just me again.

"Alright, buddy, time for bed," I murmur, dropping down to his level. His large brown eyes gaze up at me, understanding and affection reflecting back in them.

And as the late-night quiet settles around the two of us, I boost Bentley up onto the edge of my mattress. His soft snores fill the room while I tuck myself in, a comforting reminder of the simple, real parts of my life.

The tiny slices of truth that I hold on to, desperately hoping they might ground me.

# Chapter Two

DAISY

"YES, THAT'S IT," I murmur to myself, gripping tightly to my board, ice-cold salt water surging around me. Despite the early hour and the misty chill, there's a massive grin on my face and laughter in my voice. It's not even five in the morning yet, but I'm back in the ocean now, exactly where I belong.

The wave crests under me, and I rocket forward, feeling invincible. As the water barrels past, my heart thumps wildly against my ribcage, the thrill of a perfect ride coursing through me. The taste of the ocean spray fills my mouth, salty and nostalgic.

It may sound strange, but this right here is my idea of heaven.

The wave subsides, leaving me bobbing on the gentle swells, my body thrumming with adrenaline. I glance back at the horizon, soaking in the pretty pinks of the lingering sunrise, when someone shouts my name.

I turn on my board to see a group of my new friends waving at me from the shoreline. Raising a hand in acknowledgment, I continue on, knowing I'll catch up with them once I've had my fill of the surf.

I've only been at Coastal U for a few weeks now, having transferred in as a junior from Dayton, but it already feels like home. Between the pretty beaches, their top-notch marine biology program, and the welcoming people I've met, it's everything I've ever wanted.

As a wave pulls me back, I paddle out further, my muscles straining, aching to keep my rhythm.

Back at my old school, I'd been landlocked and desperately missed the ocean. I grew up in a beach town not too far from here. And as far back as I can remember, this has been my therapy, my escape, my happy place.

Another wave builds behind me, and a quick glance over my shoulder tells me it's a good one. Without wasting another second, I reposition my board and paddle to meet the wave head-on. As it lifts me, I pop up to stand, finding my balance as the world blurs around me.

The wave propels my board toward the shore, the wind whooshing past me, carrying my laughter along with it. This is freedom, I think, unadulterated fucking joy. My heart soars with each moment that I'm out here, each second that I move with the water.

Eventually, my wave runs its course, depositing me near the shoreline where my friends have all congregated. I grab my board and wade the rest of the way in, my smile never wavering.

Barefoot, I pad my way across the sun-warmed sand to where they're gathered, the rhythmic crashing of waves filling the silence. I drop my board a few paces away and stretch my arms above my head, sore as hell from the morning surf.

Sadly, it's been a while since I've been able to get out there, and I'm no longer used to the constant muscle fatigue. It feels good, though. A familiar sort of pain that lights me up from the inside out.

Once I finish my lackluster attempt to stretch, there's a bottle of water thrust into my hand. I gratefully accept it, taking a long, refreshing sip. Then I flop down onto a towel spread across the sand, the damp fabric sticking to my skin.

I've always been energized by big social groups, a quiet sort of extrovert, and moving to Coastal has only opened up a new avenue for friendships. I think it's in my nature to be drawn to crowds or something.

And the bunch I find myself surrounded by now—Max, LJ, and Gracie—are an assorted mix of personalities that blend perfectly together.

"You looked like a fucking queen out there, Daisy, as per usual," says Max, the oldest of the group. He's a grad student with a penchant for sarcasm and a habit of showing off his abs at every possible opportunity.

His girlfriend, LJ, sits beside him. With her soft, auburn hair and love for morning yoga, she's as fiery as she is flexible. And then there's Gracie, my new roommate, so tiny and sweet, her demeanor as calming as the ocean we all love.

"This has been a blast, guys. But I need to get back to the real world now." Max gestures wildly, his dark eyes wide with exasperation. "You know, if I didn't have Khatri as an advisor this year, I'd surely fucking lose it," he says, and I can't help but giggle at his theatrics.

Next to him, LJ rolls her eyes, her curls bouncing with the motion. "Max, you need to chill. How about joining me for a class tomorrow? We're focusing on inversions this week."

Max groans, leaning back on his beach towel. "I told you; I can't bend myself into a fucking pretzel like the rest of you." He flicks a thumb in my direction. "I can barely get myself up on the board with Miss Junior Champion over here."

A wry smile tugs at the corners of my mouth, but inside, it stirs up a whirlwind of emotions and memories.

"Miss Junior Champion," he says, as if that title were still an inseparable part of me, as if those words could erase the past two years I'd spent twiddling my thumbs at Dayton, choosing my studies over the professional circuit.

I'd spent nearly three years participating in the Junior Series competitions before I turned eighteen and gave it all up for a more traditional lifestyle. I've still been surfing, but not at the competitive level that I used to. And although I'm picking it up again, I certainly couldn't carry my weight with the pros in the WSL.

Across from us, Gracie chuckles softly, her hands wrapped around her knees as she stares out at the waves. "You never know, Maxy Poo. It might actually help you relax for once."

Caught in the middle of it all, I roll my eyes, a secret smile playing on my lips. It feels nice to be out here with them, just listening, basking in their conversations. I don't even have to say a word, yet these three always ensure I'm included.

Luckily, I have a knack for making new friends despite my quiet nature. It's a trait that's followed me from childhood, and it's one I'm grateful for, especially now. Coastal U may be nestled in a small town, but it's a big university, a state school where it's easy enough to get swept up in the crowd.

It's not that I *wanted* to leave my boyfriend behind at my old school, but I came here for so many different reasons. My affinity for the ocean being only one of them. There are more opportunities for me here, a better marine bio program, and much easier access to my first love—surfing.

A small part of me is still nervous about starting over somewhere new, especially after two years of living right across the street from my high school sweetheart. But mostly, I'm excited. It's a new chapter in my life, one where I have the chance to rediscover myself.

Besides, I put my full trust in Logan, and I know it's better to carve our own paths while we're still young.

As the sun climbs higher in the sky, signaling the end of our morning session, I stand up, shaking sand off my legs. It may still be early, but there's a whole day ahead of me now—classes, exploring campus, and settling in to Gracie's and my apartment.

The rest of the group joins me, with Max wrapping an arm around his girlfriend. My roommate, ever the mother hen, reminds us to keep ourselves hydrated as we all part ways. And already, I'm feeling a bit warm and fuzzy inside, like the four of us might truly have something special here.

Maybe, if I'm lucky enough, they'll let me think of them as my stand-in family, as my home away from home.

AFTER CLEANING up from the beach and grabbing some breakfast with Gracie, we trudge back to our apartment. It's a cute, if small, place that we share, nestled only a short walk from campus and a breezy drive from Amber Isle. It's not a palace by any means, but it's still sweet and comfortable.

I push open the door to my room, stepping into organized chaos. Boxes lie half-unpacked, their contents spilling over onto the floor. Clothes—some folded, others crumpled—are strewn across the chair, all thanks to the whirlwind of settling in.

Despite the mess, there's a distinct homey vibe to the room, a comforting sense of belonging that tugs a smile onto my face.

As I wade over to the bed, my gaze lands on my nightstand, where a picture of Logan and me sits. It's from our second anniversary, a perfect summer day spent laughing under the sun. We're both smiling, eyes pinched shut and crinkling at the corners.

A fondness sweeps over me as I trace the edges of the frame.

But then, my phone buzzes, pulling me from my thoughts. I glance down and see Logan's name flashing on the screen. A smile pulls at my cheeks, warmth filling my chest.

"Hey, Daisy," he says as I pick up the FaceTime, voice low and rough just the way I like.

"Hey, you," I say softly, fondly. Even though we've been keeping close contact, nothing beats seeing him, even if it's only over a screen.

The two of us quickly fall into an easy conversation, updating each other on our week. He talks about baseball and the new drills their coach is introducing in the off-season. I gush about my morning surf and my newfound friends.

Despite the distance, we find a way to share our lives. But there's still a tinge of sadness, an undertone of longing that underlines every word. It's been over two weeks since I've seen him in person, a far cry from the last two years when we were inseparable.

"I wish I could be there," Logan says after a pause, a hint of frustration in his voice. "You on your board again? It's like . . . you're part of the ocean. You always have been."

His words warm my heart, and I can't help but smile. "I know. I wish you were here, too."

The conversation continues, a gentle ebb and flow of familiarity. I can hear the excitement in his voice as he talks about his chance at securing team captain this spring. I listen, my heart filling with pride for him. I share my excitement about my new courses and gush over how beautiful Amber Isle is.

Our conversation is comfortable, easy, full of the shared understanding and affection that we've always had. But just as Logan starts telling me about a mishap with one of his teammates, I hear something else entirely. It's the unmistakable sound of a girl's laughter, faint but clearly audible over the call.

If I didn't know any better, I'd guess that the two of them were in the same room.

I frown, my confusion cutting through our bubble. "Do you have someone there with you?"

"No, that's just . . . uh, someone here for Scott," he deflects, referring to his new housemate. "She dropped by to give him some notes."

"Oh, alright, a new girl he's seeing?"

"Just a friend."

The explanation makes sense, but there's a distinct hint of awkwardness that's now draped over our conversation. I shrug it off, reminding myself there's no reason for Logan to lie to me.

"Anyway, I should let you get to class," he rushes to say, tilting the screen, his usual smile a bit strained now. "And I should get going, too. My schedule's really busy."

His words bring me back, the reminder of the day ahead acting like a splash of cold water. "Yeah, you're right. Love you, Lo," I manage to say, keeping my tone light.

"Talk later, Daisy." Then, he ends the call without another word.

The silence that follows is a stark contrast to our once lively chatter. In the past, I could've easily brushed it off as nothing. But I don't know Scott or the rest of his new housemates very well at all.

Things are changing for him—new house, new friends, new spot on the team—and I'm not there to witness it. Instead, I'm left alone in my room, gaze focused on the hand that's come to rest on my lap . . . that old, frayed picture of us staring straight back at me.

# Chapter Three

ELIO

I'm LATE, way too fucking late.

Rushing up the stairs to a fourth-floor apartment, I barely register the carpet's worn-out pattern beneath my boots. The hallway is dimly lit, the air thick with a musty scent. The late-night hour casts an eerie quiet over the apartment complex, the silence punctuated by the sound of my ragged breath and the pounding of my heart.

That's when a jolt of pain slices through my chest. My steps falter, one hand reaching out to clutch the railing as my vision blurs at the edges. It's like my heart is a drum, beating a rapid, chaotic rhythm against my ribcage.

A gasp escapes my lips as I collapse onto the stairs, fighting to catch my breath. But it's like trying to inhale through a straw —my lungs can't seem to draw in enough air. Beads of sweat trickle down my forehead, seeping into my eyes and blurring my vision further.

This isn't normal.

It's not my usual anxiety or a simple adrenaline rush. It's different. Scarier. It's a whirlwind of fear and confusion, everything around me suddenly too big, too loud.

Curling in on myself, I try to ride it out. The minutes tick by as I hunch over, clutching at my chest.

*Breathe, Elio, just fucking breathe.*

I try to use the calming techniques that Kaia taught me—

deep breaths, distracting thoughts. I close my eyes, willing myself to believe it's a panic attack, but the erratic beat of my heart argues otherwise.

I force myself to glance at the phone gripped tightly in my other hand. *Thirty minutes.* I've been sitting here for half a fucking hour already. My screen is filled with messages from my scene partner for tonight, the anxiety-inducing pings forcing my heart to pound even harder.

With trembling fingers, I manage to type a vague excuse. *Something came up. Can't make it. Sorry.* It's a shoddy reason, but the alternative—telling her I'm half-dressed, sweating, and reeling on her building's staircase—doesn't seem any better.

With one last look at the apartment door I never reached, I force myself up, each step an arduous task. It's embarrassing, leaving like this. I feel like a deserter, a coward. But at this moment, all I want is to get home, to escape the terrifying confines of this hallway.

I manage to get the Jeep back to my apartment building, parking it in my assigned spot under the hazy glow of the security lights. The moment I kill the engine, my head drops against the steering wheel, the heavy silence swallowing me whole.

The sweat-slicked fabric of my shirt sticks to my back, a stark reminder of the phantom marathon I've just run. It's like my heart has been hammering away in double time for hours, and despite my best efforts, I can't seem to slow the damn thing down.

I've been feeling like this for weeks now, my heart beating faster than normal, easily worn out by simple tasks. But tonight? Tonight's a whole new level of fucked-up.

In the rearview mirror, my own reflection stares back at me. The dark circles under my eyes and the pallor of my skin are concerning, to say the least. And even though I keep telling myself it's just stress, just anxiety, the nagging fear that something's seriously wrong refuses to back down.

After what feels like hours, I finally glance at my apartment window from the car, the faint glow of Bentley's night-light bleeding out into the quiet night. I think of his soft snores, the rhythmic rise and fall of his furry chest, the lullaby that usually grounds me.

Perhaps I could use that right now.

With a shaky sigh, I climb out of the Jeep, the night air cooling my fevered skin. The familiar journey from the parking lot to my apartment door feels like a pilgrimage, each step heavier than the last. But as I slip inside, the sight of my dog, sprawled out in his bed, offers a small comfort.

I kneel down beside him, ruffling his golden fur, and his sleepy eyes blink open, a low groan rumbling in his throat. I'm worn-out, probably looking worse for wear, but Bentley just thumps his tail gently against his bed.

The minutes stretch into an hour, the quiet of the early morning wrapped around the two of us. And yet, my body refuses to slow down. I keep circling back to the staircase, to the dizzying sensation of my heart threatening to burst from my chest.

The steady tick of the wall clock nudges me back to reality. It's far too early, the sky outside still a blanket of stars, but it's clear I won't be getting any sleep for the rest of the night.

"Walk?" I ask Bentley, my voice a gravelly whisper in the still room. His ears perk up at the familiar word, and he's on his feet in an instant, the sleepiness all but gone.

"Alright, buddy," I murmur, pushing to my feet.

Maybe the fresh air, the open beach, will help clear my head. Maybe it will give me a chance to breathe. At the very least, I'll be doing something other than sitting here, stuck and empty.

We make it over to Amber Isle in just a few short minutes. It's been nearly a week since our last visit, and both of us have clearly missed the place.

The cold breeze brushes against my face as we walk along the beach, Bentley trotting carefully at my side.

Growing up in Boyer, a small town just off the nearest exit, has led me to take this place for granted over the years. But something about being here now just feels right. Again, I'm alone, cast away before the sun has risen.

It's the calm and quiet I need to soothe my mind and reset my racing heart.

But as I keep walking, the pounding in my chest returns. This time, it's coupled with a dizzying sense of fatigue, each step a calculated, grating effort. My legs feel like they're made of lead, my body heavy.

Barely managing to catch my breath, I drop down onto the sand, pulling my knees close to my chest.

*In, two, three, four, out.*

I desperately count, working to ignore the urge to pass out. Bentley pads over to me, a low whine escaping him. It's something of a feat, but I manage a weak smile, reaching out to scratch behind his ears.

"It's okay, buddy," I tell him, lacking conviction.

Bentley seems to understand despite my own confusion. He curls up next to me, his golden head resting on my lap. His soft snores are soothing, the steady tempo a stark contrast to my erratic pulse.

And then, before I know it, my eyes are heavy, my body weak. Exhaustion pulls me under, and I let it, my last coherent thought being the hope that this will all pass by the time I wake up.

"Hey, are you okay?"

The question, soft but insistent, pulls me from the edges of sleep. I squint against the sun's early glare, glancing up at a figure casting a tiny shadow over me. As I blink the sleep from my eyes, her features slowly come into focus.

She's a girl, probably around my age, with sun-kissed blonde hair swept up into a ponytail. A pair of light brown eyes peer down at me, crinkling at the edges with concern. She's dressed in a wet suit, her surfboard wedged up behind her like some oversized prop.

"Yeah," I manage, my voice a gravelly echo of sleep as I boost myself up on one elbow. I blink away the sleepiness, trying to gather my scattered senses. "Just . . . didn't sleep very well."

Her gaze briefly flickers to Bentley, who's curled up by my side, his rhythmic breathing a testament to his undisturbed sleep. "Is your dog okay?"

"Yeah, he's good. Aren't you, buddy?" I ask, laying a reassuring hand on Bentley's side. My faithful companion stirs at the touch, lifting his head and opening his eyes to regard the stranger. After a careful assessment of about two seconds, he gives her a friendly wag of his tail.

"Isn't he just adorable?" A smile warms her face as she squats down, giving him a quick scratch on the neck. "What's his name?"

"Bentley," I mutter, working to stifle a yawn.

The encounter, though unexpected, isn't entirely unwelcome. Now that I think about it, it's been a long time since I've had any kind of normal face-to-face conversation, especially outside of my work.

"He's a lucky dog." She hums in approval, turning her attention back to me. "And you're out here awfully early."

"Could say the same for you," I say, meeting her comment with a raise of my brow. The girl—she hasn't given me her name yet—just laughs, the sound so sweet and soft.

"Fair point. But I've got to be if I want to catch the best waves," she says fondly, that smile never fading. There's a quiet certainty in her voice, like this is a ritual she wouldn't trade for anything.

I stand, brushing off more sand from my clothes. Despite my towering height, I'm oddly self-conscious beneath her unwavering gaze. She rises to her feet, effortlessly matching my pace as Bentley leads the way.

"I haven't seen you around here before," I say, half statement, half question.

"You wouldn't have. I'm new, just transferred in from Dayton. It's my first semester," she says, her tone bright. I catch the sparkle in her eyes, the reflection of the morning light making them appear almost golden.

"Been here a few weeks, and you're already out on the beach before the birds?" I ask, a reluctant curiosity sneaking into my tone. She chuckles, a light, airy sound that blends in with the soft lull of the waves.

"No better way to start the day."

Her easygoing nature is infectious, causing the ghost of a smile to pull at my lips. But as I watch her laugh, a strange sense of unease creeps inside of me. Something isn't right here.

It's not her; it's the situation. Talking to someone like this—someone so bright and full of life—is a sharp detour from the night I've just had.

"I should get going," I say, more abruptly than I intend to. But I need to get away, go back to my apartment, retreat into my careful solitude.

Her smile wanes a little, replaced by a slight furrow of her brow. "Oh, okay," she says simply. But instead of stepping back, she keeps pace with me, her footprints trailing beside mine in the sand, Bentley happily prancing on ahead of us.

"So, do you live around here?" she asks, her voice pulling me back from the edge of my thoughts.

I nod, keeping my gaze fixed on the path ahead.

"And what's your name?"

"Elio."

"Nice to meet you, Elio," she says with a bright smile. The name seems to roll off her tongue easily, as if she's known it forever. "What brings you here so early?"

I gesture down at Bentley, who's eagerly sniffing at a patch of sand. "Just fell asleep after walking my dog."

"Hm, any chance you surf?"

A dry chuckle escapes me. "No, I don't surf. Never have, never will."

"I don't know about that. There's always a first time for everything."

From there, her chatter continues—a stream of consciousness that keeps the silence at bay. *It's such a pretty morning, don't you think? How often do you come here? Does Bentley like to swim?*

Each question's met with a monosyllabic answer or a noncommittal grunt, a poor substitute for a real conversation. And yet, she keeps talking, her words filling up the quiet morning air.

I'd usually hate this—prefer the quiet, the peace, especially with a stranger. Yet for some reason, I let her talk.

Maybe it's the change of pace, or maybe it's just her, but I find myself not minding the company. Her presence offers a distraction from my fears, my worries, my racing heart. For the first time in a long while, I'm not alone with my thoughts.

And it feels . . . strangely nice.

# Chapter Four

## DAISY

I CAREFULLY TREAD inside my apartment, a scattering of sand from my shoes tracing my path to Gracie. She's absorbed in a thick law textbook, her brow puckered in concentration. It's a sight I've grown used to over the past few weeks, one that provides a comforting sense of normalcy after my unexpected morning.

"Hey," she greets me without looking up, her attention unwavering from the book. "You're back early."

With the memory of the mystery man still fresh in my mind, I dive right into it. "Yeah, I met someone new this morning," I say, kicking off my shoes and padding into the kitchen.

Gracie's gaze finally leaves her book, and her brows shoot up. "Hmm, someone else wakes up as early as our dear Daisy Grey?"

"Well, no. Not exactly."

I recount the morning's events, describing Elio with as much detail as I can remember—his intense gaze, the protective way he hovered over his dog, Bentley, and his reserved, yet oddly inviting, demeanor. The way I found him, curled up and shivering, sleeping alone without a blanket at 4:30 in the morning.

How at first, I assumed he might be houseless, but he claimed to live in an apartment nearby. How, for some unknown reason, I couldn't stop asking him an endless stream of questions.

As I talk, Gracie listens, sipping her coffee and encouraging me with nods and thoughtful hums.

"And you let him just walk away in the end? Didn't immediately rope him into a lifelong friendship?" she asks when I finish up, a playful smirk twisting her lips.

I shrug, my cheeks flushing. "What was I supposed to do, Gracie? Lasso him?"

Her laughter fills the room, a welcome sound that helps to diffuse the strange tension that's built up inside me. "Well, at least you know where to look if you want to run into him."

Heat creeps up my neck. "I'm not going to, like, stalk him or anything, if that's what you're suggesting."

She chuckles, closing her textbook to give me her full attention. "Who said anything about stalking? Just a coincidental meeting. You both seem to be early risers, after all, so a chance encounter is pretty likely."

Her words, though in jest, plant an idea in my mind. It may sound silly, but part of me thinks I should work to make that happen. It's just . . . Elio seemed like he could use a friend. And while I'm not exactly short on those myself, it never hurts to widen the circle.

I glance out the window—the desolate parking lot a sharp contrast from the quiet, sandy stretch of my new favorite beach—and let out a sigh. A mischievous smile plays on my lips as I turn back to face her.

"Oh, would you stop that?" she asks, running a wary hand through her soft, brown curls.

"Stop what?"

She rolls her eyes at my act, leaning against the counter as she folds her arms. "You've got that look on your face. The one you get when you're scheming."

"You've only known me for a few weeks now, Grace, and I don't scheme," I say, the corners of my mouth lifting. "I just . . . ponder possibilities."

She arches a brow as she gets up, leaving her half-finished breakfast on the table. "You're right, you love to *ponder*. Besides, I suppose it'll be good for you to make more friends at Coastal outside of our little group."

"Hey!" I protest, my mock offense earning me a chuckle.

With Gracie now in the kitchen, I trade places and plop myself down at the table, my eyes scanning the cluttered surface. Her law textbooks are stacked in one corner, while my own bio papers are spread out on the other.

It's only now that I realize I haven't checked my phone since late last night. So, I pull it out, half expecting to see a classic good-morning text from Logan. But the other—much more self-aware—part of me knows that he's been too busy this week to remember to message back.

"Speaking of *friends*," Gracie starts, pulling me back into the conversation. She leans against the kitchen counter, a thoughtful expression on her face. "You haven't mentioned Logan as much this week."

I shrug, not bothering to meet her eyes. "He's just been busy with practice."

"But isn't it off-season?" she asks, brows furrowing. I have to give her credit—she's more observant than I thought, especially considering her distinct lack of interest in all things sports.

"They've been ramping up practice, and . . . other stuff. You know, with Logan vying for the captaincy and all," I explain, brushing off her concern.

Despite my words, there's a knot of unease forming in my

stomach, a nagging doubt I've been trying to ignore. But now, with Gracie's pointed questions, it's becoming harder to push away.

"Hmm," is all she says, but I can tell she's not entirely convinced, and I don't blame her one bit.

It's not just that random girl's voice I heard over the phone that unsettles me but also the growing gap between us: unanswered calls, unread messages, and a sense of disconnect that's crept in over the last five days.

I'm usually not one to stress over the small stuff—a few unanswered texts and a handful of days—but it's never been like this before. Not between us.

Maybe it's just a phase every long-distance relationship goes through, a rough patch due to the physical separation. At least, I hope that's all it is.

LATER THAT NIGHT, Gracie and I join Max and LJ for a late-night bonfire at the beach. A few of their other friends are here, too. Some people Max knows from his graduate cohort, a few of the other girls in LJ's classes, and even Gracie brought along someone new.

It would be the perfect Saturday evening if not for the glaring absence of one person. Logan, who might be physically hundreds of miles away but should, in theory, feel much closer to me than he does tonight.

I've tried my luck at a couple of texts throughout the day, hoping to not sound as desperate as I feel, but my phone remains eerily silent. He's busy, I tell myself. Baseball, his friends at Dayton . . . it's a different world, and it's not like we have to be in constant communication.

But as the crackling fire casts shadows over our little group and the sea whispers stories to the night, his silence weighs heavy on my mind. This isn't like him, like us.

I sneak out my phone, pretending to be absorbed in some conversation about a recent football game. *No new message.* I swallow the disappointment that trickles in and find myself scrolling through Instagram. A few taps later, I'm on Logan's profile, his smiling face and silly captions working to bridge the distance.

But then, my stomach bottoms out.

It's a tagged picture, candid, of his teammate. But what leaves me cold is the background. Logan is there, a girl laughing, curled up on his lap in a familiar sort of way.

I have no idea who she is, never seen her before in my life, but she's extremely pretty. Long, dark hair and a tiny little outfit that's bunched up on her thighs.

My gut twists, my mind freezes, and I can't tear my eyes away from the sight.

With a lump in my throat, I mutter something about needing some air, the sounds of the fire and laughter fading as I head toward the murmur of the waves. It's just an innocent picture, a new friend that I haven't met before, I try to reason, but my heart pounds in disagreement.

Pulling up Logan's contact, I hit Dial. The line rings, every tone echoing my anxiety. It's an eternity and a half before he finally picks up, and I'm not even sure how many times I hit the Call button.

His voice is drowned out by the sound of music and laughter, but I can still hear him ask, "Hey, you okay?"

"Yeah, fine." I force myself to speak, my voice unsteady. "But, um, Lo, where are you?"

He sounds surprised, almost caught off guard. "I'm at a get-together with the team."

"Ah, you didn't mention that before."

"We trained all day, and they wanted to unwind a bit. I thought you'd be hanging out with your new friends, so I didn't want to bother you."

His words hit me harder than I expect, a cruel reminder of the distance between us. But the picture flashes back in my mind, forcing me to confront the nagging doubt.

"Oh, I saw a photo of you just now," I manage, my voice hushed by the crash of the waves beside me. "You're at a party, and there's some random girl on your lap."

There's a pause, a stretch of silence that makes my stomach sink. I hold my breath, clutching my phone, as the sea whispers comfort I can't feel.

This isn't how the night was supposed to go, not with me walking alone on a beach hundreds of miles away from Logan, waiting for an explanation for a picture that might mean nothing at all. But as the silence stretches, it feels like it's the only thing that matters.

When Logan finally speaks, his voice is a jumble of noise against the background chaos. "Babe, that's just . . . she's just one of Scott's friends."

His words hang in the silence between us, an echo of the doubt gnawing at my gut. "Then why is she sitting on your lap, Logan?"

He exhales loudly, a static huff of frustration that sends a shiver down my spine. "There weren't a lot of places to sit, and it was only for a few minutes. It's not a big deal."

"But—"

"Daisy, if you were here, you'd see it's nothing. It's just a party." His voice is quiet now, softer than I've heard it in a while. It's a plea, a desperate grasp at the trust that's suddenly so thin between us.

"You know I wish I could be there with you," I confess, my voice choked with the sorrow I've been fighting to hold back. "But I thought you were okay with all this, with me transferring to Coastal."

"I was. I am." His answer is immediate, but it's devoid of the warmth I'm used to. "I just didn't realize how hard this would end up being."

It's my turn to go quiet. I can hear the underlying accusation in his voice.

*Is this my fault? Am I the one ruining us?*

"Maybe it wouldn't be so hard if you just picked up your phone a few times this week," I finally retort, frustration replacing the creeping guilt.

He scoffs, and it grates on my heart. "So, it's my fault that you decided to put all this distance between us?"

"That's not what I meant, and you know it." My voice rises, anger and hurt tingeing my words. I don't realize I'm shouting until his silence slams into me.

"I don't like this, Daisy. I don't like this at all," he finally says.

"What, then? What do you want?" I challenge, my voice breaking. "Do you want us to break up?"

"No, that's not what I want," he says quickly, almost defensively. "But I think we need to talk about this when we're not . . . when the tension isn't this high. We'll talk tomorrow, okay? That gives us the night to cool down and think about what we truly want."

Before I can reply, the call ends, leaving me with the echo of his words. I stand there, phone clutched in my hand, as the world spins around me.

I don't feel well at all.

In fact, I'm growing more and more nauseous with every second I stand here, alone beneath this starlit sky. There's something heavy settling in the pit of my stomach—a growing realization that our next conversation could change everything.

# Chapter Five

## ELIO

"I'm just feeling a bit ragged and run-down, that's all," I try to explain to Kaia, my voice rough from sleeplessness, cell phone plastered to one ear. "It's just the stress getting to me."

Through the line, my oldest friend sighs, a mixture of concern and frustration. "El, this has been going on for weeks now. Actually, it's been since last school year. You're always tired, always wound up. That's not just stress we're talking about here."

I scrub a hand over my face, staring at the silent parking lot outside my window. I know she's worried. Hell, I'm worried myself. But I'm not ready to face what that might mean.

Not yet, anyway.

"You should talk to someone again, a professional," she says, her voice marked by a touch of hesitation, likely anticipating my resistance. "I've started seeing this new therapist over at Dayton. Maybe there's someone you can see back home. They have free counseling at the health center, don't they?"

"I don't need a therapist, Kai," I retort, the taste of frustration sour on my tongue.

The idea of discussing my demons with a stranger is far from appealing. The few times I had to attend therapy sessions during rehab—back when I was freshly eighteen—they left me feeling exposed, like a raw wound poked and prodded at.

Not exactly my idea of healing.

"What about your brother?" she suggests after a beat, her voice gentle. "He used to see someone there at Coastal, didn't he? Maybe he could give you some recommendations."

My mind flits back to Luca, always the beacon of strength and stability. I'd forgotten he'd weathered his own storm and that he'd sought professional help to guide him through it. In a way, we share a lot of similarities, but our differences have always caused a divide.

My brother's journey isn't mine; I know that much.

He worked with a counselor here nearly six years ago, righted his ship, and then married the love of his life. He's doing better now, has been for years. The man's a pillar in the NFL, a diligent athlete, the hardworking and dependable type. The perfect father, husband, brother, and son.

But that's not me, never will be.

I'm stuck in the shadows, lost in the crowd of perfection. As the middle sibling in a family full of achievers, it's always been easy to feel like the misfit. I've watched my older siblings forge paths that were lit with success, and even my two teenage sisters are carving their own way now.

The twins, Mia and Vivia, just started their first semester of college, both out of state on merit scholarships.

And then there's Georgie, our youngest, the sweetest kid you'll ever meet. In a family like mine, it's hard not to feel like the one who's got it all wrong.

I was lucky enough to meet Kaia when I did. Her older sister used to date my brother, and she's always felt like an outsider in her own family. We share a similar mindset, and our friendship has helped to keep me sane, to keep me stable, over the past ten years.

"Maybe. I'll think about it, okay?" I say, more to placate her than anything else.

Before Kaia can respond, there's a muffled sound from her end, a distinctly male voice that's filled with laughter.

"That Beck?" I ask, a reluctant smile curling my lips. There's no denying that Holden Becker, despite his obnoxious humor and persistent showboating, has been a good influence on my best friend.

"Yep," she says, her voice noticeably brighter. "He was just leaving, though."

Another chuckle slips through the line, low and sultry. "Yeah, leaving your bed to go make us some breakfast."

My brows shoot up at his comment, a shake of my head following suit. Typical Beck, a flippant remark just when things are getting heavy.

"Alright, lover boy. Your humor is appreciated, as always," I tell him, forcing cheer into my voice.

There's another bout of laughter from him, a joyous sound that takes the edge off my own worries, if only for a moment. Then, Kaia's back on the line, her voice low. "I mean it, E. Think about therapy. And talk to Luca. He'll understand."

"I will, Kai, I promise," I reassure her, though I'm not sure I can keep it. I'm still wrestling with my own stubbornness, a reluctance to admit that I might need to look outside myself for once.

"I hope so," she says quietly. "We worry about you, you know? You're not alone in this."

Her words stick with me, long after the call ends. It's comforting to know I have people who care about me outside of my own family. But it also magnifies the reality of the situation.

*You're not alone*, she said. But as I sit here in my empty apartment, with the early morning light trickling in, I've never felt more isolated.

Shoving my phone back into my pocket, I head to my

bedroom. There's an uneasiness clawing at my gut, the ghost of Friday night's panic attack still too fresh in my head. I know I should take Kaia's advice, maybe even talk to my siblings about it.

But I'm not sure that my ego can take the scrutiny.

With a heavy sigh, I wander over to my workspace and flip open my laptop, a familiar routine to start my Sunday. Everett's world, as usual, is a contradiction to mine, a realm where I'm always wanted, always needed.

And right now, I could use that reassurance.

My screen lights up, AfterDark's familiar interface coming into view. My inbox, usually a quiet corner, is abnormally crowded today—live one-on-one requests pouring in from users I don't recognize. But one message, in particular, catches my eye.

SapphireDream.

"Really enjoyed our last session," she writes. "I may have shared your profile with a few of my friends. Hope that's okay."

A spark of gratitude lights inside of me, tinged with a layer of apprehension. The attention is welcome, but it also equates to higher stakes.

The second part of her message nudges at the boundaries I've carefully constructed around my work. "I was wondering if we could try something different. Something personal this time?"

*Something personal.* Well, fuck. I don't do personal, not in this world. Everett's no more than an invention, an illusion, not meant to be tangible or real.

My gaze flickers across her request once more. It's daunting, the idea of stepping out of my carefully curated persona. But there are realities I can't ignore.

My sisters need the little extra I send their way each

month, next semester's tuition isn't going to pay for itself, and Bentley's recent health decline has led to more vet visits and a special, expensive diet.

And then there's my fucking heart issue to top it all off.

I'm still trying to chalk things up to anxiety, a simple series of panic attacks, but I've been feeling faint since Friday night, making it impossible to film any new scenes with a partner. If this keeps up, who knows when I'll be able to return to my usual tempo.

Swallowing hard, I hover over the Reply button. I can't afford to turn away business, especially when it's something this promising. The solo pleasure sessions can only keep Everett—keep me—afloat for so long.

With a deep breath, I type my response. The truth is, I need this just as much as she appears to, maybe even more. "So, you want something more personal," I write. "I might be able to arrange that. What did you have in mind?"

Later in the day, Bentley and I head over to a nearby café. It's a place I used to visit with Kaia back when she was a student here. There's this little blue door that leads to an outdoor courtyard, and it's dog-friendly, making it a perfect study spot for the two of us.

I secure Bentley's leash to a pole and assure him, "I'll be back, buddy."

He responds with a contented huff, and I keep an eye on him while I head inside.

Returning from the counter, my Americano and a muffin in hand, I find the blonde girl from the beach kneeling down beside my dog. Her face is a picture of delight as she showers him with affection.

Clearing my throat, I slowly approach them. "Hey," I say, my voice sounding gruff even to my ears.

She glances up, brows furrowed, but her features soften when she recognizes me. "Oh, it's you! I knew this one looked familiar." She pushes onto her feet, giving him one last pat to the head. "Such a sweetie pie."

I snort lightly. "Yeah, he's a good boy."

She bounces on her heels, hands tucking into her pockets. "So, are you here all by yourself?"

"Yeah, er, just me and my dog."

"Do you mind if I join you, then?"

"Ah, I actually need to study this morning." Her face instantly drops, so I rush to add in, "But you can sit with us if you want."

I drag another chair to our table, leaving it untucked for her to take a seat. Despite the hesitation, her company doesn't seem like the worst idea in the world. It could be nice . . . just to have someone to sit with while I pore over my books.

As we settle into a comfortable rhythm, her cheerful chatter begins. "Have you been to this place before? The muffins are to die for," she says, pointing to the pastry on my tray.

"I'm more of a coffee guy," I tell her, trying to focus on the screen of my laptop. But it's hard to ignore her energy, so infectious and bright. "You can have the muffin, though. If you want?"

She giggles, a pleasant melody that seeps into the silence around us. "You know, you're much softer than you let on."

I give her a sideways glance, lips curled. "Think so?"

"Yeah, I do. It's not a bad thing, though. Makes you more . . . interesting."

Something inside me stirs. Her words are simple, but they

hold a strange power. I swallow it down. "Yeah, and how about you? Do you ever run out of things to say?"

She shrugs, leveling me with a sheepish grin. "Actually, I'm usually the quiet one in a group. But with you, it's like I can't seem to keep my mouth shut. Maybe I'm just looking for a distraction or something." She twirls a strand of her blonde hair between her fingers, nails painted a soft periwinkle blue. "Got a lot on my mind these days."

A knot of understanding lodges itself in my chest. I'm all too familiar with the sentiment. "Yeah, I know what you—"

"Daisy?" a foreign voice interrupts us, heavy and weary.

I glance up, meeting the gaze of a man who appears out of place, a stark contrast to the calming atmosphere of the café. The sound of her name hangs in the air, a question wrapped in a statement, seeped in confusion.

*Daisy*, huh? It suits her. Bright and sweet, a wildflower in a field of mundane green. But even still, I'm struck by the realization that I never asked for her name.

"Logan?" Her reaction is swift and startling, body stiffening, eyes wide, as she rises to her feet. The easiness of our conversation dissipates, replaced by an undercurrent of tension that prickles at my skin.

She turns to me, then to the man, a silent plea flickering in her gaze.

"Who's this?" Logan asks, shifting his attention, suspicion in his eyes.

"This is Elio. We just met the other day," she finally introduces, her voice a threadbare whisper in the sudden quiet. "Elio, this is Logan, my boyfriend."

The word falls between us like a dead weight, plunging the moment into an even deeper awkwardness. The silence stretches, lingering, until she finally snaps it.

"I think I need to go. But I'll see you around, right?" She sounds hopeful, sincere. "And Bentley, too?" She gives him a quick ruffle behind the ears, and he seems to accept her departure with more grace than I do.

I nod, managing to find my voice. "Yeah, you'll see us around."

Then she turns and walks away, Logan following in her wake like a lost little puppy. Logan, *her boyfriend*. I say the words in my head a few more times, trying to reconcile the man in front of me with the images I'd already constructed in my mind.

And somehow, the two of them, it just doesn't fit.

# Chapter Six

DAISY

THE MOMENT we step out of the café, Logan wraps an arm around me, pulling me into his side. He's usually affectionate when we're together, but in this moment, the gesture feels empty, like a desperate attempt to reclaim something we've lost.

Despite the uneasy feeling, I let myself lean into him.

"Where's your car?" he asks, glancing across the rows of street parking.

"I walked here."

His eyes flash with suspicion, a brow arching. "Sure that guy in there didn't give you a ride?"

I flinch at the accusation, my lips pressing into a tight line. "What are you doing here, Lo?"

He sighs heavily, running a hand through his thick, blond hair. "I just . . . we needed to talk."

*Well, that's just great.* Everyone knows that's the worst way to start a conversation. I'm willing to talk, to hear him out, but I'm not listening to another word until we're safely tucked inside my space.

The drive back to my apartment is painfully silent, each tick of the clock an echo in the void between us. Logan's hand reaches for mine, his thumb rubbing circles on the base of my thumb. I allow him the comfort, though it does little to ease my mind.

When we arrive, I lead him inside. Gracie's in the living

room, scrolling through something on her phone. But at the sight of Logan, standing so stiff and awkward beside me, her eyes widen.

"Everything okay?" she asks, voice cautious. I give her a nod, but the look on my face must say otherwise because she quickly retreats. "I'll be in my room if you need me, alright?"

Once she's gone, Logan falls onto the couch, head in his hands. He looks defeated, the normally confident, handsome man I'd fallen for seeming so lost.

"Logan . . ." I start, uncertainty threading my voice.

"Daisy, I . . ." He struggles to find the words, a pain etched onto his face that I've never seen before. "I really fucked up."

A lump forms in my throat, a premonition of what's to come. "What happened?"

"I . . . God, this is really fucking hard. Baby, I, *fuck*, I slept with someone last night." The words hang in the air, heavy and heart-wrenching. My whole world tilts on its axis.

"What?" My voice comes out as a whisper, his betrayal sinking deep into my bones.

"It was a mistake," he rushes to explain, his hands reaching for me. I recoil, the touch I once sought now tainted. "I love you, Daisy, I really do."

"But . . . Why, then?" I ask, tears pricking at my eyes.

He looks down, a deep breath trembling through him. "I've missed you so fucking much," he confesses, voice barely a whisper. "This girl . . . she was just there. Everywhere I turned this past week, she'd be there, flirting with me, and it felt good to have that kind of attention again. I let my guard down."

"We've been apart for less than a month, Logan." The words slip from my lips, laced with disbelief and pain. His confession burns, searing a hole straight through my heart.

"I know, I know." He rubs his face with his hands, his voice thick with regret. "But you know, with the team and all, I've always been surrounded by this type of attention. And I've tried, I've really tried to keep my focus. But when you're not around, it's . . . it's harder to resist."

I squeeze my eyes shut, desperate to make sense of his words. "But why would you throw it all away for some fling?"

Logan looks down, and I can sense the battle waging inside him. "You know I love you, Daisy. More than anything. But . . ." His voice trails off, he swallows hard, and then, "When we—the two of us . . . look, our sex life, it's always been very careful, reserved."

My heart slams into the walls of my chest, each beat echoing his words. "Did you enjoy it, then?" I ask, my voice a choked whisper. "Being with her, was it . . . better for you?"

He swallows, thick and heavy, a look of anguish crossing his face. "It was different," he finally admits.

His words are a punch to the gut. *Different.* I'd always thought we were enough, that we were good. His confession shatters that belief.

"You know I can't forgive you for this," I whisper, the tears stinging as they pool in the corner of my eyes, dripping down my cheeks, and flooding the neck of my T-shirt.

He nods, gaze never leaving his feet. "I know."

A heavy silence fills the room, the sting of his betrayal still ringing in my ears.

Slowly, I rise from the couch, every ounce of pain and heartbreak radiating through me. Wordlessly, I open the door for him, my hand shaking as I turn the knob. He walks out without a backward glance, leaving behind a silent apartment and a shattered heart.

The door closes with a click, the finality of the sound resonating in the empty space.

And just like that, it's over.

The silence Logan leaves behind rings through the apartment, making the walls feel colder, the light dimmer. Like he's taken with him all the warmth, all the vibrancy, leaving behind a stark, empty shell.

The reality of the situation hits me hard. My body feels numb, the weight of the heartbreak rendering me immobile. I sink onto the couch, folding myself into a tight ball, as if trying to shield myself from the agony that's yet to come.

The tears follow suit, hot and heavy, a silent stream that won't relent.

When Gracie emerges from her room a while later, her expression is one of deep concern. She takes one look at me, crumpled on the couch, and instantly knows. Words aren't necessary; the sadness hanging in the room is testament enough.

"I'm calling LJ," she announces, fishing her phone out of her pocket. "We need reinforcements. This calls for an emergency girls' night."

I want to protest, to argue that I'd rather be alone, but I can't find the energy. Instead, I just nod, too spent to disagree.

A short while later, our living room is transformed into the perfect movie night scene courtesy of Gracie. The TV screen casts a dim light over the room, corny movies playing in the background, snacks laid out on the coffee table. It feels familiar, almost comforting, if not for the constant reminder of why we're here.

LJ joins us shortly after, her usual bright smile replaced with a sympathetic frown. The three of us huddle together on the couch, a massive tub of Rocky Road ice cream placed strategically between us. It's an unspoken agreement to eat our feelings away.

As I dig into the tub, the sweet, creamy flavor doing little to ease my turbulent thoughts, my mind still centers on Logan. My first boyfriend. The first man I'd ever been with, the first man I'd ever loved.

The connection between us had never been electric or instant. Instead, it was a slow, gentle simmer, gradually heating up until it was impossible to ignore.

We'd taken our time, explored each other at a leisurely pace. And I loved that about us. The first time we'd slept together, it was sweet, slow. More about the connection, the intimacy, than the act itself.

It felt right. More than just right, at the time.

"I just can't believe it, you know?" My words shatter the silence, barely above a whisper yet thunderously loud in the quiet room.

Gracie's arm snakes around me, pulling me into a side hug. "I know, hon," she says softly. "It's a real dick move."

Yet, I can't fully process her words, lost in a whirlpool of my own thoughts. Logan's confession keeps replaying in my mind, his words reverberating through the silence. His dissatisfaction with our sex life, his confession that he wanted more. It gnaws at me, makes me question my own desires.

"Do you think I should've been . . . more interested?" I ask, hating the vulnerability in my voice. "In that stuff?"

Gracie looks at me, confusion knitting her brows. "What do you mean?"

"In . . . in sex, in general," I clarify, my cheeks warming up. "Should I have been more adventurous? Done more to keep him interested?"

"Daisy," LJ cuts in before Gracie can reply. Her voice is

firm, the reassuring tone I've come to associate with her. "Don't ever let someone else's actions make you question your worth. You're not responsible for his decisions. You shouldn't have to change who you are or what you want because of what he did."

I know she's right, but the gnawing guilt is harder to ignore. *What if things could've been different? If I'd been more adventurous, shown more interest, would he have stayed despite the distance? Would he have still had the thought, the inclination to stray?*

Gracie seems to sense my thoughts. "Daisy," she says, her voice softer this time. "Everyone has their own pace, their own desires. You shouldn't feel pressured to change that for someone else."

I give her a pitiful nod, forcing the lingering doubts to the back of my mind as another scene unfolds on the screen.

The rest of the night passes in a blur. The sad movies continue to roll, our tub of ice cream quickly depleting. But amidst the comfort of my friends and the forced distraction of the TV screen, the sense of loss is inescapable.

Logan was my first in many ways. My first boyfriend, my first love, and now, my first heartbreak. The pain is fresh, a deep wound that will take time to heal. But as I glance at my friends, their faces reflecting my own sorrow, I'm reminded that at least I'm not alone.

And for now, that'll have to be enough.

THE DAYS of the following week melt into one. I fall into a monotonous routine, a robotic state where I'm just going through the motions. I attend classes, mechanically jotting down notes, but my mind is a million miles away.

The moment I'm back in my apartment, I find myself

crawling into bed, pulling the blanket over my head as if it can shield me from the crushing reality. My appetite has dwindled down to almost nothing. I've been living off sips of water and the occasional piece of bread that Gracie insists on me eating.

My phone keeps lighting up with notifications, a constant stream of messages and missed calls from my friends back in Dayton. They all heard about the breakup but have no clue about the real reason behind it. According to their messages, they seem to be questioning my motives and immediately taking Logan's side.

Apparently, he made it seem as though I transferred to Coastal and dumped him after a few weeks apart. My stomach dips every time I think about it. How easily he managed to paint himself as the victim while the truth is the exact opposite.

But what hurts more is the radio silence from Logan himself. There hasn't been a single text or call from him since he walked out of my apartment. Not a single word of regret or even a pathetic attempt at an apology.

In fact, the realization dawns on me that he never once said the words "I'm sorry" following his confession.

And now, my friends' well-meaning messages of comfort and misunderstandings just feel like salt on an open wound. None of them truly know what happened, none of them know about the deep-seated betrayal I feel.

And then there's surfing. My board lies untouched, collecting dust in the corner of my room. It's strange how something that used to give me so much joy now feels like a reminder of all that I've lost.

I haven't had the heart to even look at it.

In these quiet, solitary moments, I allow myself to feel the pain, the heartbreak. Tears stain my pillow, my chest heavy with unshed sobs. Yet amidst all the despair, I find myself trying to hold on to a tiny sliver of hope. A silver lining in the midst of it all.

Logan was a significant part of my life, but he wasn't my whole life.

His betrayal hurts, but it doesn't define me or shape my worth. I'm more than this heartbreak, more than this pain. I'm Daisy Grey—friend, student, surfer. I'm a girl who's strong enough to overcome this, who deserves someone who can match that strength, someone who will respect and love me the way I'm worthy of.

I hold on to this thought like a lifeline, a glimmer of hope amidst the sea of sorrow I find myself in. My strength may be a tiny spark right now, but I know it will grow. As they say, time heals everything.

The nights are the hardest. The silence of the darkened room allows my thoughts to run rampant, every "what if" and "if only" echoing louder in the stillness. The ache in my chest intensifies,_the tears fall easier. But I let them, each salty droplet a small part of my healing process.

My thoughts continue to wander back to that moment. Logan's confession, his raw and uncomfortable honesty. His words play back in my mind, their implications sinking deeper each time. The feeling of inadequacy has a way of creeping back, bringing with it a fresh wave of pain.

And on Saturday night, when I'm curled up alone in my bed, my phone lights up with another message from a friend. This time, it's Nessa, and she's wondering when she might see me again. I consider replying, to let them all know that I'm okay or, at the very least, that I will be.

Instead, I clear my notifications, silencing the unending

stream of concerns and condolences. It's not their fault they don't know the whole truth, but right now, their misguided sympathy feels more like an intrusion into my healing process.

I need time and space away from anything—everything—that reminds me of him. Time to heal on my own terms.

# Chapter Seven

ELIO

THE USUAL CALM of my apartment feels too oppressive tonight.

Late-night filming, usually a solace in its own way, is off the table until my heart gets its act together. The emptiness around me echoes louder than it should, pushing me out of the four walls closing in on me.

So, Bentley and I head over to Amber Isle.

Our late-night strolls have become an escape route for me. The quiet hum of the ocean and the feel of the cold sand under my feet are grounding in ways I never thought possible. Bentley, of course, revels in the freedom to sniff out every little thing without distraction.

But tonight, the solitude I crave is disrupted.

In the distance, there's a figure hunched over on the beach. Her silhouette is bathed in the soft glow of the moonlight. A surfboard lies abandoned next to her. The wavy hair cascading down her back catches the light, making her stand out against the dark sand, and my chest tightens with recognition.

*It's Daisy, out there all alone.*

Bentley, who never fails to pick up on my unspoken thoughts, pulls at his leash, eager to greet her. "Alright, bud, let's go," I concede, realizing I'm not completely averse to the idea myself.

As we approach, I see Daisy in a new light. Her usually

radiant face is cast downward, shoulders trembling. She's crying, sobbing by the looks of it. And the sight of the tearstains on her cheeks, those red-rimmed eyes, yanks at something inside of me.

"Hey," I say, lowering myself onto the sand beside her.

She looks up, surprise flashing in her eyes. "Elio? What are you doing out here so late?"

"Just couldn't sleep," I say with a shrug. "And what about you?"

A heavy silence descends upon us, broken only by the soft lapping of the waves nearby. She's hurting, and I want to say something, *anything*, to make it better. But the right words evade me.

Finally, she speaks, a sniffle and a hiccup preceding her words. "Logan cheated on me."

Her confession hangs heavy in the cool night air. *What a fucking loser*, is all I can seem to think. But I scramble for other words, for some way to comfort her. "That's . . . really shitty. I'm sorry."

She merely shrugs, her gaze distant, lost in her own world as her toes dig into the sand. "He . . . he was my first real boyfriend, you know?" she adds. Her words are so soft they nearly drown in the sound of the ocean. "We'd been together for over two years . . . went to college together at Dayton. He even seemed fine with the long distance, said it was no problem, that we could make it work."

"Fucking hell."

Her voice trembles, her gaze far-off, lost in a memory. "And it hadn't even been a month since we'd been apart, and he . . . he just slept with someone else."

The words sit between us, a painful reminder of human fallibility, of betrayal. I watch her, the way her body shivers slightly at the admission, the way her eyes grow glossy with a fresh set of tears.

"He drove all the way here last weekend just to tell me he did it. I don't know if it's some twisted version of 'honesty is the best policy' or if he was just looking for an easy way out," she adds bitterly, the hint of a sarcastic chuckle escaping her lips.

I swallow, my throat suddenly dry. "I . . . dammit, I'm sorry. I'm not sure what else to say, but what I do know is that you didn't deserve it."

It's all I can offer her in this moment, my own past experiences having taught me that sometimes, the most comforting thing you can do for someone is just to be there.

"Has anyone ever told you you're a great listener?" she asks after a moment, her tone hinting at a sliver of her usual lightheartedness.

The question rattles me, ripping a surprised chuckle from my throat. I meet her gaze, the corners of her mouth tugging upward into the faintest semblance of a smile.

"My friend Kaia says that sometimes, but I always feel like she's lying."

"Well, she's not." She laughs, the tears catching in her throat. "You just . . . sit there and listen. You don't try to fix things or pretend you have all the answers. It's . . . nice."

"I'll be sure to put that on my resume."

She laughs again at that, a tiny, breathy sound, like the first warm ray of sun breaking through a cloudy morning. Her chuckle dissolves into silence, her gaze distant as she watches the waves crash against the shore.

"I really thought he loved me," she finally whispers. There's a raw, open vulnerability in her voice, and it sends my gaze flickering back to her.

I take a deep breath, the taste of salt and sea filling my

lungs. This isn't my field of expertise. *Hell*, I'm probably the last person who should be giving relationship advice, but I find myself drawn to help her, to offer some small comfort where I can.

"Hey," I say, my voice steady. "Being cheated on says more about him than it does about you. You're more than enough for the person who deserves you."

There's a beat of silence, the world holding its breath. Then, slowly, she gives me another smile. It's small, it's fragile, but it's there. "You're sweet, Elio. Really."

A surprised laugh escapes me, my usual wall of sarcasm momentarily crumbled. "I'm not. But for you, right now, I sure can try."

AFTER A FEW MORE MOMENTS OF peaceful quiet, of shared comfort staring out at the shore, Daisy and I part ways. She promises to make it home safe, and Bentley leads me back while she returns to her abandoned surfboard, the tears finally at bay.

Now that I'm tucked back inside my bedroom, the image of her sitting there all alone on the beach still lingers in my mind. It's sad, disheartening, to witness someone so full of life become so brokenhearted.

But she'll bounce back. I know she will.

To distract myself from the thoughts, I lie down on my bed, that familiar blue glow from my laptop the only source of light, and scroll through my AfterDark messages. The request from Sapphire still sits in my inbox, unanswered.

I agreed to something more personal, and she came back with an offer that's hard to ignore. She wants to take things further, to transition our live sessions to two-way video chats.

The amount of money she's proposed is more than tempting, but I've told her I need time to think about it. And now, that time's running thin. A decision needs to be made one way or another.

I switch tabs, browsing through the backlog of one-on-one requests that have piled up throughout the last couple of days. Thanks to Sapphire, the demand for web chats is sky-high.

Since my heart issue sidelined me, I've done back-to-back live sessions all week in place of filming scenes. The immediate financial benefits are good, but the longer-term income that comes from partner videos and shoots is far more consistent.

The decision is a gamble. The promised windfall from Sapphire could secure me for a while, allowing me to recover and return to filming with professionals—the people in this industry who know how to separate the work from the personal.

But I don't know if her request is a boundary I'm willing to cross.

I pinch the bridge of my nose, the strain of the decision taking its toll. And yet, Daisy's heartbreak remains heavy in my thoughts. She loved the man she thought she knew, trusted him, and he betrayed her. I know what that feels like, to trust someone only to have them hurt you in the worst possible way.

My thoughts stray to Jackson Ford, a person I haven't thought about in years. My old friend who, in a way, set me on this chaotic path. Back then, we were just two high school students living life on the edge. The whole world at our feet.

He was the one who introduced me to the party scene, to the thrill of letting go.

But it quickly spiraled out of control. Alcohol, then cocaine. And Jacks, my first real friend outside of Kaia, became an unpredictable whirlwind. We both did.

But that's the thing about me and Jacks. At night, he'd put his hand on my thigh. But the next day, he'd tell me he was just drunk. He'd kiss me and then claim he was high out of his mind. I didn't realize what was happening until it was too late. Until I was staring at my brother broken down on the pavement and chose to run away.

I thought I was protecting someone I cared about, someone who cared about me. But I was wrong. Because Jacks didn't want me; all he ever wanted was to get high.

He used me to take money from my siblings, to support him with his reckless decisions, and then he left me high and dry, never to be heard from again. The end result was me spiraling down an uncontrollable path—a path that would take me years to recover from.

When my brother, Luca, first confronted me about everything, I didn't know how to act. All I knew was that I didn't want Jacks to get in trouble. And so, we fought, harder than we've ever fought before. I shoved him down on the pavement outside of Jackson's house during a party, and I left him there all alone.

He was injured, and he could've lost everything—his shot at the NFL, the love of his fucking life. It was the wrong decision, a misstep that I wish had never happened. But it did, and it's because I was clouded by what I thought was love.

I blink, dragging my thoughts back to the present, away from the haunting ghosts of my past. The cursor on my AfterDark message box blinks mockingly at me, reminding me of the unresolved decision.

My gaze drifts back to the blank walls of my apartment, and they seem to be closing in on me now more than ever. I'm caught in this crossroads, questioning the path I've chosen, the decisions I've made, and the ones that are yet to come.

My line of work, the persona of Everett, provides a safe space for other people to explore their sexuality, their desires, but it also requires me to compartmentalize my own life. The boundaries I've established to protect my sense of self have prevented me from experiencing any real, honest intimacy.

So, there's the truth. I'd like to have a physical connection that isn't hidden behind a computer screen or a pseudonym. But it's not exactly compatible with my current lifestyle, my chosen profession.

As I lean back against the headboard, I close my eyes, letting the silence seep in. The questions linger in the back of my mind, an echo bouncing off the walls of my solitude: *Is it even possible to have both? And if so, is it worth all the effort, the potential for another heartbreak?*

A soft whine from Bentley draws my attention, his big brown eyes looking up at me with a kind of understanding that's all too human. A faint smile pulls at my lips, and I close the laptop, deciding to postpone the decision for another day.

The irony isn't lost on me. Here I am, a man who's built an entire online persona to provide a sanctuary for people's fantasies, yet struggling to navigate my own reality.

With a resigned sigh, I rise from the bed, Bentley immediately on my heels. "Come on, boy," I mutter, giving him a scratch behind his ears. "Let's let you out before we call it a night."

# Chapter Eight

## DAISY

As I MOVE into a new week, the initial shock of the breakup dulls. It doesn't go away, not by a long shot, but it's less overwhelming now. The void Logan left behind is still there, a painful reminder of our shared memories, of the love I once thought was real.

But it's also a reminder of his betrayal, of the pain he inflicted without a second thought.

Every day, I wake up, and for a moment, I forget. I reach for my phone to send him a good-morning text, to tell him about a funny thing I saw, or just to say I love him. And then reality hits, each time a little less gut-wrenching than before.

The insecurities he sparked are still fresh, raw, and uncomfortable, and I worry that maybe there's something fundamentally wrong with me. At least, when it comes to sex, that is.

But I remind myself of LJ's words. I'm not responsible for his decisions. His actions aren't a reflection of my worth. And I certainly shouldn't question or change my desires based on his inability to stay faithful. I have the right to want what I want, to take things at my own pace, and I shouldn't have to feel guilty about it.

And, as Elio so kindly pointed out, Logan cheating on me says more about him than it does about me. But there's still a small part of me that's curious about exploring my own sexuality on a deeper level.

Not for Logan, but for myself.

Sex, or even sexual attraction, has never been something I've thought about consciously. Not until Logan and I had been dating for quite a while. Our relationship felt so right, our connection so deep, that sex just was a natural progression for us.

I wasn't just attracted to him physically; it was more than that. I was attracted to him as a person, to his humor, his kindness, his soul. Once I got to know him, once I fell in love with him, that's when the physical part clicked for me. When he initiated, I found myself reciprocating, eager, turned on.

But I've never felt that way with anyone else, and it's a difficult concept for me to fathom.

Wrapped up in these thoughts, I migrate toward Gracie's room, my palms sweating. I feel like a nervous teenager seeking advice, but I know Gracie—so calming and nonjudgmental—is the best person to talk to about all this.

Drawing a deep breath, I tap lightly on her door. As she opens it, her expression shifts from surprise to concern. "Hey, what's going on?"

"I just, I have some questions for you." I gulp low in my throat. "About . . . sex."

"Well, uh . . . sure. Yeah, okay. I mean, I'm definitely no expert on the subject, but I suppose I can try to help." Her brows arch up, and a smirk graces her lips. But then, as she studies my serious expression, that smile slowly fades. "Wait, you're not just trying to change yourself because of what Logan did, are you?"

"No, not at all," I assure her quickly, the mere thought making my stomach churn. "This is for me. I just want to understand a little more about myself."

"Okay . . ." She draws out the word, her eyes reflecting concern. "So, what's on your mind?"

"I know I'm not ready to have sex with someone else, and I'm not even sure I could do so outside of a relationship. But I want to explore, learn more about my own interests and desires. Do you have any ideas?"

She nods, understanding dawning in her eyes. "There are a few ways you could go about it. I mean, toys are always an option."

Heat creeps up my neck, and I quickly shake my head. She chuckles and slides an amused hand down her cheek before swiftly moving on. "Alright, that might be a bit much to start. But there are other avenues you can explore. Um, have you ever thought about watching porn?"

"I've seen a few things . . . But isn't the whole industry, like, super exploitative and all that?"

"I mean, a lot of it is. But there are subscription sites where sex workers can be self-employed." She pulls out her phone, scrolling for a few quick seconds. "There's this one site called AfterDark. It's supposed to be really good."

"AfterDark?" I give her a soft giggle. "That's kind of clever, actually."

"Mhm, and there are a lot of different types of creators on there. They all offer tier levels based on what you're looking for. You might find some you like, maybe subscribe to them. It'd be a safe, healthy way to explore your sexuality."

Her suggestion hangs in the air, not as daunting but more so intriguing. "Um, yeah, I think I might take a look later on. Thank you, Gracie."

"Of course." She gives me a reassuring smile and a quick hug. "Take it at your own pace and do what feels right for you.

But I'm here if you want to talk about anything else. You know, outside of the sex bomb your ex just dropped."

"I appreciate that."

With her reassurance and support, I retreat to my room, feeling slightly empowered. This isn't about Logan anymore but about understanding myself and my desires on a deeper level. It's about taking control of my narrative, and in its own way, that feels liberating.

I curl up on my bed, pulling my laptop into the space beside me. There's a sense of thrill, a touch of apprehension, and a burst of curiosity as I type in the URL: AfterDark.com. It feels almost symbolic, like a key turning in a lock, and it may be silly, but I can't help but hold my breath as the page loads.

Once I'm in, I click over to create a new profile. I contemplate my username for what feels like a ridiculous length of time before eventually settling on WildFlower. It's fitting for me, simple but anonymous, and it makes me feel like maybe I'm the one in control here.

Like I'm free to explore this part of myself without judgment or expectation. And despite feeling sad about how things ended with Logan, I'm finally excited to start fresh.

As the twilight fades, my friends and I huddle together under a dimly lit sky. We're back on Amber Isle, our beach blanket stretched out on the sun-warmed sand. Sparks dance up from our bonfire, illuminating our small group as the evening grows dark.

The scent of salty sea air and food from the Surfbreak waft around us. I swear, they have the best burgers and beer in the whole state. And it's a good thing that stuffing my face with junk food always makes me feel better, even if it's only temporary.

Max, LJ, Gracie, and I sit comfortably in the soft light, our laughter dancing alongside the crackling fire. They've planned this evening for me as a midweek distraction, a buoy to keep me from sinking too deeply into breakup-related thoughts.

LJ, her auburn hair glinting in the firelight, wears a mischievous grin on her face. "You know, I decided to try out that shoulder stand pose the other day—the Salamba Sarvangasana, right?"

"Repeat that?" Max interrupts, feigning confusion, his brows raised in an exaggerated arch.

"Come on, Max. Keep up," LJ fires back, smirking at him. He chuckles, taking the jest in stride, and waves for her to continue.

"So," LJ resumes, mimicking her struggle with an elaborate hand gesture, "I'm all balanced, legs in the air, thinking, 'This isn't too bad.' And then—"

"Let me guess, you face-planted?" Max interrupts again, his voice laden with amusement.

"No, *Maxwell.*" LJ rolls her eyes. "That would've been a blessing compared to the entire bookcase I knocked over. Let's just say my yoga mat and my favorite collection of hardcovers aren't on speaking terms anymore."

"You never did know how to pick the right spots," Gracie says, giving her a consoling pat on the back. "Remember when you held that class in Brook Valley Park? They were hosting a protest against new tech and wouldn't stop blasting all those old hip-hop tapes."

"Yeah, that was bizarre." LJ runs a weary hand through the ends of her hair. "It wasn't even, like, the original tapes, either. I'm pretty sure it was just Mac Miller on cassette for some reason. But yeah, at least I didn't break anything that time. I may have accidentally ruined a signed edition of *Little Women* the other day."

Max gives her an amused snort. "And here I was thinking my wipeouts were bad." He turns to me, a playful challenge in his eyes. "Which reminds me—Daisy, you've got to get back on your board soon."

I take a gulp of my wine, the sweet tang giving me a spark of courage. "I'll do it this weekend. Okay?"

Gracie gives me a pointed look, her voice gentle but insistent. "Promise us, Daisy. I think it'll do you a whole world of good."

"I promise," I affirm, raising my half-empty bottle. For me, it's a silent toast to new beginnings. For them, it's an assurance that I'm making progress.

Our conversation continues to flow, seamless and carefree, until I spot a familiar figure walking along the beach, a golden dog bounding happily around him. I swear my heart gives a little leap at the sight.

"It's Elio," I murmur mostly to myself.

Without waiting for a second, I push up from the sand and head toward them. I leave behind the safety of my friends, drawn to the silent pair like a moth to a flame. As I approach, Bentley bounds over to me, his tail wagging in pure joy.

"Hi!" I exclaim with more enthusiasm than intended. The echo of my voice hangs in the air between us as Bentley circles around my feet.

Elio's dark eyes twinkle under the starlight, amused as he glances at the bottle in my grasp. "Hey, Daisy," he says, his voice a low rumble in the quiet night. "What's that you've got there?"

"Wine," I say. It's a challenge to steady my voice as the

alcohol and my racing heart conspire to make me giggle. "Would you like some?"

He laughs, soft and low, the sound washing over me like a warm wave. "I think I'll pass. But thank you for the offer."

I shrug, a grin playing on my lips as I take a long swig, the sweet liquor warming my insides. "More for me, then."

Noticing my slight sway, he reaches out, his fingers lightly circling the neck of the bottle. "Maybe we should save the rest for later?"

I mock gasp, feigning offense as he pulls it away. "What, don't trust me with it?"

A teasing glint lights up his eyes. "Well, I don't know. Can't be too careful around a girl with a bottle of strawberry wine."

I shake my head at him. "Are you implying you don't have faith in your new friend?"

His brow quirks. "We're *friends*, huh?"

"Yeah, aren't we?" I ask, an unintentional vulnerability coloring my words.

He studies me for a moment, his expression softening before breaking into a gentle smile. "You want us to be friends, Daisy girl? I think I could manage that."

I smile to myself, not bothering to hide it. There's a comfortable silence between us, me swaying gently to an imaginary rhythm, Elio steady and solid beside me.

"You're out late again, aren't you?" I finally ask, kicking at the sand as I stumble on my feet.

"The beach is always better in the middle of the night," he says. "It's nice, quiet and lonely, helps me clear my mind."

"I haven't been able to clear my mind much lately," I confess, my words slurring slightly, an embarrassing hiccup squeaking out of me. "Last time we had a bonfire here, I saw that picture of Logan with a girl on his lap. That's why my friends decided to have this little gathering tonight. To kind of erase that awful memory and help me get back on track."

His expression shifts, softening further. "That sounds like a good idea. And your friends seem like a good group."

"They are." I nod enthusiastically, warmth spreading through me. "They've become my anchor in all this, really. They've even convinced me to get back on my board this weekend. It's been a few weeks now since I last surfed, but they think it will make me feel better."

"And do you agree?

"I guess so, yeah," I say, my gaze falling on the shimmering ocean. "I mean, I love surfing. It's a big part of the reason why I transferred here in the first place. But ever since that night . . . it's just been hard to do . . . literally anything. I make it to my classes, but outside of that, I just feel kind of numb most of the time. I don't know, it probably sounds dramatic."

"It doesn't," he says softly. "I feel like that a lot of the time, too. But I hear it's supposed to help—you know, facing our fears and reclaiming what we love."

"Yeah," I affirm, my decision solidifying with his words. I turn to look at him, my smile bright. "And what is it that you love?"

"I'm still figuring that out myself."

"Oh," I murmur. "Well, let me know if you need any help, okay?"

He tilts his head, clearly amused. "Yeah, alright. You'll be the first one I come to."

I pat him on the bicep, ruffle Bentley's fur, and glance over my shoulder to where my friends are sitting. "They're probably missing me. So, um, I better get back."

"Okay." He lifts up my bottle, and as I reach out to accept it, our fingertips graze. The contact is fleeting, a barely there touch, but it brings a subtle warmth to my skin. "Don't forget your wine."

As I sway back toward the bonfire, Elio's soft chuckle lingering in the air, a spark of hope flickers inside my heart. I feel ready to step into a new chapter, to release the weight of the past, and to open myself up to future possibilities here at Coastal.

# Chapter Nine

ELIO

I GROAN, stretching the sleep from my muscles, and force myself out of bed bright and early. It's Friday already, meaning we're almost through another week of the semester.

My calendar's haphazardly marked with the day's assignments and lectures, and a tiny sense of pride fills me at the sight.

One more week into my final year at Coastal, one more week of perfect fucking attendance. Last year's slacking version of me is starting to feel like a distant memory, a shadow that I can finally put behind me.

It's not that I wanted to skip my classes before, but I was running myself ragged, wearing myself down to the bone. I was forcing myself to stay up all night to film scenes, to edit. Not to mention the anxiety and the pressure I was feeling.

It all piled up until it was too much for me to handle.

If I wasn't forcing myself to slow down now, I'd be having the same issues this term. But I'm taking it easy for once, and it's finally starting to pay off. At least in terms of my health, my sanity, my schoolwork, that is. The financial piece is a whole other issue.

As per usual, my classes stretch throughout the day, a blur of seminars, assignments, and lecture notes. It's a rigorous routine, but it's a price I'm willing to pay to earn my degree. To make a living doing something I'm actually interested in.

Once the school day is over, I head home, attending to Bentley before I settle down with my own work. He busies himself with his special meal while I open my laptop, pulling up my calculus assignments first.

It takes a few grueling hours of dedication before I can finally switch over to AfterDark.

Once I log in, I sift through my new followers and reply to DMs, prioritizing web chat requests. But I consciously steer clear of Sapphire's messages until the last possible minute. I've yet to resolve my decision about our two-way chats, and her patience appears to be dwindling.

***SapphireDream:*** *Please let me know your decision, Everett. I'm waiting.*

I wish I could give her a definitive answer, but I can't seem to make up my mind one way or the other. I've been distracted, to say the least. A little bit careless with my time this week. My mind keeps straying, drawn to the lingering echoes of Daisy's voice from the other night, the raw curiosity in her words.

*What is it that you love*, she asked.

I didn't have a clear answer then, and I still don't, even though a part of me wishes it were different. There's something in me that wants to feel that intense passion, that unshakable dedication. To love something with the kind of desperation that borders on clinical—the way that Daisy loves surfing or the way that Kaia loves studying the human brain.

But I don't think I'm capable of that level of commitment. Not anymore.

My phone vibrates, and my best friend's name flashes on the screen. She asks a simple question that jolts me back into the present.

KAIA

hey El, how are you?

While I'm grateful for Kaia's presence in my life—her constant check-ins despite the distance—I don't feel like opening up that can of worms. So, instead of pouring out the whirlwind of my thoughts, I tap out a quick, meaningless reply.

ELIO

just fine, thanks. saw holden lost both his games last weekend. tell him it really bummed me out

no, thank you. and stop deflecting

I'm honestly okay, mother. don't worry

mhm. I'll check back later, then

*saluting emoji*

It's a surface-level response, barely scratching the depth of what's actually been gnawing at me. But it's easier to keep my feelings under wraps, to not admit out loud the concerns about my health, about my work.

Not to mention the strange tug that Daisy's heartbreak is having on me, the way she's somehow stirred up emotions I'd long attempted to bury.

To distract myself, I continue working through my string of requests, editing another pointless solo scene before moving on to my web chats. And when I finally step away from the screen, hours later, it's not the dimmed images of AfterDark that linger.

Instead, it's the echo of Daisy's laughter, the ghost of her tipsy smile that follows me into the silence of the night.

. . .

As THE FIRST light of Saturday spills into my apartment, I fasten Bentley's leash and bypass my phone sitting on the counter. We hop in the Jeep, and the two of us make our way over to Amber Isle in record time.

As we walk together, there's an unfamiliar stirring in my chest, a subtle thrum that matches the rhythm of the waves—not the unsettling pulse of anxiety I've grown used to, but something more like anticipation, excitement.

I shake off the thought, attributing it to the rising sun, the promise of a peaceful walk, but as Bentley and I amble closer to the shore, there's no denying it. Somewhere in the back of my mind, I'm hoping to cross paths with Daisy again, the girl cradling stars in her eyes.

The prospect of seeing her back on her board, to witness her reclaiming that passion, strangely nudges at my curiosity. She mentioned she'd be back here this weekend, and without fully realizing it, I find myself eager to see her ride the waves again.

As we walk along the shoreline, I spot her there in the distance—Daisy in all her glory, her wet suit glistening under the early morning sun. She rides the waves, her body moving with a grace that contradicts her recent heartbreak.

When she finally paddles back to shore, salt water dripping from her beachy blonde hair, a flush across her cheeks, she doesn't take long to spot Bentley and me. Her eyes instantly brighten, and my heart all but fucking stutters.

"Hey, stranger!" she calls out, panting slightly as she approaches. "Didn't expect to see you here this morning." She wedges her board into the sand, moving to give Bentley a scratch behind his ears.

"I could say the same," I say, although I know I'm lying through my teeth.

I wanted her to be here this morning—I was hoping for it—and it's half the reason I even trudged out here in the first place.

"I did tell you I was gonna get back on my board, didn't I?" she teases, nudging me with her shoulder as she wipes a droplet of water from her cheek.

The corner of my mouth twitches upward. "You did. Woman of your word."

We fall into a comfortable silence as Bentley trots along beside us, chasing after a tiny crab. It's easy, the way Daisy seems to fit into our quiet morning routines, our late-night strolls. And I find myself not missing the solitude so long as she's the one filling it.

"Thought you preferred to take your walks in the middle of the night?" she asks, giving me a curious stare.

"It's five in the morning." I huff a laugh. "That's practically the middle of the night if you ask me."

"Not usually an early riser?"

"These days, more often than not. But that first morning I ran into you? That was a bit of an accident. I, uh, I actually passed out here after a rough night."

"Late-night partying?"

"Nah, just tired from school, from work." I shift the conversation to something decidedly less heavy. "Not everyone can absolutely smash a bottle of strawberry wine and then still wake up for classes the next day."

"That was more of a onetime thing." She gives me a soft laugh as she bends forward, squeezing a bit of sea water from the ends of her hair. "Yesterday was rough for me."

A smirk tilts my lips. "I'm sure it was."

"Hey." She gives me a humorless snort. "Life's too short to stick to our safe, little routines. Don't you think?"

"If you say so."

"You know, I'm curious," she says, her gaze sweeping across my features. "What is that you're studying?"

"Electrical engineering." I scrub a hand across my forehead, blowing out a heated breath. "I'm in my final year of the program now. Took a year off after high school."

"So, that makes you . . ."

"Twenty-two."

"Hm, I just turned twenty-one over the summer."

I angle my head and give her a knowing look. "Should've guessed you were a summer baby."

"That's right." She beams at me, her soft, amber eyes sparkling in the sunrise. It's invigorating. Warm. All-encompassing. "And what are your plans after graduation? Any big dreams?"

My smile fades a little, and I scratch the back of my neck. "Don't know, really. Get a decent job in my field, move out of my apartment, get Bentley a yard to putz around in if he's still kicking."

"That sounds nice," she says sincerely, her eyes meeting mine. "What about in the far future?"

"Far future?" I quirk a brow. "You mean, like, retirement?"

"Yeah, like that."

"Never put much thought into it." I let out a breathy laugh. "Maybe a small house by the beach, a cottage in the woods, a steady job to keep me busy. Nothing fancy."

"That sounds perfect," she says softly, wistfully.

"What about you?"

"Maybe academia, research of some kind." She shrugs out of the top half of her wet suit, raking a hand through her damp hair. Then she pats the sandy spot next to her, a silent invitation. "I'd like to teach marine bio at the college level, I think."

Sitting down next to her, I unclip Bentley's collar, watching as he slowly dashes toward the receding waves. "That's your major?"

"Yeah. Fitting, right?"

"Very." Clearing my throat, I venture a bit further, "What's, uh, do you have a favorite thing about it?"

Her features brighten as she turns to face me. "I really love sea turtles."

"Yeah?"

"Yeah, well, all animals, really." She looks out at the ocean, her gaze softening. "But I think sea turtles are my favorite thing to study. Did you know that they use the Earth's magnetic field to navigate?"

"I didn't. But that's pretty cool."

"Right? It's incredible. I love how the ocean's full of so many mysteries." She stretches her arms high above her head, spine stiff from her morning surf. "Did you know that over ninety percent of its species have yet to be classified?"

My brows shoot up. "Really? That's fucking terrifying."

"No, it's amazing."

"I don't know, something about all that mystery kind of freaks me out."

"You mean, like, the universe in general?" Her eyes spark with mischief. "How it's constantly expanding? How there are probably three hundred and fifty billion galaxies out there just like ours, yet to be discovered."

I lean back on my hands, shooting her a wary look. "Jesus Christ," I mutter, the enormity of her words sinking in. "See, when you put it like that, it's pretty scary shit."

She tilts her head, looking at me curiously. "Why does that scare you?"

"Because we're all just so tiny, so meaningless."

"No, Elio, we're infinite." Her voice is soft, her expression sincere.

"I suppose that's a sweet way to look at it." My throat inexplicably tightens. "Very optimistic."

"For me, it's the only way to look at it." Her gaze flits back to the horizon, and a moment of silence stretches between us before she continues. "You know," she says, her voice dropping just a notch lower, "These moments with you. They're the first time in a while I've felt . . . calm. Serene, actually."

I shift in my spot, digging the toe of my shoe into the sand. "Yeah? I'm, uh, glad you could get yourself back out on the water."

She chuckles, shaking her head slightly. "Yeah, it's not just surfing, though. This . . . us, talking, not worrying about anything else." Her eyes meet mine, a vulnerability laid bare. "I'm really glad I met you."

Her honesty reaches into me, leaving a knot of emotion in my throat that I struggle to swallow. "Me too."

LATER THAT NIGHT, sleep's nearly impossible for me to come by.

Daisy's honesty, her resilience, her infectious passion—it all blends into my usually compartmentalized life. Somehow, she's already blurred the lines for me. The ones I've painstakingly drawn to separate myself, my family, and my personal life from everything else.

For the last five years, I've been living inside the Reynolds bubble, with Kaia being the only exception. And now, I'm not quite sure how to feel about popping it.

The reflection does bring me some clarity about Sapphire, though. I've realized that I can't extend her anything beyond what I'm already offering. I need those boundaries, those clear barriers that prevent my work life, Everett's life, from bleeding into the rest.

No matter how much I might like the proposed financial buffer, I can't afford to make an exception here. I also can't afford to overwork myself—not again.

So, I schedule a partner scene for next weekend. It's something local, a small commitment, with a woman I've worked with a handful of other times.

It should be simple and straightforward. And after allowing myself some much-needed rest, I'm finally feeling up to filming again. Besides, if it all works out, then the end product should tide me over for a few solid weeks.

# Chapter Ten

DAISY

I HAVEN'T LOGGED into AfterDark since the day I set up my account.

I've been distracting myself with surfing, with school, with my friends. It's been good, finding my balance again. Slipping back into the familiar rhythm of the ocean, the hush of the waves as they break against the shore. The pull of the current beneath my board.

It's home. It's healing.

There's a local surfing competition that I've been thinking about, too. It's nothing major but enough to keep my mind busy outside of classes. Their next big event isn't until April, six months away. Plenty of time to get myself back in tip-top shape. And who knows, I might even snag a trophy if luck's on my side.

Late at night, when the memories of Logan creep in, I remind myself about why I'm here—to be closer to the ocean, to pursue my dreams on my own terms. And a competition like this—setting an achievable goal—could help keep me focused, to remind me of my life's purpose.

That aside, there's still that nagging part of my brain pushing me to explore uncharted territories. My sexuality, my preferences, the pieces of me I never even thought to question before.

So, I decide to do something I haven't done since I first created the account—I log back in to AfterDark.

The site is just as I left it, filled with whispers of promises, hints of hidden desires. I browse through some profiles, my eyes scanning their bios, their likes, their kinks.

There's an adrenaline rush, a thrill in the unknown. It's new, it's exciting, but it's also kind of terrifying. I don't dive in headfirst, though. I take my time, skimming through profiles, taking notes of the ones that interest me the most.

It's kind of silly, but it helps me feel better to be so organized, so methodical about the process.

There are a lot of attractive men on here. Some that are young, some that are much older than my preferences, and some that don't fit with what I'm looking for at all. I still don't know if I should push myself out of my comfort zone from the get-go or if I should simply move toward what feels most natural.

After a while, I find a few that are definitely worth a closer look. A couple that pique my curiosity, tickle my interest. So, I jot down all their details in my notebook, and then I take the plunge, subscribing to them without looking back.

But just as quickly, I shut down my laptop, the reality of the situation sinking in. I'm not quite ready to watch any videos yet, to start up a web chat or join a texting room. I think I should just give it some time, take it slow.

Logan's parting words are still flitting around my head, and I don't want them to be the driving force behind all of this. Pushing me to explore this side myself just to prove him wrong.

Besides, the journey is the fun part, right? And it will always be there waiting for me when I'm ready.

. . .

THE NEXT MORNING, I'm up before the sun again. Slipping out of my car in the empty parking lot, I grab my New Flyer board, the leash bouncing against my leg as I make my way toward the beach.

The cool morning air nips at my skin, late summer finally giving way to my favorite season. Although it's chillier now, it's still so beautiful and fresh out here in the early morning—the stillness, the way everything feels suspended in time before the world wakes up.

Once I reach the shore, I take a moment to appreciate the scene before me. The water's a dark, tranquil blue under the pale dawn light. It's vast, open and free, and it feels like there's a world of possibilities stretching out before me.

Off to my right, there's a fishing pier that extends a few hundred feet into the water. At this hour, it stands desolate and quiet, its usual bustle of activity yet to come alive. But I've bumped into the guy who runs the place a couple of times, and he carries a certain charm that's impossible to ignore—always ready with a warm smile and a friendly wave.

Plus, he seems to have a soft spot for the lifeguard who works the weekend shifts. It's pretty cute, watching them steal quick glances at each other from across the beach, trying—and failing—to hide the way they flirt well into the late-morning hours.

I'll admit, I love the prospect of people-watching, especially following my morning surf. The silent exchanges, the quiet connections, stories being told in every smile and gesture.

It's not a busy scene at this time of day, but when someone inevitably shows up, it adds a touch of color to the hush of the beach.

Hoisting my board under my arm, I slowly wade into the ocean.

The initial chill of the water is stark, but soon, my body heat works in tandem with the insulation of my wet suit, gradually warding off the cold. It's a feeling I've come to love, to cherish, over the years.

It all brings me clarity—the cold touch of the sea, the slow warming of my heart.

With a deep breath, I paddle out, pushing through the familiar dance of waves. As I navigate through the rolling water, the mental fog lifts, washing away everything but the pulse of the ocean and the thrill of what's to come.

In the gentle lull of my movements, my thoughts inexplicably find their way to Elio. Our little talks, his quiet company, his soft brown eyes that seem to hide a world of stories. I'm hoping to see him out on the beach again, to share another morning under the hazy glow of dawn.

But after a few hours, when I've finally caught my breath on the beachfront, half peeled out of my wet suit, there's still no sign of him. And for the next three days, I find myself in the same predicament—constantly getting my hopes up for nothing.

Over the next couple of mornings, I make it a habit to visit the café where I ran into Elio, hoping for another chance encounter. By now, the staff likely recognize me—the early bird with the stack of textbooks, nursing a London Fog, along with a strawberry-and-cream-cheese muffin.

But despite my attempts, I keep coming up empty. No signs of Elio in sight.

I catch myself glancing at that blue doorway more often than I should, hoping to spot a mop of dark hair. Although it's only been a few days so far, his absence has left an odd sort of emptiness inside me. I've come to value our easy, flowing conversations and the comfortable silences we share.

Things feel simple between us, easy, like maybe we were meant to meet all along.

So, when Friday night rolls around and Max and LJ join us for a movie night at our place, I decide to probe for information.

Max was part of Coastal's engineering program as an undergraduate. He only finished his courses this past year, which makes it likely that they knew each other, at least in some capacity.

"Max," I say, my gaze flickering from the glow of the TV to his focused profile.

We're all huddled together in the dimmed living room, LJ curled into Max's side next to me, Gracie on her own in the reclining chair. The air is thick with the smell of buttery popcorn and the warm scent of our pumpkin spice candle.

He grunts a nonresponse, eyes still glued to the screen, tracking Cady Heron's every movement. You'd think he'd never seen *Mean Girls* before, but I know for a fact that it's at least his third time watching it.

"You knew some of the EE students here, right?" I ask, tucking my hands underneath my thighs.

He tilts his head away from the screen, sparing me just an ounce of his attention. "Yeah, we shared a lot of classes. Why?"

"Do you remember when I ran off on the beach last week to talk to that guy?"

He arches a skeptical brow. "Yeah, of course."

"Well, I can't seem to run into him again," I say, nervously picking at a loose thread on the couch cushion. "He said he's in his final year, part of the engineering department. His first name's Elio, so I thought maybe that's unique enough to—"

"You're talking about the Reynolds kid?"

"That's his last name?" I blink in surprise. "Reynolds?"

He chuckles, a smug grin curling the corners of his lips. "Yeah, it's Luca's little brother."

"Luca . . ." I murmur, my mind scrambling to connect the dots.

"Reynolds, Daze," he says. "He's been the star linebacker for the Bobcats for the past five years. An absolute unit on the field, over six feet tall, weighing around 230 pounds. Coastal alum—I mean, the guy's practically a local legend."

"Oh my God, really?" My head jerks back, and I don't even bother to question his alarming knowledge of Luca's stats. "You know, his wife, Harper, used to babysit me. We grew up in the same town near Cape Casserat."

"No shit?"

"Yeah, I don't know if she'd remember me, though. It was only a few times, like, ten years ago."

He slings an arm over the back of the couch. "You know she's the athletic trainer for our hockey team, right?"

"I know." I pull out my phone to set a quick reminder for myself. "And I've been meaning to go catch up with her but haven't quite had the time."

"Huh, it really is a small world, after all."

"Truly." I nibble on my lower lip, circling back. "So, is he, uh, do you know if Elio's into sports, too? Like his brother?"

"No, not exactly." He snorts, a faint smile playing on his lips. "Let's just say his interests lie . . . elsewhere."

"Like, he's just really into math and circuits?" I continue, leaning forward on the couch, eager to piece together his meaning.

He chuckles, rubbing the back of his neck. "Yeah, that's part of it. But what I meant is . . ." He trails off, his gaze drifting as he stumbles for the right words. After a moment, he turns back to me, his expression contrite. "Daisy, are you planning on pursuing something with this guy?"

Across the room, Gracie pauses mid-chew on her popcorn, glancing our way with a raised brow. Even LJ, who's been engrossed in a dog-eared paperback beside us, lifts her gaze, her interest officially sparked.

"No! Of course not," I blurt out, heat creeping up my cheeks. "I just got out of a long-term relationship. But Elio . . . he's cool, nice. Actually, he's really sweet, and like I already told Gracie—I feel like he could use a friend right now."

"Cool, nice, and sweet." He gives me a humorless snort, throwing a handful of popcorn into his mouth. "Sure. I mean, a friend could be good for him, especially since his partner in crime just went off to Dayton."

"Partner in crime?"

He nods, popping another kernel into his mouth. "Kaia Karras. His friend, his girlfriend, whatever she was at the time. They were practically attached at the hip up until last year. I thought she was aiming for our grad program, but she chose Dayton's instead. And now she's dating some hockey superstar, another graduate from our department."

"Interesting." I hum thoughtfully. "I think he may have mentioned her once before."

"Yeah, so . . . just be careful around him, will you?"

"Why?" I ask, knitting my brows. "You don't seem to know him all that well, Max."

"Let's just say I've heard a few things," he says abstrusely. "So, just . . . have your guard up."

"God, babe, can you stop being so cryptic for two seconds?" LJ chimes in, swatting his arm with her book.

"Yeah, I guess you're right." He sighs, his shoulders dropping. "You should make your own judgments about him, Daisy.

All I know is what I've heard through the grapevine. Once you really get to know him yourself, you'll figure things out."

"Okay." I nod, slightly unsettled by his words. "Do you . . . know of any way for me to contact him, then?"

"Well, you know his last name now," he says, rubbing his chin thoughtfully. "You could just email him through our Coastal accounts. Or I think I have Kaia's number from a project we worked on. I could ask her for his number?"

"Would that be too weird, though? Too stalker-ish?" I rub nervously at my temples, second-guessing myself.

"Up to you." He shrugs. "You're the one who's spoken to him the most. Do you think he'd mind?"

"No, I don't think so." I shake my head, slinking back into the couch. "He seemed to like talking to me well enough. Besides, we're all at a big school in a tiny town. We've got to make connections where we can."

"Alright," he concedes, pulling out his phone. "I'll text her for you, then."

As Max taps out his message, Gracie and LJ exchange a subtle glance, a silent form of communication I can't quite decipher. I'm sure they think they're being protective of me in their own way, but they can save their judgments for someone else.

I know what I'm doing, and I'm certainly not afraid of a little challenge.

# Chapter Eleven

## ELIO

Sapphire's on my ass, and I can't seem to catch a break.

She isn't taking my rejection kindly. My inbox has been overflowing with her incessant demands, her ill-informed complaints, all week. She's relentless, even roping in some of her friends to make the same requests, as if to catch me in some kind of lie.

It's twisted, fucked-up how she can't seem to grasp the simplest of concepts.

I've tried reasoning with her, explaining that there are boundaries I've decided not to cross—not with any subscriber, not with any client. But she exploded on me. The anger seeped through her messages, eventually devolving into desperate pleas and guilt trips.

So, I blocked her, hoping to put an end to it all.

But the internet is relentless, and she keeps returning—new accounts, fresh subscriptions, and more messages laden with different demands. It's as if I'm being stalked in my own domain—well, Everett's domain—and the pressure is starting to get to me.

It's so bad that I've shut down this week's web chat requests altogether. It's the first time I've done something like that since I started my channel, but I need space. My professional cool is slipping, my detachment eroding.

My carefully constructed life—separate boxes for academics, AfterDark, and my personal life—is bleeding into one mess of a battleground. Now, just when I thought I was finally regaining my footing, I'm starting to lose control.

Even Bentley is affected by the changes. We've fallen into a comfortable routine over the past few weeks—our late-night strolls, our early morning walks—but all of that's been thrown off now. And I can tell he's just as unhappy about it as I am.

After another exhausting day of navigating through the chaos, I slump onto the couch, feeling defeated. Bentley jumps up beside me, his tail wagging as he nuzzles his head into my side. I stroke his soft fur, my movements slow and gentle, and it's oddly calming.

"Hey, buddy," I mutter, running my fingers along the length of his spine. "This whole thing is just . . . It's all a fucking mess."

Bentley just looks up at me, his ears perked, his eyes wide and attentive as if he's trying to understand. I know it sounds absurd, talking to a dog about my problems, but Bentley's a great listener. He's always there, ready to lend an ear without passing judgment.

He may be just a dog and only half-mine, but I've never been more glad to have him by my side. Over the past year, and especially now with Kaia gone, the good ol' boy has become my rock.

When my older sister, Taylor, first asked me to take him in, I wasn't certain it was the right choice for either of us.

I didn't know if I'd be able to care for him the way he deserves, considering his old age and my busy schedule. But now, we depend on each other. I've tried my best to be there for him, to give him everything he wants and needs. And I'm happy, lucky even, that I was tasked with his care.

Because right now, with my world feeling more like quicksand than solid ground, I need him more than ever.

As I mindlessly talk to him, stroking his thick fur, I find myself gradually relaxing, the tension seeping from my shoulders. His eyes eventually close, his body goes slack against mine, and before long, we both drift off to sleep right there on the couch.

I WAKE UP WITH A START, disoriented and cramped from an uncomfortable night. Bentley's half-sprawled on top of me, his snoring filling the quiet living room. Wriggling out from under him without disturbing his sleep, I grimace at the stiffness in my neck and back.

*Mental note: Never sleep on the fucking couch again.*

I grab my phone off the coffee table and squint at the too-bright screen. It's just past seven in the morning, and there's already a new message waiting for me. My pulse kicks up a notch as I open the text, worried that Sapphire's already found another way to track me down.

Thankfully, it's not from her or any one of her other creepy pseudonyms. It's from someone I'd never expect to be seeking me out.

UNKNOWN

hey, stranger. this is daisy. you know, from the beach. I hope you don't mind but I asked around for your number

ELIO

I don't mind. hi, daisy.

DAISY

oh! hi! I missed seeing you around this week! we should meet up if you're not too busy

I'm not sure how she managed to get my number, especially since I've been keeping a low profile ever since Kaia left. But I don't find myself annoyed or put off by it—quite the opposite, actually.

There's a sense of warmth in her message, a sincere effort to connect that's vastly different from my experiences with Sapphire—her relentless demands and expectations. In contrast, Daisy's approach feels genuine. Endearing, even. She's not intruding, not invading my privacy.

She's just . . . simply reaching out.

As I think about my answer, there's a flicker of peace that I haven't felt in a while. It's been an intense week, to say the least, and the prospect of seeing Daisy—of spending time outside the constraints of my work life, my academics—seems like it could be a nice distraction.

ELIO

what did you have in mind?

DAISY

want to go on a bike ride to this little ice cream place? I've been craving something strawberry

you mean the golden cone? I actually don't have a bike

yes! & no worries, you can borrow my friend max's

I stir, shaking off the lethargic weight of sleep. A bike ride with Daisy could provide a much-needed change of pace, but there's a small part of me that's already worrying about the work I've yet to do.

Tonight, I'm supposed to film my first partnered scene in a long while. It's a step I've been reluctant to take after my last panic attack—or whatever the hell that was—which sidelined me out of nowhere. But it's a move I need to make, if only to tide me over for a while and keep my subscriptions steady.

It's not that I'm wholly unprepared for it; I've been doing this for long enough to know what needs to be done. But it's not something I can rush through. I'll need to pace myself, focus on staying relaxed and comfortable. If I wear myself out during the day, then there's no guarantee I'll be on my A game when the time comes.

I tap out a quick response to Daisy, reminding myself that I can just take it easy on the ride. It's a simple enough combination—biking, ice cream, and a girl who helps my brain relax. There's no chance of this derailing my plans.

ELIO

yeah, okay. send me your address and I can be there by lunch

I send off the message, already picturing the warm sun, the gentle coastal breeze, and the company of someone who just wants me for me. Elio Reynolds, not Everett Rain. Someone who isn't asking anything more of me than a bike ride and a scoop of strawberry ice cream.

THE DAY IS HEATING up when I arrive at Daisy's place, the sun high and bright in the clear sky. I've donned my usual casual attire—dark jeans, a simple T-shirt—but this time, I've swapped my boots for a pair of old sneakers better suited for bike riding.

Daisy looks exactly like I remember. Her amber eyes are sparkling with anticipation, her bright, blonde hair loose and tousled from the breeze. She's wearing these little denim shorts and a loose white top that highlights her sun-kissed cheeks.

When she spots me, her smile is as warm and welcoming as the Carolina sun.

"Hey, El," she greets, her voice light, wistful.

I give her an easy grin, and she points to the pair of bikes resting against the side of her complex. Hers is bright yellow with a little basket hanging off the front, while Max's is a plain blue—sleek and discreet.

"You up for an adventure?" she asks.

"Not sure I have another option."

As we mount our bikes, she laughs while I stumble, working to regain my footing.

"Try to keep up, okay?" she says, already pedaling away. I follow her as closely as I can, navigating around parked cars and pedestrians to make our way toward the road.

We ride together for a while, quickly falling into a comfortable silence. The soft hush of tires against asphalt, the distant hum of traffic, the occasional birdcall—all merge into a calming backdrop. It's the first moment of genuine peace I've felt all week, and I revel in it.

Every so often, Daisy glances back at me, a cheeky smile on her lips. "Are you sure you can ride that thing? You look a bit wobbly."

"I've got it all under control," I call back, steadying myself. The fact that I haven't ridden a bike since middle school isn't something she needs to know.

"Really?" she asks, a teasing lilt in her voice. She swerves slightly, almost causing me to veer off the sidewalk. "Because it looks like you're about to crash into that tree."

I shoot her a faux scowl, adjusting my course just in time to avoid it. "Funny. You ride like a feral child, you know that?"

She just laughs, pedaling even faster. "Life's too short for safe biking. Live a little."

Her words echo in my mind, and despite everything, I find myself snorting a laugh. This is exactly what I fucking needed —a real, honest break. A hint of carefree normalcy for once.

"So, where were you this week?" She tosses the question over her shoulder. "I thought for sure I'd catch you on the beach or maybe the café again."

"Just busy with work, with school."

"Work, huh?" She glances back at me again, brows tightly knit. "What do you do for work, anyway?"

Her question rings in the air, and I hesitate for a moment. It's not that I'm ashamed of my job. Hell, it's not even that I think Daisy would judge me for it. It's just that . . . work is work. It's not who I am, not who I want to be when I'm with her.

And it can be a lot to explain to someone who's not familiar with that world.

"I work online," I say, giving her a half-truth. "Freelance stuff. It keeps me busy."

"Sounds mysterious." There's a pause, and I can tell she's trying to read me. I don't blame her for being curious. But it's a curiosity I can't quite meet, not yet. I want to keep things simple between us, easygoing, for as long as I can.

"And didn't you say you like mystery?"

A laugh bubbles from her throat. "Exactly," she calls back to me, pedaling on ahead.

For the next few miles, Daisy and I continue biking down the quiet streets of our small coastal town. The casual chatter, her laughter echoing in the otherwise quiet morning, it all feels *normal* . . . so damn normal that it takes my breath away.

Unfortunately, reality has a way of cutting in when I least expect it.

We're only three blocks away from the Golden Cone when

I feel it—a sharp, stabbing pain right in the center of my chest. My heart hammers erratically, the world tilting sideways as I lose my balance and tumble off the bike.

I hit the asphalt hard, pain radiating from my shoulder where I landed, but it's nothing compared to the thundering ache inside my rib cage. It's like someone is squeezing my heart in a vise, each heartbeat jarring, unnatural, like it's ripping me apart from the inside out.

"Daisy," I manage to choke out, my vision blurring at the edges. I press a hand to my chest, trying to bring myself back to Earth, but the pain doesn't subside. It only gets worse.

I can vaguely hear her calling my name, but her voice sounds so far away, as if I'm underwater. She's at my side in an instant, her hand on my shoulder.

"Elio?" she sounds panicked, her eyes wide and frightened. I try to tell her I'm okay, that I just need a moment, but the words won't come.

Instead, everything goes dark.

# Chapter Twelve

DAISY

It all happens so fast.

One moment, we're laughing, racing toward the ice cream shop, and then, in the blink of an eye, Elio's gripping his chest, gasping for air before he tumbles onto the asphalt.

His bike skates away, careening into the distance, but my attention is riveted to his prone form. Braking abruptly, I barely manage to keep my balance as I scramble to help.

"El!" I yell, dropping to my knees beside him.

His eyes are closed, his face ashen, lips slightly parted as he takes in shallow, irregular breaths. His pulse is quick under my trembling fingertips, erratic and stuttering, like a drummer with a shitty sense of rhythm.

I pull my phone out of my pocket with my other hand, dialing 911 with shaking fingers.

"You'll be okay," I whisper to him, hoping he can hear me even though his eyes remain shut.

I tuck my phone away and gently position his head in my lap, his dark hair soft under my touch. He's flushed, semiconscious but still stirring, so I pour a bit of water from my bottle onto his face, hoping the coolness might rouse him.

"Elio," I murmur, stroking his sweat-damp hair back from his forehead. "Can you hear me?"

The minutes stretch into what feels like an eternity, the silence between his gasps punctuated by the sound of my pulse pounding in my ears. Then, finally, his eyelids flutter open. They're heavy, dazed, but it's the most beautiful sight I've seen all day.

"Wha' happened?" he manages to rasp out, his voice so faint I can barely hear him.

I squeeze his hand gently, relief flooding through me. "Oh, thank God. You, um, you just fell out of nowhere. But don't worry, I called an ambulance," I rush to add. "They'll be here soon."

He attempts a weak nod, closing his eyes again as he takes a shaky breath. I can still feel his heartbeat fluttering under my palm, too fast, too uneven, but at least it's there.

Sirens wail in the distance, growing steadily louder until it fills our quiet street. An ambulance rounds the corner, lights flashing. Two EMTs jump out, equipment in hand, as I call out, "Over here!"

They rush toward us, their movements quick and efficient as they kneel down next to Elio. One of them is talking to me, asking questions about what happened, but my attention is fixed firmly on the broken boy beside me.

His eyes are closed again, his face pale and sweaty.

It's strange seeing him so vulnerable, so unlike the carefree guy who'd been teasing me just minutes ago. But one thing is clear: I need to be strong for both of us now. Elio needs someone to be there for him, and I'm not about to let him down.

"Just hold on," I whisper, brushing his hair back as the EMTs begin their work. "It's all going to be okay."

Once he's stabilized, strapped down, and placed inside the ambulance, they all head off to the hospital. And I'm left here, alone, standing in the middle of the deserted street. I scramble to pull out my phone, my hands trembling as I dial Gracie's number.

"Hey," I begin, my voice breaking. "Can you come pick me up from Pacific Street? Elio . . . he's been taken to the hospital."

"Oh, my God. Yes, just drop me a pin, and I'll be there as soon as possible." There's a distinct rustling in the background and then the sound of a car door opening. "What happened?"

I explain the best I can between hiccups and shaky breaths. I tell her about the bike ride, the sudden collapse, and all the air squeezing out of my lungs.

"Could you take me to Harbor Point Hospital?" I finally ask, my throat tight as her ignition turns.

"Okay," she says, voice steady and reassuring. "I'll be there as fast as I can. And hey . . . he's gonna be okay, you know? You did everything you possibly could."

"I really fucking hope so."

Hanging up, I sit on the curb, cradling my head in my hands. The uncertainty of the situation crashes over me, leaving me numb and confused. But I try my best to hold my shit together for the time being.

When Gracie arrives, I've managed to calm my breathing and push down the panic. She doesn't ask any questions, just wraps an arm around me and helps me into her car. The drive to the hospital is silent, save for the occasional reassurances she whispers in my direction.

"I'm sure he's fine, Daze. It's probably just a little scare." Her words don't quite soothe the ache in my chest, but they're enough to keep me going for now.

Unfortunately, Harbor Point's waiting room is just as terrifying as I'd imagined. The sterile scent of antiseptic, the muted hush, the intermittent whispers—it all adds to my anxiety.

Time seems to stretch out before me, each second feeling like a lifetime.

"I'm here." Gracie's voice pulls me from my thoughts. "It shouldn't be too long now."

We stay seated in the rigid plastic chairs for what seems like an eternity, although in reality, it's probably just a few agonizing minutes. Every once in a while, Gracie tries to engage me in light conversation to take my mind off the situation, but her words barely register.

It feels wrong thinking about anything else when Elio's lying in a hospital bed. I don't fully know what happened out there, and my mind keeps playing the worst-case scenarios on a loop. Even though we just met a few weeks ago, it's like he's already slipping away from me, evaporating like smoke in the wind.

I'm not sure I know him well enough to provide him the comfort he needs. So, I contemplate reaching out to Kaia.

In a moment like this, he could find solace in the presence of someone familiar, someone he knows well and trusts. But then again, I don't know where they stand, and I don't want to intrude on an unfamiliar dynamic.

Thankfully, I don't have to make a decision right now. A nurse has just entered the waiting room, and she's here calling for me. "Daisy Grey?" she asks, and I nod my confirmation, standing from my seat. "Mr. Reynolds has been asking for you."

Gracie and I follow her, and she leaves us at the door of his room, telling me to call if I need anything. Before I enter, I turn back to my friend.

"You should go home," I tell her, "I want to stay with Elio for a while, and I'll find us a ride later on. Thank you for bringing me here, for waiting with me."

She looks like she wants to protest, but she only nods, squeezing my hand just once before she leaves.

Taking a deep breath, I step into Elio's room. The sight of him lying on the hospital bed, looking so vulnerable and fragile, wraps my insides into a tight coil. But I swallow it down and force a smile.

"Hey, stranger," I greet him, trying to keep my voice light and steady. His eyes flicker toward me, and the relief that washes over his face tugs at my heart. I pull a chair up to his bed and reach for his hand, holding it gently in my own.

"Jesus, what happened?" he finally asks, his voice a raspy whisper.

I squeeze his fingers, trying to offer some sort of comfort. "I don't really know. You were gasping for air, and you . . . you just fell. It was like you couldn't breathe, and then . . . then you just went limp." I choke on the words, my throat tightening as I relive the horrifying moments. "I called 911. They carted you away."

There's a silence between us then, a heavy pause that fills the air as Elio absorbs my words. His gaze flits over to the machines beside his bed, to the wires and tubes that extend from his arms, then back to me. He's quiet for a long moment before he speaks again.

"I'm sorry, I didn't mean to scare you," he says, and there's something about those simple words that cuts right through me.

He didn't ask for this. He didn't want to end up in a hospital bed any more than I wanted to see him here. And yet, he's the one apologizing.

Before I can say anything else, a knock sounds at the door and a doctor strides in, clipboard in hand.

"Hello, Mr. Reynolds. I'm Dr. Foster." He glances at me

then, a hint of surprise in his gaze. "Would you prefer if we have this conversation in private?"

Elio doesn't miss a beat. "No, it's okay. She can stay."

The doctor nods, then turns his attention back to Elio. "You gave us quite a scare there, young man. We ran some tests to determine what might've caused your collapse."

"Was it . . . a heart attack?"

"No," the doctor responds, flipping through the pages on his clipboard. "Your blood tests and initial EKG don't indicate a myocardial infarction."

"Then what was it?"

"We're still trying to figure that out," Dr. Foster says. "The paramedics noted an irregular heartbeat when you were brought in, but we'll need to do further testing to determine what might've caused it. I do see in your records a history of drug use, specifically cocaine."

"I've been clean for five years," Elio interjects, his voice firm.

"Even past use of such substances can have long-term effects on the heart," he says, gaze narrowing slightly as if he's not fully convinced.

I can't help but chime in then, feeling the need to defend him. "Isn't there something else you can do? Another EKG or a cardiac MRI, maybe?"

The doctor turns his attention to me, his gaze softening a bit. "We've already conducted the EKG upon his arrival and will perform further tests. As for the cardiac MRI, we'll have to see if his condition stabilizes first. In the meantime, we'll monitor him closely."

He leaves us then, promising to return with any further updates.

Elio lies back against the hospital pillows, the energy

completely drained out of him. His hand reaches out in search of mine, and I give it willingly, letting our fingers curl together.

"I'm sorry for dragging you into this shit," he murmurs, his thumb stroking the back of my hand.

I shake my head, swallowing the lump in my throat. "Don't apologize to me. I'm just glad I was there with you to help. I'm sorry . . . If I pushed you too hard with the bike ride and—"

"None of this is your fault, okay? We couldn't have known this would happen."

"Yeah, okay."

We fall into silence, the steady beep of the heart monitor filling the room. But it's not an uncomfortable silence. It's the kind that feels safe, warm.

This is where I'm meant to be, with him, even though it scares the hell out of me. But whatever I'm feeling now, it's different than anything I've felt before—for my other friends, even for Logan.

It's fear and concern, yes, but it's also something deeper. Somehow, some way, it feels a lot like . . . attachment.

# Chapter Thirteen

## ELIO

I WAKE up to the alarming sounds of medical machinery, the smell of antiseptic, and a sterile, white ceiling hanging above me. A sickening sense of déjà vu hits me, the familiarity of the scene unsettling, to say the least.

My head throbs, and I wince at the memory of the pain from earlier, hoping that it was another random fluke and not a forewarning of things to come. But then, there's a comforting squeeze on my hand, and I turn my head to see Daisy—her warm brown eyes, the tiny little scar above her left eyebrow, and that soft, blonde hair that halos around her face.

*Fuck*, she sure is a sight for sore eyes.

"I'm sorry," I rasp, the words scratchy in my dry throat. "How long have I been out?"

Daisy takes a deep breath, the corners of her mouth twitching upward in a piss-poor attempt at a smile. "Just about half an hour. Don't worry about me, though. You need your rest."

"Okay," I croak out, reluctantly turning onto my side, not bothering to fight the drowsiness any longer. Because no matter how hard I try, I can't seem to keep my eyes open in this place.

I'm in the hospital for the rest of the day, drifting in and out of a restless sleep. They run some more tests, wheel me in a meal, and then I pass right back out. Through it all, Daisy remains by my side, a comforting presence in the cold, clinical room.

With her help, I manage to get in touch with my brother, Luca. He's the only one I trust to not blow this whole thing out of proportion. Our parents tend to overreact, and the last thing I need right now is more fucking stress.

"Hey, I'm at Harbor Point," I tell him over the phone, trying to sound nonchalant. "Had a bit of a scare, but I'm okay now. They're still not quite sure what happened—some heart issue, I guess."

"Fuck, El," he says roughly. "You're good now, though? You're stable?"

"Yeah, for now. Just about to get discharged. If you're not too busy, er, if you're around, that is—could you give me and my friend a lift home?"

He agrees without hesitation, and an ounce of tension seeps out of my body.

I spend the next hour waiting for Luca in a haze, my mind running wild with questions. *Why did this happen? How did this happen? Will it happen again?*

Dr. Foster's still uncertain, just as useless and confused as I am. He continues to assure me that I didn't have a heart attack, that I'm stable for the time being, but that's where his comforting words end.

Instead, he's sending me home with a parting gift—a Holter monitor. It's a simple-looking device that carries the heavy responsibility of cataloging my every heartbeat. I have to wear it constantly for the next two weeks, and while I hate the idea, I know it's a necessary evil.

But it also means I have two more weeks of waiting, two more weeks filled with uncertainty.

I'm supposed to go about my daily activities as much as

possible while avoiding any unnecessary strain. If it wasn't immediately obvious, partner scenes are off the table for the time being.

"Alright, Mr. Reynolds," Dr. Foster begins, snapping on a pair of latex gloves. He rolls over to me on a squeaky stool and searches beneath my shirt to attach the monitor. The whole ordeal is uncomfortable, not because of the cold gel or the slight tug as he attaches the leads, but because of the look of worry in Daisy's eyes as she watches from across the room. "Remember, any chest pain, difficulty breathing, or severe weakness needs to be reported to us immediately, okay?"

I nod, acutely aware of how quiet the room has gone. It's just the three of us: me, Daisy, and Dr. Foster, who's focused on my chest as he attaches the monitor.

Daisy's eyes are locked onto me, filled with something I can't quite decipher. Worry, definitely, but also a strange, fierce determination that catches me off guard.

"Do you live alone, Mr. Reynolds?" Dr. Foster's question cuts through the silence like a knife, his eyes still focused on the monitor.

I nod, finding my voice. "Yeah."

He clicks his tongue, finishing up with the wires. "I'd strongly recommend having someone stay with you for a little while. The next two weeks are crucial. If you experience a recurrence of today's episode and there's nobody there to help, the outcome may not be the same as today. Do you have a partner or a family member who could stay with you?"

A lump forms in my throat. I don't have a roommate or a partner, and the thought of having my family hovering over me for the next two weeks isn't exactly comforting. Before I can answer, Daisy stands up, the chair scraping against the linoleum.

"I can stay with him," she offers.

I whip my head around to look at her, my chest tightening. "Daisy, you don't have to—"

"Really, it's no problem," she insists, crossing her arms as if that could fortify her position.

I want to argue, to tell her she's done enough for a guy she barely fucking knows, but the words catch in my throat. I feel like I'm teetering on the edge of a cliff, one wrong move from tumbling into a chasm.

Dr. Foster raises his eyebrows, looking between the two of us. "Well, if Ms. . . . ?"

"Grey," she offers, her gaze never leaving mine.

"Right, if Ms. Grey is willing to stay with you and you're comfortable with it, I think that's an excellent plan," he says, peeling off his gloves and tossing them into a nearby bin. "It's essential to have someone nearby in case there are any complications, especially during the first few days. Ms. Grey, I'm sure the nursing staff can provide you with basic instructions on what to look for and what to do if he has another episode."

Daisy nods, her gaze flickering between Dr. Foster and me, her determination unwavering. It's a look I've come to recognize in the past few weeks, a look that tells me she's not going to be easily dissuaded.

She's essentially offering to uproot her life to stay with me, to help me during one of the most uncertain times of mine. The gratitude I feel is overwhelming, but there's also a strange twinge of guilt mixed in.

"Are you sure about this?" I ask her quietly once Dr. Foster has left the room.

She gives me a small, understanding smile. "I'm sure, Elio," she says softly. "I've got you. Besides, you're not, like, a murderer or anything, right?"

"I suppose you'll find out soon enough."

Her soft snort of laughter fills the room, easing a fraction of the tension. "I'll take my chances," she says, standing up. "I'll go find a nurse for those instructions."

Left alone in the room, I find myself staring at the ceiling, the events of the day weighing heavy on my mind. My chest feels strange, not painful, but definitely not normal, either.

This Holter monitor is just an unfamiliar weight. And its wires, hidden under my shirt, feel like a leash, a constant reminder of my condition.

When Luca finally arrives, he opts to call me from the parking lot to avoid disturbing the other patients. An NFL player showing up at a hospital, seemingly out of the blue, is generally a cause for commotion. So, I'm glad he had the forethought to keep things discreet.

With Daisy's help, I settle into the wheelchair provided by one of the nurses, her every move exuding care and caution. As we approach Luca's truck, he remains tight-lipped, but the concern glinting in his eyes speaks volumes.

The ensuing car ride is largely silent, each of us wrapped up in our own thoughts. I can practically see the gears turning in Luca's head as he navigates both the road and his concern. Eventually, though, he cuts through the quiet. "Still no concrete answers?"

I shake my head, glancing down at the monitor under my shirt, patting it with a firm hand. "Yeah, they still don't know what caused it. Might just be stress, a panic attack, a random spike of adrenaline. Who the hell knows? But they're hoping this will give them some answers."

His gaze is fixed on the road, but his fears hang heavy in the air. "And this has nothing to do with . . . coke or anything like that?"

The abruptness of the question feels like a sharp slap to the face. I know he has every right to ask, but it still stings. I've been clean for years, and hearing the question brings back a surge of unwanted memories.

"I'm clean, Luc," I assure him, meeting his gaze in the rearview mirror.

He blows out a breath, and the relief in his eyes brings me a strange sense of comfort. It feels good to know that he still takes me at my word. "Good. Stay that way," he says, his voice carrying a brotherly sternness I haven't heard in years.

As we reach my apartment, he claps me on the shoulder before stepping back toward his truck. "Call me if anything changes, okay? Don't make me regret not telling our parents."

I give him a small smile, hiding the fear creeping into my heart. "I promise."

"Good to meet you," Daisy squeaks out, her sweet voice carrying across the lot.

Luca turns, as if he's just now realized we've had company this whole time. A flash of red heat creeps up the back of his neck, and he awkwardly clears his throat. "Right, sorry," he says. "Good to meet you, too. Take care of my brother, will you?"

She gives him a beaming smile. "I'll try my best."

As he pulls away, we're left standing alone in the parking lot.

"Daisy," I begin, her name sounding oddly formal in the cool night air. "You know you don't have to do this, right? If you just said all that to get Dr. Foster off our backs, I don't blame you."

She glances up at me, surprise etched on her face. "Elio, I wasn't fibbing," she says with such conviction. "It's really no trouble. My roommate will barely notice I'm gone. And I can just sleep on your couch."

"You're okay camping out with a near stranger?"

She chuckles. "You're hardly a stranger. By now, I feel like I've known you forever. Besides, I'll let my friends know where I am and how to get in touch. It's not as if I'll be disappearing off the face of the planet."

"I could just get one of those Life Alert devices or something."

She shakes her head, adamant. "You're not getting out of this that easily."

"Okay," I say. "But I don't want to feel indebted to you . . . If there's anything you want, anything you need, you just let me know."

Her playful smile widens. "I'll think of something, don't you worry about that."

"Alright." I run a ragged hand through my hair, clear my throat, and then, "That's good."

"I need to go and grab a few things from my place, though," she says, pulling out her phone and tapping out a quick text. "Gracie's gonna pick me up, but not until after you're all settled in."

"I can handle one measly flight of stairs and a quick sprawl onto my couch."

She gives me a stern look, one that's all too endearing. "Just humor me, alright? Besides, it wouldn't hurt you to have an extra pair of hands."

"Fine," I say, fighting a grin.

As we climb the steps to my apartment, the absence of daylight presses on my consciousness. I'm supposed to be filming a scene with Alex in less than twenty minutes, and my phone is a fucking dead weight in my pocket.

Once again, I'm the unreliable one, the flake, ducking out on a coworker without any notice. And this time, I didn't even have the decency to send a quick text first.

Not to mention, my apartment is a mess. I'm not at all prepared for a guest—let alone one who's about to become my temporary roommate. I know there are probably forgotten pizza boxes, strewn laundry, and miscellaneous items scattered around my living room.

We finally reach my door, and I fumble with my keys, an echo of the nerves creeping up my spine. I can't ignore the reality of what's happening here: Daisy's going to be living with me, in my personal space, for fourteen long days.

For better or worse, there's no going back now.

As I push the door open, I cast a quick glance back at her. She smiles at me again, something so soft and so sweet. And under the faint hallway light, she seems wholly unfazed, her constant presence soothing the doubts churning inside me.

"Welcome to my little corner of the world," I mutter, struggling to keep my voice steady. "And, well, our home for the next two weeks."

# Chapter Fourteen

## DAISY

As the night closes in, I settle into the passenger seat of Gracie's car. The streets are barely lit, but she navigates the route to our apartment with the ease of familiarity. It's quiet between us for a while, my mind spinning while Gracie obviously attempts to hold her tongue.

"So, you're really doing this, huh?" she finally asks, her voice barely audible over the hum of the engine.

"Yeah, it looks that way."

"You know, I have nothing against Elio, personally. But you barely know him," she says softly, carefully. "Staying at his place for two weeks feels a bit extreme, don't you think?"

"I know it sounds bizarre, but . . . it just feels right to do this," I say, struggling to find the right words. "He's not in a good place, Grace, and he's basically all alone. I can't just abandon him. Besides, you're the one who was surprised I hadn't roped him into lifelong friendship."

She sighs, the sound filled with unspoken words. "It's just—you're just so trusting, Daze," she says, but she doesn't push the matter any further.

Once we get home, I pack a bag, shoving in some clothes, my toothbrush, and a couple of books. Just when I'm about to zip it up, my gaze lands on the bottom drawer of my dresser . . . the same one I've been avoiding for weeks now.

My fingers twitch, itching to yank it open, to confront the

past hiding within. The smiling faces of Logan and me, frozen in a moment of pure joy and blissful ignorance. We'd been so happy once, so foolishly in love.

But that feels like a lifetime ago now.

With a shaky breath, I pull the drawer open, the old photo frame catching the faint light in the room. I toss it into the trash bin beside my desk, and a pang of longing hits me as I slam the drawer shut, the ghost of what we had lingering in the air.

Taking a deep breath, I hoist my bag over my shoulder, forcing myself to focus on the task ahead. This isn't about me; it's about Elio. I don't have room to dwell right now.

I drive back to his place alone in my own car, my mind buzzing. I remember how eerily quiet it was when I left, how defeated Elio seemed. The image of him sitting inside his apartment, so vulnerable and exhausted, has my stomach reeling.

When I make it up to the entryway, it's dark and silent. I knock a couple of times, but there's no answer, so I fish the spare key out of my pocket and let myself inside. And there's Elio, all curled up on the couch, fast asleep, with Bentley tucked snugly against his side.

As I close the door, tiptoeing through the living room, Bentley's wide brown eyes flicker open, his tail wagging at the sight of me. I pet him for a bit, but my gaze is fixed on his owner. His sleep is fitful, his brows furrowing even in slumber.

Tenderness washes over me, and before I know it, I'm kneeling down beside him, pushing back a few unruly strands of hair from his forehead. His skin is warm under my touch but not quite fevered like it was before.

"Elio," I whisper, hating to disturb his rest but knowing it's necessary. "You should really sleep in your bed."

"Nah," he mumbles sleepily. "You take it."

"No way. I'll take the couch."

He groans, running a hand over his face before reluctantly sitting up. He looks so adorable, all sleepy and ruffled, and it takes everything in me not to audibly coo at him.

"Yeah, wait," he rasps. "I need to put fresh sheets on the bed before I let you sleep in it."

As we make our way to his bedroom, I notice the slight hesitation in his movements, a flash of something that might be embarrassment in his eyes. But he doesn't say anything, just leads me to a small closet where he keeps his linen.

Together, we strip the bed and replace the sheets. Elio's so focused on tightening the corners that he doesn't notice my glances or how I watch the way his muscles flex when he tugs the fitted sheet into place.

It's an oddly domestic moment, one that's shared in a quiet, half-lit room. A certain kind of intimacy I hadn't expected.

"Please take the bed. At least for tonight," I say, gathering my hair and pulling it behind my shoulder. "You just got out of the hospital, and you need a good night's rest."

"Okay." He scrubs a hand across his forehead. "But I'm only doing this because I'm so fucking tired, and I don't have the energy to argue with you." Then, visibly exhausted, he sinks onto the freshly made bed, his eyes already drifting closed. "Just give me a few minutes," he murmurs.

I chuckle, tucking the blanket around him before retreating to the living room. Of course, Bentley's still waiting for me there on the couch. I whisper a soft good-night, pat him on the head, and curl up beside him, quickly falling into my own fitful sleep.

. . .

When morning comes, I wake up early, my internal clock set by years of surfing. Honestly, the couch is kind of comfy, especially because my shorter height allows for the perfect fit.

I spend a few minutes freshening up in the guest bathroom. Then, I try my best to keep quiet while maneuvering around Elio's kitchen. His fridge is nearly empty, his cupboards bare save a box of Cinnamon Toast Crunch cereal.

So, I grab my jacket and head out, deciding to pick up breakfast from my new favorite café.

The morning air is crisp and cool as I make the short drive down the street, windows cracked, the quiet coastal streets slowly coming alive. The Seashell is just opening, and I put in an order for an Americano, a London Fog, two strawberry muffins, and a half dozen bagels.

From a flower stand on my way back, I pick up a single, vibrant sunflower—a burst of color to brighten up our morning.

When I return to the apartment, I quietly unlock the door, careful not to make any loud, sudden noises. Instantly, I'm met with Elio's familiar scent, something warm and spicy that I've come to associate with him.

I take my time setting the food out on the table, neatly arranging everything. The bagels and pastries are set out on plates, coffee cups filled, and the tiny tubs of cream cheese opened.

Now, I'm on the hunt for a vase. I rummage through his cabinets but come up empty. Not one to be defeated, I grab a tall drinking glass, fill it with water, and place the sunflower right smack-dab in the center.

Once everything's set, I step back and survey my handiwork. The small table in Elio's kitchen is transformed, and I can't help but smile at the sight. It's warm and homey—a sweet reception for someone who's just had one hell of a day.

Smoothing out the wrinkles in my dress, I head down the hallway to knock on Elio's bedroom door. There's a faint shuffling sound before it swings open. And then, the man of the hour appears.

His hair is wet and tousled, droplets of water trailing down his neck and disappearing under a towel that's slung low around his hips. My breath catches as I take in the sight—his toned torso, beads of water accentuating every vein and muscle, and the intricate linework tattoos decorating both arms.

There's a lifelike butterfly above his right elbow and a small flock of birds taking flight from his bicep. Both thick arms are intertwined with vines, accentuated by sequences of the number 3. A little broken dog bone lies near his wrist. And on his inner forearm, there's a detailed drawing of a woman, with a snake that slithers on beside her.

Symbols of luck—a horseshoe and a four-leaf clover—are etched beside a small collection of the sun, moon, and stars. And then, there's this small buzzing bee near his elbow—it's tiny and easily overlooked, but somehow, it feels significant.

I could stare at the artwork for hours, lost in every small, intricate detail. I want to know what they mean, where they came from, and how many there are in total. But it's impossible to see everything, to take it all in, from just one angle.

It's tempting, though, to grab hold of him—to turn his arms every which way—until I've catalogued all the pieces. But instead, I swallow hard, forcing myself to meet his eyes.

"Morning," I manage to say, the word sounding more like a croak.

He laughs at me, his dark eyes warm and sleepy. "Morning, sunshine," he says, running a hand through his damp hair. "You're up early."

"Yep, as per usual. You feeling any better?"

"Loads."

"I, uh, went to the Seashell Café." I gesture behind me with a flick of my wrist. "Got us some breakfast."

He peeks around the corner, gaze locked on the spread all laid out on the table. "Damn, you didn't have to do all that."

"I wanted to," I say, sheepishly rubbing my arm. "Besides, you need to eat, especially with the day you had yesterday."

The smile he gives me is one of the most genuine I've ever seen. It lights up his face, softening his features and making my stomach flutter. "Thank you, Daisy. You're quite literally a lifesaver."

Once Elio's dressed for the day, we sit down together to eat, and he tears through his muffin like he's never seen food before. It's funny, cute, and ridiculous all at once. I can't help the laughter that bubbles out of me at the sight.

He shoots me a self-conscious look, swallows it down, and then his gaze turns all serious. "So, I've been thinking," he starts, "about us . . . cohabitating for the next couple of weeks."

I raise a brow, leaning back in my chair. "I already told you, there's no backing out now."

"No, I just think . . . I mean, we probably need to set some ground rules, y'know? Just so we're not stepping on each other's toes and all."

I let out a chuckle. "Ground rules? Like what?"

"Like, first off, you're sleeping in the bed. No arguments."

"How about you give me one more night on the couch, just enough for you to recover a little bit. Then I'll take the bed for the rest of my time here, okay?" I ask, negotiating despite the firmness in his gaze. "What's next?"

"Fine." His cheeks turn a subtle shade of pink as he continues. "Also, I work from home, and some of it . . . it's private." He glances away briefly before his eyes meet mine.

"I'll need a few hours alone in my room throughout the week."

His request is odd, but I don't question it. Everyone has their quirks, after all. "That's fair. I'll be out for a good chunk of the day anyway—surfing, errands, hanging with some other friends. Just as long as I can get back here to check on you."

"Yeah, that'd be great," he says.

And then we spend the next half hour caught up in a playful discussion about the rules of our shared living space. We assign Bentley, who's been sitting patiently by our feet, the power to choose the TV channel—after all, who can resist those puppy dog eyes and his natural affinity for wildlife documentaries.

The next rules are simpler: first person to wake up brews a full pot of coffee, last to sleep checks the lock on the door, and both of us, of course, are required to provide unlimited snuggles to the dog.

We remain at the kitchen table long after our cups are empty and the dishes have been cleared away. When it's finally time to part ways to get on with our respective days, I stand, and Elio surprises me by gently brushing his hand across my forearm.

His warmth seeps into me, and I briefly close my eyes, savoring the comforting scent of him—clean soap, a subtle hint of spice, and the faint sweetness from the strawberry muffin.

"Thanks again," he murmurs, his voice a soft rumble. "For everything."

His fingertips trail down, then tap against my wrist—just one barely there touch—before he pulls them away. I give him a small, heartfelt smile. "It's no big deal. That's what friends do."

His eyes spark with something I can't quite decipher, and then he says, "Yeah, Daisy girl, they do."

# Chapter Fifteen

## ELIO

"Hey, E." Luca's voice is deep, comforting through the phone line.

It's still early, the sunlight barely peeking through the gaps of the kitchen blinds. And I'm sitting at the dining table, nursing a mug of black coffee while Daisy sleeps peacefully on the couch.

Her legs are tucked beneath her, her arm hanging off the edge of the cushion, fingers twitching slightly in her sleep.

"Hey," I murmur back, my voice hushed so as not to disturb my house guest.

I glance over at her, the morning light playing with her hair, turning it into a golden halo. A fucking angel if I've ever seen one. I have to tear my eyes away, the sight leaving a weird ripple in my chest.

"You doin' okay?" Luca asks, concern in his voice. I don't blame him; my sudden collapse and subsequent hospitalization is enough to rattle anyone.

"I'm okay. Better." My gaze flits back to the couch. "Getting there, I think."

There's a stilted pause, and then, "You know, my team has a home game next weekend, and I thought you might want to come." He clears his throat, and I can almost picture his ears burning bright red. "Harper and Juney are dying to see you."

"You didn't tell them, did you?"

"No, E." He sighs, long and heavy. "I didn't tell my three-year-old daughter that her uncle had a fucking heart attack."

"It wasn't a *heart attack*. Christ," I mutter. "And you know what I meant."

"Yeah, I told my wife." He gives me a humorless snort. "I had to tell her, El. We talk about everything."

"Is she freaking out?" I groan, rubbing at my temples. "Oh, who am I kidding? It's Harper—of course she's freaking out. Worried I'm gonna fall off the deep end, isn't she?"

"As she rightfully should. You were in the hospital," he grinds out. "You have a fucking monitor strapped to your chest recording your every heartbeat. This is serious shit."

I work to steady myself, tapping my fingers quietly against the side of my coffee mug. "I'm *fine*."

"Yeah, fine." Junebug's delighted little squeals play out in the background, and it makes my heart clench. He's right; it's been ages since I've seen my niece, and I need to remedy that as soon as possible. But I don't know if a fucking Bobcats game is the best place for me to do that. "So, I'll see you at the game, then?"

"Come on, man."

"Didn't you hear me say Juney misses you?"

"Yeah? She tell you that herself?"

"Swear on my life. I can put her on the phone right now if you don't believe me."

"Fuck, fine," I mutter, shutting down the idea. I don't need to hear Juney's sweet, little voice reminding me how shitty of an uncle I've been lately. "I'll come."

"Bring your friend along if she wants. It'll be good for you to get out of the house."

"Yeah, maybe." The thought of being outside, amongst a crowd of people, doesn't exactly appeal to me right now, but the idea of doing something normal, something routine, is slightly tempting.

We exchange a few more words—mostly about Bentley and his wife—before hanging up, leaving me in the quiet apartment, Daisy still dozing peacefully on the couch.

I finish my coffee and go about my morning, all while trying to avoid waking her. Her peaceful slumber seems sacred, something not to be disturbed. So, I go about my tasks with extra care and catch up on some neglected tasks inside my room.

Work, for me, is fluid, unpredictable these days. When I first joined AfterDark, I didn't know it would evolve into all this. I thought it was a quick way to make money, to support myself without needing to rely on my family.

But then, it turned into something much bigger, much more demanding.

It all began when I was freshly nineteen, and that shady offer in the back of a van turned into a lifeline. Back then, it felt simple, inconsequential. All I had to do was show up, fuck a stranger, ensure the pop shot, and the money started rolling in.

It wasn't supposed to last forever. It was supposed to be a temporary fix to a permanent problem. But now, as I sit here, I realize just how naive I was.

When I first started, I craved the independence, the ability to make my own money doing something that, on the surface, seemed relatively harmless. The temptation of the unknown, the adrenaline rush of stepping in front of the camera, the power that came from knowing that people wanted me enough—found me attractive enough—to watch me fuck.

It was a different kind of intoxication.

But three years down the line, it's turned into something else. Something that fuels my restless nights and fills my days with anxiety. It's like living in a constant state of dread, waiting for the next shoot, the next web chat, the next payment to go through.

And it's not just the role-play—the forced persona of Everett—or the sexual acts that bother me. It's the constant reminder that to these people, I'm just a screen name, an object of desire.

It's the lack of real human connection, the isolation.

As a sex worker, we deserve our rights, our safety, our dignity just like anyone else. A job's a job, and I respect anyone who's out there hustling. But it's not all sunshine and roses. Burnout, dissociation, dehumanizing messages, the pressure of keeping up a persona—it all takes a toll.

And no matter who you are, it's impossible not to feel it, not to be affected by it.

My subscribers are good, fine, for the most part. They've supported me, monetarily and otherwise. But none of these people know the real me, and none of them are people I can call on when I'm having a hard day.

I feel detached, jaded. I know that it's fucking embarrassing, but I've never even had sex without being paid for it, without it technically being a performance. And that's why I feel so disconnected from the act itself.

Sex, for me, has become nothing more than a job. And over the last three years, I haven't felt much desire or sexual attraction to anyone outside of what I do for work.

I don't know if I can rewire that part of myself once all this is over. Despite craving a real relationship, wanting intimacy, I don't even know how it all might work.

All I know is that I'm tired. Tired of pretending, of putting on a show, of maintaining a façade.

But again, I'm not in a position to quit. My income is tied up to this site, to the persona I've created.

And now, my heart's fucked-up, too. This unexpected health issue has eliminated all my partner scenes for the last month. So, I'm left with the lower-earning tasks for the time being—solo scenes, web chats, photo shoots—and it's all so time-consuming.

The pressure, the uncertainty, the loneliness. None of this can be good for my health, either. But for now, I'm stuck. I need the money. I need to keep my head down until I finish school and secure my degree.

I need to keep going, to push through.

All I can do is hope that I'll make it through. That I can find myself again—maybe for the first time—once all this is over.

AFTER SPENDING some time catching up on work, my attention is yanked away by a soft knock on my door. "Hey, you heading to campus soon?" Daisy's voice rings out, muffled by the wooden barrier separating us.

"Yeah, just give me a minute," I call back, already swiveling my chair around and standing up. Time has a funny way of slipping by when I'm holed up in my room.

Stepping into the bathroom, I splash some cold water on my face. It's a poor attempt to wash away the remnants of the world I've just escaped from. With a sigh, I push my fingers through my hair, raking it back with a dollop of gel, and then change into a clean T-shirt.

When I open my bedroom door, I find Daisy standing in the hallway, cheeks flushed and eyes shining. As one of our established ground rules, we agreed to carpool to classes when it suits us. Of course, I volunteered to drive, given the fact she's done so much for me already.

"I'm sorry I slept in," she says, wrapping her arms around her middle. "I just . . . I don't know, I must have been really tired."

"Don't apologize," I say, brushing her off. "You've been doing a lot lately. You deserve a break."

A genuine smile lifts her lips, chasing away any lingering guilt. For a moment, I let myself bask in it. This girl, she came into my life like a whirlwind, all bright eyes and infectious laughter. And now she's here, looking after me, caring for me, simply out of the goodness of her heart.

It's new, different, and hard to accept. Aside from Kaia and my family, I'm not used to other people caring about me like this. And the last thing I want is for her to overwork herself, to spend all her time and energy focused on someone like me, and subsequently burn out.

After letting Bentley outside, we hop in my Jeep and head to campus together.

For some reason, I can't help but sneak glances over to the passenger side, drinking in the sight of her every chance I get—the way her lips curve into a soft smile as she hums along with the radio, the glow of the setting sun lighting up her face, the innocent look in her eyes as she gazes out the window.

I'm starting to realize that I'm not just grateful for her help, but I also care about her, almost too much—as a person, a friend, a girl who just picked up the broken pieces of her heart and shared them with someone new.

By the time night falls and we're back at our apartment, the stillness of the evening wraps around us like a cozy blanket. We're tucked on the couch together, Bentley curled up between us. And Daisy, of course, is the first one to break the silence.

"Do you need to . . . I mean, I can give you that privacy you mentioned before. Maybe run to the store for a bit or something?"

I shake my head. "No, I finished my work for the day while you were sleeping in." The relief in her eyes is clear, and I can't help but offer her a half-smile. It's easy, comfortable—this mutual understanding, this respect we already have for each other's boundaries.

"I can't believe I did that," she mutters, a frown creasing her forehead. "I haven't slept that late in forever . . . well, no, that's a lie. I was basically glued to my bed the first week Logan and I broke up, but other than that, never."

The mention of her ex sends an odd pang through me, but I push it aside. "It's been a wild weekend, and you needed the rest. How are you . . . I mean, are you feeling okay about it now? About Logan?"

Her shoulders shrug, a slight smile tugging at her lips. "Yeah, better. It doesn't hurt as much anymore. Maybe it's all the distractions, but I don't wake up thinking about him. I don't reach for my phone expecting to see his name and then feel disappointed when it's not there."

There's a quietness in her voice, a rawness that makes my chest ache. I curve an arm around the back of the couch, barely brushing a hand against the top of her shoulder. The contact is light, fleeting, but I hope it conveys the comfort I'm trying to offer.

"You know," I say. "I've been thinking about something."

"What is it?"

"It's just . . . I know I said you didn't deserve what happened, what he did to you. And that's the honest truth. But *God*, Daisy, I just hope your next love isn't one you have to heal from."

She turns to me, her eyes wide and full of tenderness, but I see a glimmer of something else there. Something that makes my heart thump a little faster, makes me hope for things I sure as shit shouldn't be hoping for.

"Yeah," she whispers, tilting her head back, cheekbone brushing against my knuckles. "Me too."

# Chapter Sixteen

## DAISY

My damp wet suit clings to my skin as I make my way back to the apartment, surfboard tucked securely under one arm. Salt water drips from my hair onto my back, a reminder of the pure bliss I've found within the waves.

Staying with Elio these past couple of days has been strangely . . . normal. Comfortable, even. We've slid into an easy rhythm of shared meals, shared car rides, shared space that feels so natural.

So normal that I almost forget about the absurdity of the situation.

He's been holding up, as far as I can tell. His heart seems to be behaving for now, but there are moments when it's painfully clear how fragile he is. Like when he huffs up the stairs after a long day of classes, his chest heaving just a little too much, his face a shade too pale.

And I catch the fleeting glances he throws my way—little checks to see if I've noticed. I pretend I haven't, for both our sakes.

"Elio?" I call out, pushing the door open. My board squeaks against the linoleum floor as I lean it against the wall. The apartment is quiet, except for the soft hum of the fridge and the faint whirring of the ceiling fan.

"I'm here," he calls out from the kitchen, his voice light. I can hear the rustling of paper and the clinking of cutlery—

sounds of domesticity that a few weeks ago, I wouldn't have associated with him.

Now, it's almost second nature.

I find him at the stove, stirring something in a pot. The smell of tomatoes and garlic fills the air, making my stomach grumble. He looks up as I enter, his lips quirking up in a small smile. "Hey, you're back already."

"Yeah," I say, walking over to the counter and leaning up against it. I watch him as he moves around the kitchen, a little in awe of how effortlessly he navigates the space. There's a grace to his movements, a certain rhythm that seems intrinsically his. "So, whatcha makin'?"

"Eggs in purgatory."

"That sounds . . . kinda spooky."

"It's basically an Italian version of shakshuka. My mom always used to make it for me. I thought . . . " He trails off, his eyes flickering up to meet mine. "I thought you might like it, too."

The simple sentiment, the thoughtfulness behind it, warms me from the inside out. "I'm sure I'll love it. Thank you."

"I thought we could eat together before classes today."

"That sounds perfect," I say, pushing myself away from the counter. "I'm just gonna grab a shower, and I'll be out in a bit."

"Take your time."

After cleaning up, I come back to the kitchen feeling refreshed. Elio has set the table, and the two of us sit down together, Bentley lingering at our feet as per usual. Unashamed, Elio watches closely as I take my first bite, and my eyes widen. The dish is rich, savory, and delicious—an explosion of delicious flavors on my tongue.

Thankfully, I won't have to lie when I tell him just how much I like it.

"Good, huh?"

"Good? This is amazing," I mumble around a mouthful, giving him a dorky little thumbs-up.

"I'm glad you like it," he says, and there's a note of pride in his voice that brings a smile to my face. "Oh, and here's something else I've been meaning to ask you. Er, you remember Luca, my brother, right?"

I nod, remembering the large, kind-eyed man who drove us from the hospital less than a week ago. "Of course."

"Well, he has a home game this weekend," he continues, his fingers drumming a rhythm against the counter. "He asked me to come watch. Would you want to join?"

I'm surprised by his invitation, and a flurry of questions whirls in my mind. But instead of voicing them, I say, "That sounds fun. I'd love to go."

"Great." He shovels in another mouthful of food, and I wait while he swallows it down. "We'll be in the family box, but Luca's wife, Harper, will be there, too. And their daughter, June. I haven't seen them in a while."

A flush creeps up my neck. "And Luca plays for the Bobcats, yeah?"

"Ah, yeah, sorry," he says, giving me a small, self-deprecating laugh. "I just assumed you knew. Most people do."

"Actually, my friend Max mentioned it to me once. And Harper . . . well, it's kind of funny, actually. She and I grew up in the same hometown near Cape Casserat. She even babysat me a couple of times."

His brows shoot up. "Really?"

"Yep, we have more in common than you might think."

"Six degrees of separation, huh?"

"Exactly." I lean forward, resting my elbows on the table. "And Luca? He's not your only sibling, is he?"

"No," he admits, his voice softer now, eyes dark and thoughtful. "I've got four others. Lucky me."

"What's that like?" I ask. "Having such a big family? A famous sibling?"

"It's . . . overwhelming sometimes. But I wouldn't trade them for anything. I fucking love my sisters. And while being Luca's brother has its ups and downs, I'm mostly proud of him. God knows he's put up with enough of my bullshit over the last twenty-two years. But I've always . . . in a way, felt like I've been living in his shadow, no matter how much he'd hate to know that."

His answer resonates with me, tugging at something inside my chest. Sure, I don't come from a big family myself, but there's a kinship in his words, a familiarity that parallels my own feelings.

"I think my little sister, Summer, feels that way about me sometimes. I've forgotten how much I've missed her over the last few months."

"Been a while since you two talked?"

"About a year, yeah."

When we were kids, things were different between us. We were close, friends more than sisters. But once I grew up and Summer entered her teenage years, we lost that fragile connection we shared. And now, she treats me as if I'm no better than the dirt beneath her shoes.

I don't know what happened, but I think it has something to do with the way we were raised. Our upbringing was similar —indifferent parents, fair-weather friends. But while I did my best to soak up every little drop of sunshine, Summer let the rain wash her out.

"I'm sorry," he says softly, sincerely. "I know how that goes, and it's a real shitty feeling to have."

The room falls silent as we let our admissions linger. A quiet understanding passes in the air, and I find a familiar sort of comfort in it—in sharing, in understanding, in simply being in the same place and time as Elio Reynolds.

"Hey, Daze?"

"Yeah?"

"I'm really glad you're here. These past few days . . . they've been better, lighter, because of you."

I look up at him, our gazes locking. "I'm really glad I'm here, too."

UNDER THE SOFT touch of the Friday afternoon sun, I push open the door to Elio's apartment. We drove separately today due to his free afternoon. And after spending a hectic morning on campus by myself, I ended up wallet-less at a coffee cart.

Hence, the detour I'm making now.

When I step inside, the first thing I notice is the quiet hush in the living room. Elio must be buried in his work by now, typing away or taking calls. And then, of course, I notice Bentley, his big fluffy tail wagging at the sight of me.

I kneel down, giving him a quick scratch behind his ears. I've only been home for a few minutes when I hear a groan ring out, soft and strained, and my heart lurches. The sound's undoubtedly coming from inside Elio's room.

*Fuck, what if his heart's giving him trouble again?*

"Are you okay, El—?" I begin, heading down the hall. And then I hear his voice, deep and husky, much different from the way he usually sounds.

"God, baby," he rasps. "I've been thinking about fucking you all day, the way your cunt feels wrapped around my cock."

I reel back from the door, the heat rushing up my neck and

spreading across my face like wildfire. He's not alone, he's not in pain. He's in the middle of having sex with someone else. I thought he needed privacy for work, not . . . *this*.

The hurt in my chest is irrational, but it takes root regardless. *Why would he bother lying to me?*

Feeling slightly numb, I grab my forgotten wallet from the kitchen counter, my mind a whirlwind of conflicting emotions —surprise, confusion, frustration. And something else. Something I don't quite understand.

*Jealousy?*

God, it's not like he owes me anything, but it feels like some sort of betrayal, a shift in the dynamics we've come to establish over the past week. So, I make a hasty retreat, the front door closing behind me with a soft click.

I walk back to my car in a complete daze. Then, without lingering too long, I flee, heading back to my own apartment for the first time all week.

When I finally arrive, it's eerily silent. Gracie isn't home yet, and I'm grateful for the solitude. The last thing I want right now is to explain my flustered state, to tell her about the compromising situation I accidentally walked in on.

Even still, I'm restless, my skin prickling with a strange, uncomfortable energy. I can't sit still, my thoughts spinning, emotions churning. The thought of Elio having sex with someone, alone in his bedroom, shouldn't make me feel this way.

Sex, in general, shouldn't make me feel this way. It's normal, natural, to have desires and to explore them when you're single. I've been meaning to do so myself, even if it's only through that fucking subscription site.

I'd signed up weeks ago now, spurred on by the idea of liberation and curiosity, but never really explored it beyond subscribing to a few profiles. I've been busy, distracted. Now—

with the taste of Elio's lies still fresh in my mouth, his moans echoing in my mind—I'm drawn back to the idea.

But first, I run a hot bath help to me unwind, to loosen the knots of tension in my muscles. I sink into the water, and it feels good, relaxing, despite the fact that I shouldn't be here in the first place. I should've gone back to campus like I'd originally planned, distracted myself with an afternoon of bio.

Instead, I'm skipping out on my last class of the week, planning to pleasure myself to some random online account. But what the fuck ever. I'm in this too deep now to turn back.

So, once I'm done with my bath, I slip into a set of silk pajamas. They make me feel sexy, confident, unlike the way I've been feeling for the past month or so. Then I slide into bed, laptop balanced on my thighs, and click on a profile—one I'd subscribed to earlier, some muscular man who hides his face.

All I know about him is that he's young, he has some visible tattoos, and he goes by the name of Everett Rain.

My heart hammers, a mix of anticipation and nerves working through my body. I try to calm my racing thoughts, to focus on what I'm about to do instead. Fishing in the top drawer of my nightstand, I grab the little toy I'd bought on a whim when I first started all this.

But just as I'm about to switch it on, my phone lights up with a call from the person I least want to hear from—Logan. I'm hit by a jolt of surprise, quickly followed by annoyance. This is the last fucking thing I need right now.

Ignoring the call, I work to refocus my attention. But then a text notification pops up, and against my better judgment, I check it.

LOGAN

can I please see you?

My heart sinks all the way down into the empty pit of my stomach. *Why now, after weeks of silence?*

I thought I was finally getting over him, finding a semblance of peace and moving on. But his simple question stirs me up inside, and I feel *everything* again—pain, longing, betrayal, anger. It derails me, the anticipation of exploring AfterDark replaced by a familiar, quiet hurt.

Sighing, I put my phone aside. Now's not the time to deal with Logan's bullshit. Now's the time to focus on me, to rediscover myself and what I want. But the magic of the moment is broken, my enthusiasm dampened.

Maybe it's just not meant to be. Not right now, at least.

I close my laptop, the empty bed and silence around me suddenly oppressive. All I can think about is Elio, alone with a random woman, his low, raspy voice carrying through the door. And then, well, there's Logan again, intruding into the new life I've created—one that doesn't include him this time, one that never will again.

# Chapter Seventeen

ELIO

The apartment is somehow too quiet without Daisy around, and I hate it more than I'm supposed to.

The monotony of the ticking clock. The whirring of the fan above my head. The faint smell of her perfume already drowned out by the essential oils I'd picked up earlier today—strawberry and citrus, because I know Daisy likes the smell—and freshly laundered bedsheets.

The thing is, I've been waiting for her to come back home for ages now. It's past seven, and she's still not here. Her last class finished hours ago. I know her schedule by now, the routine and rhythm of her life after spending the last five days together.

I'm not exactly worried, but there's something uneasy prickling at my skin, a tension that makes Bentley whine softly from his spot on the couch. I pick up my phone again, tapping on the screen.

*Nothing.* No calls, no texts.

And Bentley, he just plops his big head onto my lap, his brown eyes filled with a quiet understanding.

"She'll be back soon, bud," I say, scratching behind his ears. His tail thumps against the couch in response, the familiar rhythm soothing my frayed nerves. I contemplate taking him for a quick walk on Amber Isle, but I hesitate, thinking of the consequences. It's highly likely that I could pass out on the beach again.

*Besides, what if Daisy gets back and I'm not here?*

She'd worry, no doubt. She's been so cautious around me all week. Always attentive, always watchful. And I can't blame her, not when her constant supervision, her vigilance, is the entire reason she's here in the first place.

Her concern is endearing, but it's also been a source of new complications, ones I didn't bother to think too much about when I first agreed to this arrangement. There's a gap, a dissonance, between my normal daily routine and what I've let Daisy see of my life this past week.

Namely, the crux of my work on AfterDark.

The monitor I've been wearing, the one tracking every beat of my heart since Saturday, has been a thorn in my side, a real pain trying to conceal during my shoots and video chats. It's become a delicate dance of angling my body just so, awkwardly shifting to keep the monitor out of view from my fans.

Sighing, I toss my phone onto the coffee table, its soft thud echoing in the quiet room. I grab the remote, deciding to drown out the silence with some background noise. The sounds of *Wings of Life* fill the apartment, Bentley lifting his head at the sudden noise.

"Yeah. It's your show, buddy," I say, readjusting myself on the couch to make it more comfortable for the both of us.

I try to focus on the screen, to lose myself in the birds and the bees. But my mind keeps wandering, my eyes drifting back to the empty spot next to us on the couch—the spot that Daisy's happily occupied for the last six nights.

Unable to resist, I push myself up and pop some popcorn on the stove. The comforting smell fills the apartment, easing some of the tension out of my shoulders. I'm about halfway through the bowl when the front door finally creaks open.

"There she is," I breathe out, relief washing over me.

Daisy walks in, a bottle of strawberry wine cradled in her arms. But something's different—her usual smile is missing, her eyes a little too bright. And she doesn't even acknowledge me, just bends down to pet Bentley and walks into the kitchen, her movements more rushed than usual.

She spends a solid five minutes rummaging through my cabinets, muttering something unintelligible under her breath. I blatantly stare at her the entire time, brows cocked, wondering what the hell has gotten into her.

"Where are your wineglasses?" she finally asks, voice strained.

"I don't have any," I cautiously say, shoving myself up from the couch and walking over to her. "What's going on?"

Ignoring my question, she pulls out a regular short glass and pours herself some wine, knocking it back with a grimace.

"So . . . everything okay?" I try again, a lump forming in my throat.

Her gaze narrows in my direction. "You know, I don't particularly like liars."

"Okay." My chest pulls tight, confusion rattling inside my brain. "Is this in reference to anything specific? Did something happen today on campus?"

"No, I'm talking about you."

"Sorry, but I'm a little lost here, Daze."

"I just think . . . if you want to bring someone here to hook up with, then you should come out and ask me for the space directly. I don't like feeling lied to, feeling deceived, especially not after what happened with Logan."

"Okay?" I manage to say, brows furrowing as I wrap my

mind around the accusation. "I haven't hooked up with anyone, and I don't have plans to, especially not while you're here."

"Right, sure," she scoffs, pouring herself a second glass.

"Genuinely not lying to you."

"I heard you, though," she confesses, her voice loud in the quiet room. "Today! I heard you in your room with someone, and you told me you needed privacy for work. Why not just be honest?"

Well, there you have it. She's just pulled the rug out from underneath my feet. The moans, the dirty talk I was doing earlier—it was all part of a live web chat, fake and fabricated, just par for the course.

"*Oh* . . . oh," I mumble, running a hand through my hair. "Fuck. That *was* for work."

"What?" she asks, brows drawing together.

"So, here's the thing—" A bead of sweat trickles down my forehead, and I wipe it away, working to gather my racing thoughts. "I wasn't exactly forthcoming when I told you what I do for work, but I didn't *lie* to you about why I needed the space."

"So, then, you were sleeping with someone for *work*?"

"Kind of, I guess."

"So, you're . . . um, sorry, I'm not exactly sure what the best term for it is?"

"You're asking me if I'm a prostitute?"

"Uh-huh," she all but squeaks out. "Then again, you said you worked online . . . doing freelance stuff."

"Yeah, I do, and I'm not actually a prostitute." I fold my arms across my chest, leaning back against the cabinets. "But I do work in the same field. I post videos, pictures on an online platform. Er, just partner shoots, live cams, stuff like that. I wasn't necessarily trying to hide it from you. I just didn't want to get into all the specifics right away."

She pulls her lip between her teeth, gnawing on it. "Ah . . . okay."

*Oh, fucking hell.* I don't know what's worse—the disbelief etched across her face or the discomfort twisting my insides into a knot. But I hold her gaze, waiting for the fallout of my confession and hoping that when it does come, it's not the end of whatever friendship we've been building here.

"Is that . . . does that bother you?" I finally ask, my throat dry. Each word feels like a stone, heavy and hard to swallow.

"Not at all," she quickly assures me, her fingers tapping on the counter. "I'm just, um, I'm just processing."

"Processing," I echo, a hollow laugh escaping me. I scrub a hand over my face, the stubble on my jaw scraping against my palm, keeping me rooted, reminding me of my reality.

I'm a content creator on an adult website—that's just part of who I am and what I do. And there's nothing shameful about it. Despite the negative aspects, despite the toll it's taken on me over the years, it's still a job just like any other.

"Ah, so the work you mentioned . . ." She trails off, her gaze flitting around the room, anywhere but me. "You put it up on a public site, right?"

"That's right."

"And what's it called?"

"AfterDark." I stretch an arm across my body, fingers finding the nape of my neck, rubbing out the tension. "It's a newer sub site, but it's skyrocketed in popularity over the past couple years."

"Oh, wow." Her eyes blow wide. "That's, yep, that's a popular one, alright."

"So, you've heard of it, then?"

"Yeah," she mumbles, cheeks flushing, fingers gripping tightly to the edge of the counter. "Ah, do you have like a stage name there or . . .?"

"A pseudonym, yeah. I go by Everett Rain." Her lips part slightly, breath noticeably hitching. "Daisy, are you . . . embarrassed that you've heard of it?"

She groans, pinching the bridge of her nose, her shoulders sagging. "No, I just, well—I think I may or may not be subscribed to you already."

I stand there, trapped in the weight of the silence that settles between us, her words ricocheting around my skull. *Daisy Grey. Subscribed. To me.* As the shock takes hold, my brows involuntarily arch, and a crooked grin tugs at the corners of my mouth.

God, that's such a Daisy thing, such an unexpected, amusing twist.

I take a moment, just watching her as she squirms under my gaze, cheeks burning as I lick my lips. "On purpose, are you?"

"No, no, I *swear*." She throws her hands up in surrender, a sudden panic flashing in her eyes. "I had no idea you were a creator when I made the account, when I subscribed to your profile. It was a complete accident. A coincidence. I would never invade your privacy like that."

"My privacy? Daze, it's a public account."

"I know, but I mean, you're my friend. And there are boundaries." She diverts her gaze again, swallowing hard. Her throat works nervously as she forces the words out. "And God . . . I swear that I've never watched any of your videos. I haven't watched anyone's yet, I promise."

"Hey, hey, you're good." I raise my hand, hoping to calm her down. "Even if you had, I wouldn't be mad at you for it."

"You wouldn't?"

"No, it's okay. I'm not ashamed of what I put up there. I just . . . I guess I'm surprised you found it. Surprised you're on the site in the first place."

"What, why?" she demands, hands resting firmly on her hips, gaze finally flickering back to me. "Because a girl like me can't get her rocks off watching porn?"

"I didn't say that."

"It's safe and perfectly ethical. Plus, I was just trying it out."

"Please don't feel like you need to defend yourself, especially not to me. I'm the one posting myself online fucking strangers, fucking *myself*."

"Elio."

"Daisy, seriously, stop. Neither of us has anything to be embarrassed about, okay? Sure, I like to keep that part of my life separate from the personal stuff, but it is what it is. I don't go to great lengths to hide it, which means people I know are bound to find out."

"I know, I'm not . . . it's not that I'm *embarrassed*. And you definitely shouldn't be, either. I just—I thought that AfterDark would be my thing. My chance to . . . explore that side of myself a little bit more. And now, with you in the mix, it's all kinds of messy."

"What do you mean by explore? Like, you wanted to get into content creation yourself, or . . ."

"No, not like that. I meant, I just mean, ugh—why is this so fucking hard?"

"You know, I just laid out some pretty vulnerable truths for you."

"I know, and that's why I'm trying to explain to you." The words are a whisper, like a secret confession, disappearing in the air between us. A deep sigh leaves her lips, and she pushes a lock of hair behind her ear.

"I signed up for the site a few weeks ago, not too long after Logan cheated. He told me that I was too safe, too reserved in bed. And the more I thought about it, the more I realized that he had a point. I mean, I know there's nothing wrong with having a low libido or having no interest in sex at all. But, for me, it just feels like something I never really put much thought into before. Like, with the act itself, with sexual attraction in general. I don't know . . . am I making any sense at all?"

"You're making perfect sense." The words are sincere, spoken with a softness I've come to reserve only for her. I understand her more than she realizes—her fears, her uncertainties, her quest for self-discovery.

"Really?"

"Yeah, I get it. I get *you*. And you're right, AfterDark is a good place for you to figure out your interests, your wants, your desires. Like you said, it's safe. A lot of people, a lot of my subscribers, go there to discover themselves sexually."

She swallows, her gaze thoughtful, her fingers playing absently with the rim of the small glass. "Okay, yeah. That makes me feel a little better."

"But Daisy, you do know that Logan's a fucking asshole, and he had no right to say that to you in the first place, right?"

"Yeah, I know."

"Good." The room seems to shrink, drawing us closer. "And also, it's not as messy as you might think it is—this situation with us. If you . . . I mean, if there's anything you want to know about the site, about sex, uh, I can try my best to help you where I can."

"You want to help me learn more about sex?"

"I want to help you learn more about yourself . . . if that's what you're hoping for." My voice drops a notch lower, softer. "I'm here for you, just like you've been here for me."

Her gaze drops to the floor, her hands nervously playing with the edge of her shirt. "I don't know . . ."

"Well, it's just an offer."

She flicks her gaze up, her cheeks decidedly less pink. "You lean on me, I lean on you?"

"That's the spirit."

A soft chuckle escapes her lips, the sound easing some of the tension in my chest. "Okay, I'll think about it." She glances at the bottle she brought with her—half-empty now—then back at me. "So, do you maybe wanna share this wine with me?"

"I'm off booze, but thank you." Averting my gaze, I gesture toward the mixing bowl resting on the coffee table. "I made some popcorn, though. You can finish watching Bentley's show with us?"

"Yeah, I'd like that." She pours herself a little more wine, then fishes around the cabinets for some Tajín to sprinkle on our popcorn. "Oh, and Elio?"

"What's up?"

"I'm sorry I assumed you were lying."

*Fuck.* Her saying that shouldn't mean quite as much as it does, but something in my chest warms up at the apology. "I should've just told you in the first place."

"You had your reasons," she says, and it's exactly what I needed to hear—a simple understanding from her. Not a dismissal but a quiet acceptance.

"Well, I'm glad it's out there now," I say. "No more secrets."

"No more secrets."

# Chapter Eighteen

DAISY

Outside of surfing, I can't remember the last time I felt this loose, this free. The world's a little fuzzy around the edges, my laughter spilling into the quiet room. I'm not quite drunk but just tipsy enough to feel all bubbly inside.

The murmur of David Attenborough's voice mingles with the lazy tumble of the sea, and I sink into the soft comfort of Elio's couch. We finished up *Wings of Life* hours ago, and now we're working our way through Bentley's second choice.

Elio has one arm slung behind me as he stares at the TV, his fingers absentmindedly skimming the tips of my shoulders. It's almost adorable how fascinated he is by this miniseries. And although I love the ocean and all its creatures, I'm only halfway paying attention, my fingers tripping clumsily over my phone screen.

"Shit," I groan, rubbing my temple, pressing Ignore for the fifth time in a row.

Elio turns to look at me, his brows drawn together. "What's up?"

"It's just Logan. He texted me earlier when I was at my apartment." I let out a sigh, probably too dramatic, and roll my eyes at my own theatrics. "I tried to ignore it, but now he keeps blowing up my phone."

He cocks his head. "You went back to your apartment earlier?"

"Yeah, just to take a quick bath."

"Somethin' wrong with the bath I have here?"

"No, it's not that. It's just that when I came in earlier, I thought I heard you . . ." I trail off, the words dying in my throat. "I thought I overheard something I wasn't supposed to. So, yeah, I was a little flustered by it, and I just needed to clear my head."

"Ah, right." He falls silent, tension visibly coiling in his shoulders. "So, what is it that Logan wants?"

"To talk, I guess," I say, shrugging. "God knows about what."

He shifts in his seat, his arm pulling away from my shoulders. "He wants you back," he says, his words a firm statement. "Guaranteed."

I huff, nearly dropping my phone. "No, he doesn't. Remember, he said I'm too *reserved*," I say, a sad smile playing on my lips. I throw my head back and give a humorless snort. "He's probably balls-deep in that girl he cheated on me with."

"Jesus Christ, Daze. Vulgar." His words hold a hint of scandalized chuckle, but I notice the tightening around his eyes.

I raise a brow, my grin widening. "Oh, you're one to talk."

"What do you mean?"

"Remember, I heard you earlier," I tease, my tone lilting. "You know, '*Oh God, baby. I've been thinking about fucking you all day*.'" I mimic his earlier groan, dissolving into a fit of giggles myself.

His jaw slackens, his eyes wide. "*Fuck*," he breathes out, looking absolutely mortified.

The sight of him, flustered and caught off guard, sends another wave of laughter through me, the chaotic sound filling the room. But just as I'm about to regain my composure, my phone lights up again.

Logan's name flashes on the screen—for the sixth fucking time—and it sucks all the joy right out of me.

"Let me answer it," he says, suddenly serious. "I'll get rid of him for you."

My heart clenches. "Oh, no, you don't need to do that."

"Come on, do you trust me?"

I pause, the weight of my decisions settling in. In the short time since our paths crossed, I've let this man into my life in so many different ways. I'd isolated myself inside of his apartment —just the two of us. I'd opened up to him about my fears, my insecurities.

And now, his steady gaze is starting to feel a lot like a guiding light, a compass pointing me in the right direction.

"Okay, fine."

"And I can say whatever needs to be said?"

I roll my eyes, tossing him my phone. "Have at it."

He catches the device in midair, pressing the Answer button and switching the call to speaker. "Who's this?"

"Uh, is this Daisy's phone?" Logan's puzzled voice filters through. It's strange hearing it after a month and realizing that it doesn't affect me the same way anymore. What once sparked intense feelings now just leaves me all kinds of empty inside.

"Yeah, but she's a little preoccupied right now," Elio's tone is matter-of-fact, casual but with a rough sort of edge to it. "If you get my drift."

"Excuse me?" Logan sputters.

"She's in my bed right now, and I need to get back to her," Elio says, his gaze raking across my features. "So, you got a message for me to pass on or what?"

"I don't know who the hell you think you—"

"Sorry, *bro*, I need to go," Elio cuts in. "My girl's waiting for me, and she's fucking insatiable."

"What the f—"

Elio ends the call, quick to cut Logan off. With a shrug, he tosses my phone back to me, a satisfied grin spreading across his face.

"There you go," he says. "Bet he won't call again tonight."

"Oh, my God."

"What, did I go too far?" His brow arches, lips twitching into a smirk. "You said '*have at it*.'"

"No, I just—thank you?" I manage, my mind still reeling.

"Yeah, well, that little shit was starting to get on my last nerve." His grin broadens, lighting up his face, and I can't help but mirror it.

I'm sure Logan's sitting there, pissed off and confused, probably with a bruised ego to boot. The thought brings a sense of satisfaction I didn't quite expect. Still, as I look at Elio, it's not Logan's humiliation that's making me grin.

It's the knowledge that this man—this ridiculously good-looking, self-assured man—stood up for me. In his own unique way, sure, but he stood up for me, nonetheless. It's comforting, and exciting, and terrifying all at once.

"You're grinning like a Cheshire cat," he comments, chuckling at my obvious pleasure.

"What can I say?" I shrug, leaning back against the couch. "You're very entertaining."

He gives me a playful nudge, that smile never leaving his face. "And here I thought you'd be mad."

I wave him off, reaching for my abandoned wineglass. "Why would I be mad? Logan had it coming. Plus, it was pretty clear you were lying or at least exaggerating."

His brow furrows. "Was it?"

"I mean, come on. *Insatiable*?" I mumble, my cheeks heating under his sincere gaze. I hide my face behind my wineglass, hoping the dim light of the room will conceal my blush. "That's not me."

"Hmm." He takes a deep swig from his water, setting it down on the coffee table before turning to look at me. "Can I ask you something personal?"

"I think we're past that point by now."

"Fair enough." He shrugs, a sheepish smile playing on his lips. "I'm just wondering, with what you told me earlier about wanting to explore yourself, is Logan the only person you've been with?"

The question catches me off guard, but I don't hesitate in answering. "Yeah, he is."

"Got it." He nods, rubbing a hand over his face. "So, here's the thing. I know you're trying your best not to do this. But Daisy, you really shouldn't take that dipshit's opinions at face value. He obviously wasn't the right person for you, and maybe with the right person, sex will be different. Or maybe it won't be, and that's okay, too."

"I know. He just gets in my head sometimes." I nervously fidget with a strand of hair, curling it between my fingers. "Did, um, did you find that with someone, then? I mean, I know you've had . . . a lot of sexual partners. At least compared to me. But does it feel different when you have feelings for the person, when you're with the *right* person, or does it all kind of blend together?"

"I wouldn't know for sure, but I can only assume."

"Oh?"

He shakes his head, rubbing the back of his neck. "I've never had sex with someone I had feelings for. It's always just been . . . a performance. From my first time to the last."

I stare at him in disbelief, a pang of sympathy hitting me at the thought. He must notice because he quickly adds, "But don't feel sorry for me. I chose this path. Kinda hard to have a relationship when fucking other people is your day job."

"But don't you feel like you're missing out?"

He gives me a humorless snort. "Can't miss out on something you've never had."

His words hang in the air, a cold, hard truth that momentarily chills the warmth between us. Behind the confident façade and the playful jabs, there's a depth to him, a solitude that he wears like an uninvited guest.

"You know, I'm feeling kind of beat," he finally says, his voice softer than before, stifling a yawn.

"Ah, okay." I rise slowly from the comfortable nook I've settled into, taking care not to disturb Bentley in the process. "I guess it's getting pretty late. I should leave the couch to you two."

He gestures to the empty glasses and the discarded popcorn bowl beside us. "We'll take care of this shit in the morning," he says. "Still on for the Bobcats game?"

"Yep." As I make my way to his bedroom, I glance back at him, offering a gentle smile. "Good night, El. Sleep well."

"Night, Daisy."

Once I'm tucked inside his room, I take a moment to unwind, to gather my thoughts. Then I brush my teeth and slip into a comfy, oversized T-shirt. As I snuggle under the covers, his words echo in my mind, and I can't help but feel a little bit sad for him.

Despite his attempts to deny it, there's a certain loneliness that clings to his skin, a sense of something missing from his life. And while I drift off to sleep in his bed, I wonder if maybe I could be the one to help him find it.

. . .

A QUIET KNOCK on the door interrupts my drowsy morning peace. "Hey, Daze?" Elio's voice drifts into the room, smooth and deep.

My sleepy mind takes a moment to register his presence before I sluggishly pull myself from the warmth of his bed, eyes still heavy with sleep. Padding over to the door, I pull it open, forgetting in my early morning haze that I'm braless, dressed only in a T-shirt—one that ends halfway down my thighs.

Elio's standing in the hallway, his hair disheveled from sleep and a hint of stubble shadowing his jaw. As his eyes meet mine, I notice them dip, slowly raking over my body in a long, languid sweep. His throat works over a silent swallow, and he blows out a breath, subtly gripping his nape.

Heat flares on my cheeks, but I hold his gaze, nibbling on my lower lip. "Morning, stranger."

He's not ogling, not really. His gaze is appreciative yet careful, as though he's committing every last inch of me to memory. And then he blinks, snapping himself out of a trance.

"Sorry, got distracted for a second," he says, a boyish grin playing on his lips. "Did you want to do a quick run to the Seashell to grab some coffee and muffins? We could take Bentley and then do a beach walk unless you were wanting to surf?"

"That's okay." I beam up at him. "It's already a busy day. But I can be ready in, like, twenty minutes for coffee. If that works?"

His eyes soften. "Yeah, that's perfect. We need to head out for the stadium around ten o'clock or earlier. It'll take us a couple of hours to get there, and then if you want to watch the warm-ups, we need to be early."

"Sounds good. I'll be quick," I say, stepping back into the room and closing the door behind me. My heart races, warmth spreading through my chest as I replay the look in his eyes, the way his gaze lingered on me.

I know it wasn't just my imagination running wild—he'd all but admitted to it. And it feels strangely good to be appreciated like that, especially after Logan knocked me down a few pegs.

I know I'm not an unattractive person, but I think being cheated on changes something inside of you, maybe on a fundamental level.

I've never been one to doubt my self-worth before, to let my insecurities get the better of me. But this past month, I've felt like a stranger inside my own body. Elio has helped to remind me—in both the small ways and the big ones—that someone out there can still see me, understand me, and want me for exactly who I am.

After a quick shower and brushing my teeth, I dress in a pair of comfortable shorts and a Bobcats T-shirt, running a comb through my hair. By the time I make it back to the living room, Elio's already waiting, leash in hand, his faithful companion sitting there beside him.

"And how are my boys this morning?" I ask, brushing a hand across Bentley's golden fur.

"Just grand." Elio passes over the handle of the leash, fishing in his pocket for his car keys. "And how's our Daisy girl doing? That strawberry wine hitting you just right?"

I give him a soft, tender smile. "Yep," I say, "never been better."

# Chapter Nineteen

## ELIO

THE BRIGHT LIGHTS of the stadium blur into a million sparks as I walk with Daisy into the family box.

"Harps," I call out, seeing Luca's wife up ahead, her sunlit hair cascading over her shoulders. She's cradling my niece, June, who's giggling and fiddling with her mother's necklace.

I give Daisy's elbow a reassuring squeeze, pulling myself from the comfortable heat that always seems to surround her. Sidling up to Harper, I reach out and scoop June into my arms.

"There's my little Junebug," I murmur into her ear, my voice rough with affection. She's heavier than I remember, the soft weight of her settling onto my shoulders a familiar comfort.

"Ello," she chirps, her tiny hands wrapping themselves in my hair as she gives a delighted kick of her feet.

At the sight of Daisy, Harper's face lights up, those misty blue eyes sparkling with warmth. She extends her arms for a hug, and Daisy steps into it with a quiet sort of joy. "It's so nice to meet you. I'm Harper, Elio's sister-in-law, and that's my daughter, June."

"Apparently, you two have already met," I pipe up, nodding toward Daisy. "You used to babysit her back in the day."

"Oh!" Harper's lips curl into a beaming smile as recognition dawns. "Daisy . . . Grey? I haven't seen you in ages! You look so different now, so grown-up," she gushes, her voice just as sweet as it usually is.

For as long as I've known her, she's always been sunshine personified, bright, welcoming, the kind of woman who can light up a room just by walking into it.

She and Daisy have that particular trait in common.

"I'm surprised you remember," Daisy says softly. "It was so long ago now."

Harper's laugh is light, the sound echoing around us. "Of course I do. You were the sweetest little kid."

"I used to look up to you so much back then." A faint pink splatters across Daisy's cheeks. "Sorry if this is a weird thing to say, but I remember wanting to be just like you when I grew up."

"That's not weird at all," Harper reassures, her voice a comforting caress, her smile gentle and sincere. "I think it's really sweet, actually."

I reach up to tap at June's tiny shoes, the soft clinking sound punctuating my words. "So, how's the hockey season going?"

"Could be better." Harper gives a lighthearted shrug. "The team lost some key players last year, so it's hard to rebound from that."

My brows quirk up. "If you're talking about Beck, please spare me."

Harper chuckles. "I thought you two were getting along lately."

"We are," I concede, rolling my eyes in a dramatic show of annoyance. "But he's still kind of a little shit."

"A little shit that's in love with your best friend," she teases. But then the mood shifts as her brows knit together, worry etching lines into her forehead. "Speaking of Kaia, does she know about what happened with you last weekend?"

"No, not yet," I mutter. I haven't bothered to tell Kaia

because I'd like to have answers for her first. She's a chronic worrier, that one. So, I'm waiting until the end of next week, when this Holter monitor comes off and the doctors are able to put two and two together.

"How have you been doing since then, El?"

Instinctively, I deflect, brushing off her concern with a shake of my head. "I'm fine," I say. "It's all good."

But my perceptive sister-in-law isn't so easily fooled. She pivots, turning her warm, inquisitive eyes to Daisy. "Now will you tell me how he's really doing?"

Daisy hesitates, her gaze flitting to me as if searching for permission. I can practically see the gears turning in her head before she finally answers, her tone threaded with honesty. "He seems to be doing well. No issues this week."

Harper takes Daisy at her word and lets the subject drop, shifting the conversation toward something more lighthearted. They quickly delve into a discussion about Daisy's major, which classes she's taking this term, and I distract myself by goofing around with Juney.

It's not too much longer before the game nears kickoff. Anticipation in the stadium builds, the crowd erupts into cheers, and I hoist June into the air again, her tiny REYNOLDS jersey bunching up at the waist. We play around, me lifting her up and down in time with her giggles.

But then, without warning, a heavy strain tugs beneath my rib cage, like my heart is trying to punch its way out of my chest. Panic surges through me, but I fight it back, passing June off to her mother and keeping my face as neutral as possible. I don't want anyone to worry, not unless they have to.

As I clutch my chest—discreetly sliding a palm over my heart—my knees buckle, and I grip the back of a chair for support. The world around me spins, the noise of the crowd dwindling into a distant roar.

Through the haze, Daisy approaches, her eyes filled with concern. Her words come to me like echoes in the fog, her touch on my arm barely registering.

My body's in turmoil, my heart pounding so hard it's all I can hear, all I can feel. And then, the rest of the night barely registers.

I remember Daisy leading me out of the stadium, her hand warm in mine. I remember the long, silent struggle to buckle me up on the passenger side, the soft glow of the streetlights reflecting on her worried face. I remember her insisting on driving me to the hospital and me, stubborn as always, resisting.

But eventually, I relented. Because it's Daisy. And for some reason, I can't seem to say no to her.

And now, we're sitting in Harbor Point's parking lot, the charged silence stretching between us like a rubber band ready to snap. I finally decide to break it, the frustration and fear bubbling over all at once.

"I can't even play around with my fucking niece anymore," I snap, slamming my fist against the dashboard. "This is such bullshit."

The words, harsh and bitter, hang heavy in the enclosed space. I glance at Daisy, expecting her to be angry or upset at my outburst. But she's not. She just looks at me, her eyes filled with concern, and slides a calming hand over mine.

"I know. But we'll get to the bottom of this," she says, giving me a reassuring squeeze. "And in the meantime, I'm here for you, El."

. . .

Hours have passed since I was first admitted into the ED. Bright, clinical lights beat down incessantly, and medical professionals continue to weave in and out of the room.

Echoes of machinery beep softly in the background, the rhythm eerily in sync with my own heartbeat—too quick, too erratic. And now, the attending physician, Dr. Hayes, is standing at the foot of my bed. My medical file is clutched in his hands, its contents betraying a reality I'm not yet ready to confront.

"Mr. Reynolds, we believe it's wise for you to stay overnight for monitoring," Dr. Hayes finally breaks the silence, his voice echoing within the sterile confines.

I steal a glance at Daisy, her features strained with worry. It's still early in the evening, but the day's events have already sapped all the energy from me.

"I'd rather not," I say through pursed lips. "Is there any way I could just . . . take it easy, head home for the night, and come back tomorrow?"

"Well, given your recent symptoms and your past medical history, it's not ideal. We're detecting some abnormal rhythms on your monitor—ones that indicate a serious underlying condition."

"What kind of *condition*?"

"Well, Dr. Foster suspected some sort of arrhythmia at your original appointment but wanted to rule out other causes first: stress, anxiety, other physical conditions that could've led to your symptoms. But based on what we're seeing now, it looks as though you're experiencing episodes of nonsustained ventricular tachycardia."

"What does that mean, exactly?" I ask.

"In simpler terms, your heart's experiencing episodes where it beats much faster than it should. 'Ventricular' refers to the lower chambers of your heart, where this is all happening. Imagine your heart's normal rhythm is like a steady drummer in a band, keeping a consistent beat. But for short periods, that drummer decides to go off on a wild solo, playing much faster than the rest.

"This isn't dangerous in the short term, especially when it stops on its own—that's why we call it 'nonsustained.' But it's still not normal, and it can make you feel faint, dizzy, or short of breath. Over time, and particularly if these episodes were to get longer or more frequent, it could put extra strain on your heart."

"Extra strain, like . . ."

He gives me a tight-lipped grimace. "Like loss of consciousness, fibrillation, sudden cardiac death."

"Jesus fucking Christ."

He clears his throat and carries on. "That is to say, if all this goes untreated, the consequences could be serious," he tells me. "There are ways to mitigate and treat the diagnosis, and it will depend on how chronic and severe your condition is."

"So, are we talking surgery here?"

"They'd likely start you on some medications and go forward from there. But that's something you're going to need to discuss with Dr. Foster at a follow-up appointment."

I take a deep breath, processing what he's saying. It sounds serious but manageable, and it's something I may be able to mitigate with medications. That's not too terrifying on its own.

But there's something else that sets off bigger alarms: admitting me to the hospital for the night.

The thought sends a wave of dread through my body. Hospitals and I don't have the best track record. It's not the sterility or the smell of antiseptic or even the fact that being here means something is seriously wrong with me.

It's a feeling much deeper than that. More personal. It's a memory—painful and vivid—that's stayed with me for the last five years.

As with many of life's problems, it all goes back to Jackson fucking Ford, who once felt like everything to me but turned out to be one of my biggest regrets.

When he was admitted after an overdose, I stayed by his side, forsaking sleep, food, and my own sanity. And when I woke up the next morning in the reclining chair, exhausted and terrified, he was gone. Discharged himself Against Medical Advice, the nurses said.

And I never fucking saw him again.

That day, that loss, marked the beginning of my worst downward spiral. It was the depth of that spiral that eventually led me to rehab and recovery. But the hospital, this place of sterilized linoleum and the relentless beep of monitors, still holds the ghost of that trauma.

"I understand what you're saying, but I—I don't want to stay overnight," I tell the doctor, my voice a ragged whisper. I see Daisy beside me, her brows furrowed with worry, her hands clenched in her lap.

"I can monitor him at home," she says suddenly, her voice steady, her gaze unyielding as she looks at the doctor. "I'll stay beside him all night, and if anything changes, I'll bring him back in immediately."

There's a tense moment as the doctor considers, and then finally, he sighs. "Alright. Given you're stable right now, we'll permit you to continue your monitoring at home. But you need to see Dr. Foster on Monday morning without fail. And if your symptoms persist or worsen, return to the emergency department immediately."

I breathe out a sigh of relief, tension uncoiling in my gut.

It's not the best news, but at least I get to sleep in my own place tonight, away from the ghosts. And with Daisy by my side, I think I'll manage just fucking fine.

The doctor leaves us then, and I'm left sitting on the edge of the emergency room bed, Daisy standing beside me, her hand finding purchase on my shoulder. Her touch is comforting, grounding, a lifeline in this confusing sea of medical jargon.

"Thank you," I whisper, leaning my head against her knuckles. "I owe you one."

She gives me a small, brave smile. "You lean on me, I lean on you. Remember?"

"Yeah," I say. "I remember."

# Chapter Twenty

## DAISY

As Bentley nudges the front door with his cold, wet nose, I swing it open, letting him back into the warmth of the apartment. We step further into the living room, and I find Elio hunched over the couch, struggling with a wayward cushion.

His face is pinched in frustration, and the thin veneer of the past few hours is slipping. He's unsteady, the imprint of the hospital still seeping from his skin. Despite the physical and emotional toll of the day, he's stubbornly insistent on setting up his makeshift bed.

"Dare I ask what you're doing?"

He glances at me, the edges of his eyes creased from fatigue. "Don't know if you noticed, but I just got discharged from the ED. I'm pretty beat, so I'm gonna call it a night."

"You really believe I'd let you sleep on the couch after the day you just had?"

His gaze turns stubborn, a glint of defiance sparkling in his eyes. "Daze, we agreed."

"Agreements can change." I cross my arms, folding them tightly over my chest. "Besides, you need a proper bed, somewhere you can fully relax without any strain on your heart."

"Couch is comfortable enough."

"You're lying." I scoff. "We both know you're way too tall for the couch."

His lips twitch into a weary grin. "Okay, you got me there. It might be a bit short for me, but it's bearable."

Not letting him off easy, I threaten, "I swear, Elio, if you don't shuffle that stubborn ass of yours into your bedroom right this instant—"

A deep, hearty chuckle cuts me off, and he raises his hands in surrender. "Alright, alright, bossy girl."

"Well, someone has to be," I say. "It's hard enough to keep you in line."

"Have it your way, then."

"But there's a condition," I continue. "I'm sleeping on your bedroom floor. That way, I can keep a closer watch on you."

His playful demeanor instantly shifts, a look of concern settling on his face. "Daisy, I can't let you do that."

"I promised the doctor I'd monitor you. How am I supposed to do that from the living room?"

"But I just . . ."

"El," I press on, "it's for everyone's peace of mind."

His shoulders sag in defeat, and he pinches the bridge of his nose, a deep sigh escaping his lips. "You know what, why don't you just share the bed with me? There's enough room. And this way, I won't feel like such a jackass for disrupting your life even further."

"Yeah, I can do that." Flames of embarrassment lick up my cheeks, but I manage to swallow my shyness long enough to nod. "And for the record, you're not a jackass."

A curious expression flashes across his face. "Why are you doing this, Daisy?"

"What do you mean?"

"All of this," he says, sweeping his arm around the room. "You're going to such great lengths to help me, and I don't understand why."

My response is almost instinctive, the words flowing from me without any premeditation. "Because I like you, because you deserve to be cared for."

His laugh rings through the room, a soft, bitter sound. "Yeah, that's unlikely."

"I'm not sure who made you feel that way, because it's so far from the truth." I snatch the cushion out of his hand, placing it back in its rightful spot. "But we can discuss that another time. Tonight, we're not dealing with heavy topics. Tonight, you're going to rest."

We move into Elio's bedroom, a familiar space that suddenly feels foreign, heavy with the day's unresolved tensions. As he undresses, the dim light of the bedside lamp highlights the muscled expanse of his body, etching the contrast between light and shadow, all those dips and ridged lines.

He's shirtless now, his jeans hung low on his hips, revealing the deep V and the spattering of hair that trails below his zipper. My eyes flit around his naked torso and land on a tattoo I didn't notice before—six tiny birds inked in a row along his ribs. Heat flares in my cheeks, and I quickly avert my gaze.

"Jesus, Elio!" I splutter.

He looks up, a flicker of confusion dancing in his eyes before realization sets in. "Ah, right. Sorry," he murmurs. "I'm used to getting naked in front of people. Didn't even register it might make you uncomfortable."

With an embarrassed laugh, we settle on a compromise, turning our backs to each other to get changed. Once I'm in my oversized shirt and a pair of comfy sweats, I turn back to face him.

"Are you decent?" His voice breaks the silence, a tinge of amusement lingering in his question. I confirm that I am, and he turns around, a small smile tugging at his lips. He takes a step toward me, fingers lightly brushing over the hem of my sleeve.

"Is this your favorite shirt?" he asks. "You wore it to bed last night, too."

I blush, staring down at the oversized T-shirt. Unfortunately, it used to belong to Logan, a fact I had nearly forgotten in the chaos of the day. "No, actually, um, it's my ex's."

He stiffens, the playful smile wiped off his face. He takes a step back and says, "Why would you keep wearing it?"

"I didn't really think about it," I mutter. "I've worn it forever, and it's big and comfy enough for sleeping."

He just shakes his head, disappearing into his closet. When he returns, he's holding a clean, fresh shirt. *His shirt.* He steps closer to me, the fabric clutched in his hand. "Change."

I raise a brow, planting both hands on my hips. "Ask me nicely."

He sighs. "Daisy, will you please remove that asshole's shirt from your body?"

I turn my back to him, peeling off the fabric and exposing my bare back to the chilly air. His body heat seeps into me as he steps closer and murmurs a soft "Arms up."

I follow his command, and goose bumps prickle along my skin. It's silent for a long moment, and then, ever-so-slowly, he slips the new shirt over my body. His fingertips trace a scorching path down my sides, stopping just above my hips before he pulls them away.

The feeling is intoxicating, unfamiliar, and it sparks a flame deep inside of me.

"There," he breathes out. "All set."

"Thanks."

He grins at me, the smile reaching his eyes, warming them.

"Anytime," he says with a wink, defusing the tension as we step toward the edge of his bed.

He pulls back the duvet. With a small nod, I gingerly slip under the covers, creating a boundary of space between us. Elio mirrors my actions on the opposite side, his back facing me.

"Good night, Daze," he eventually murmurs, his voice a low rumble in the quiet of the room.

"Good night, El."

We lie there, backs to each other, separated by the chasm of the king-sized bed, each enveloped by our own thoughts. As the minutes tick by, Elio's breathing deepens and slows, a clear sign of him drifting into sleep.

And then, he turns onto his side, his body gravitating toward mine as if by instinct.

His hand, warm and heavy, finds its way to my hip, curling gently around it. The contact is barely there, yet it sends a jolt of warmth right through me, tethering us.

It's such an innocent act, almost unconscious, and it leaves me staring at the ceiling, a tender smile on my lips. A soothing calmness washes over me, an unfamiliar but welcome sensation.

It's as if, in this moment, everything else falls away—our worries, our pasts, our fears—and it's just us.

Slowly, my own eyelids grow heavier, sleep beckoning me. Despite the events of today—of the last few weeks—I feel safe, cocooned in a sense of comfort I hadn't anticipated. So, I let myself drift off, the last thing I remember being the gentle pressure of Elio's hand on my hip and the soft beat of his heart next to mine.

. . .

I'M WARM, content, all cozy in bed as the first rays of morning light filter into the room. It's still too early, but I blink open my eyes anyway, my mind foggy from sleep. A warmth radiates from my side, and I glance down, finding Elio's arm draped across my waist.

His chest rises and falls against my back in a slow, steady rhythm, his breath a warm whisper against my hair. His fingers twitch slightly against my belly, sending tiny jolts of awareness down my spine.

I freeze, holding my breath, hoping to delay the inevitable awkwardness. And just for a moment, I allow myself to enjoy the comfortable silence, the intimacy of the situation, and the rhythmic sound of Elio's deep breathing.

But then, my phone vibrates from the bedside table, shaking me out of the spell. I glance at the screen, my heart sinking when I see Logan's name. Quickly, I silence the call, sending it straight to voicemail.

"Who was that?" Elio's voice is rough with sleep, the vibrations rumbling through my back.

"Just Logan," I say, brushing it off. I don't want to think about him, not when I'm here, entwined with someone who's starting to mean a whole lot more to me.

His body stiffens against mine, but his arm remains draped across my waist. "You should think about blocking him. It's not healthy to keep someone around who's just going to cause you pain. I've had to do it before."

"You blocked someone?" I turn to face him, my brows furrowed.

"Yeah. Sometimes people don't get the hint, or they just don't relent. You need to protect yourself, Daze."

"I know. I just . . ." I trail off, the silence stretching between us. "We were together for so long, our lives so intertwined.

What if something happens to him or his family? I'd want to know."

His gaze softens, his thumb absently stroking the back of my hand. "I get that. But there's a line. You have to figure out where to draw it."

Before I can respond, my phone vibrates again, the screen lighting up with a picture of Gracie this time. With a quick apology to Elio, I answer it.

"Hey, little problem here," she rushes out before I even get a word in. "Logan's waiting outside of our apartment for you."

My heart drops to my stomach. I pull away from Elio, sitting up abruptly. "What? Why?"

"I don't know, but he seems desperate. He says he needs to talk to you about something important." Gracie sounds worried, her voice a notch higher than usual.

A pang of anxiety jabs at my chest. I glance at Elio, whose face has grown serious. His eyes meet mine, the question unspoken but clear.

"Alright. I'll be there soon," I tell Gracie, hanging up the phone. Elio's sitting up now, his back resting against the headboard. His eyes are guarded, the playful spark from earlier replaced with a soberness that makes my chest ache.

"I'm guessing you heard that," I say, my voice faltering.

He nods, running a hand through his tousled hair. There's a silence that stretches between us, heavy and full of unspoken questions. He doesn't push, doesn't probe, but the tension in his jaw tells me he's not as indifferent as he'd like me to believe.

I scramble out of the bed, gathering up my purse. "Are you, um, feeling okay after yesterday?"

"I'm fine," he grits out.

"Then I should go. He . . . he wouldn't be there if it wasn't important."

Again, Elio nods, his expression unreadable. I wish he'd say something, anything. I wish he'd voice his thoughts instead of letting me guess.

"You want me to come along?" he finally asks. "I can be your buffer."

"No, you should stay and rest. I don't want anything to screw with your heart today." I glance at the mirror above his dresser, smoothing my hair back into a quick ponytail. "I'll be back in a couple of hours, tops. If you feel anything bad start to happen, call me right away."

"Yeah, alright. Just . . . be careful, will you?"

The words hit me harder than I expect, their weight heavy with unsaid meaning. I give him a small, grateful smile, promise him I will, pat Bentley on the head . . . and then I leave, shutting the door quietly behind me.

I head out to face Logan, but my heart remains with Elio, still curled up in his bed, his gentle caution ringing in my ears.

# Chapter Twenty-One

ELIO

Bentley's nose against my cheek is a gentle, insistent poke, nudging me out of my groggy morning mope fest. I don't want to get up, but it's not because I'm too drowsy or tired. It's Daisy. Or, more accurately, the lack of her.

I rub my eyes, taking in the stark numbers on my phone screen: 7:37 a.m. I squint at it, as if that would somehow change the fact that Daisy's only been gone for less than fifteen minutes. She's off to find out what Logan wants, a meeting that leaves me here twiddling my thumbs, tracing the path of sunlight as it dances across my ceiling.

The spot beside me is empty. But the sheets still hold a hint of Daisy, a whisper of strawberry and something a little sweeter —a distinct scent that's all her. I throw an arm across the other side of the bed, the cold linen a stark reminder of her absence.

"Damn," I mutter to the empty room. Bentley, my loyal partner in this wait, glances up at me. His puppy eyes mirror my sentiment, and I can't help but give him a half-hearted smile. "I know, buddy. It fuckin' sucks."

I sit up, stretching, every joint popping in protest. Bentley seems to take that as an invitation, climbing onto my lap and offering his furry comfort. I ruffle his fur absentmindedly, my thoughts still on Daisy and that asshole ex of hers.

My gaze roams around the room—she has clothes and books scattered in the corner, her little yellow notebook thrown casually onto my desk. Everything is exactly as it was last night, but it all feels different now. Silent, oppressive, nerve-racking for some strange fucking reason.

That is, until the soft buzzing of my phone interrupts the silence.

DAISY

just reached the apartment. wish me luck

ELIO

good luck. Bentley's missing you already

I'm missing both of you. stay in bed until I get back, okay?

And just like that, the weight on my shoulders seems a little lighter. She should be worrying about herself right now, but somehow, she's still hung up on taking care of me. An involuntary grin breaks out on my face, and I swear Bentley's tail starts wagging in direct response to my mood shift.

"Alright, bud." With a sigh, I push myself up off the mattress. "Let's take you out and then crawl right back into bed. Daisy's orders."

After a quick walk to the grass patch downstairs, Bentley and I drag ourselves back under the covers. Reaching for the laptop on my nightstand, I slide it in front of me and boot up the system. My fingers move mechanically over the keys, navigating to the AfterDark homepage.

Thankfully, there's been no sign of Sapphire or any of her minions all week, no creepy remarks or thinly veiled threats. It's been a welcome change, especially with everything that's been going on lately, but it also feels a little too good to be true.

Maybe it's the calm before the storm.

And just because it's quiet doesn't mean I can fully relax. There's work to be done, requests to review, content to shuffle around in the absence of something new. My subscribers wait for no one, least of all a fictional man caught up in real-life drama.

Time seems to slip by, my focus on work distracting me from my own thoughts. It's only when my stomach growls, reminding me of a skipped breakfast, that I check the time—over an hour now since Daisy left.

She said she'd be back soon enough, and I can't focus anymore, so I choose a new path of distraction in the meantime. Mustering up the nerve, I dial Kaia's number, and she answers on the second ring.

"Hey, El. What's up?"

"So, I may or may not have a heart condition," I blurt without warning, my words a sharp interruption to her friendly greeting.

She falls silent for a moment before erupting into a flurry of questions. *How long have you known? How serious is it? Are you going to be okay?*

I do my best to answer them all, my words tumbling out in a rushed explanation about the hospital visit, the episodes of VT, my impending appointment with Dr. Foster, the entire chaotic storm that's become my life recently.

Through the line, her worry washes over me. It's as tangible as a cold, strong wind. In true Kaia fashion, she immediately offers to put her life on hold, to take some time off school and come here to stay with me.

"I already have a friend staying here," I assure her, my tone steady. I can almost picture her brows knitting together, gaze narrowed in utter disbelief.

"What *friend*?"

"Her name's Daisy," I say, a strange warmth creeping up my neck at the mention of her name.

"Daisy, huh?" Her voice is teasing, laced with a note of satisfaction. She prods further. "Is this . . . someone you know from work?"

"No, not at all. She's a Dayton transfer, a surfer from Cape Casserat."

"Huh, a surfer?" There's an awkward pause, and then, "It's been a long time since you mentioned another friend."

"Yeah, she's been good for me, though," I confess, my voice softening. "I, er, I really needed to lean on her these last couple of weeks."

"I'm sorry I couldn't be there for you."

"It's hardly your fault. I didn't bother to tell you anything was wrong."

"I know, and I'm pissed at you about it. But at least you let *someone* be there to take care of you," she says. "This Daisy—is there more going on between you two than just friendship?"

I sigh, pressing into the headboard. "No."

"Do you want there to be?"

"She's one of the best people I've ever met," I say gently, honestly. "She reminds me of you, in a way. Really caring, kind of an overthinker, but she's much more sunshine than your grumpy ass could ever be."

She scoffs. "Hey! I've been very much on the sunnier side these days."

"Yeah, did Beck inject you with something?"

"Love, commitment, stability." Her voice is half-serious, half-teasing. But then she sobers up, asking the one question that I've been avoiding. "El, could this be someone you might settle down for?"

"Don't get me wrong, anyone would be lucky to be with

her," I say, my voice firm. "But she's not looking for that right now. She just got out of a long-term relationship about a month ago. And Lord knows she doesn't need to be with someone like me."

My best friend's response is instant, firm, her fiery spirit making itself known even through the phone. "Shut up, E. There's nothing fucking wrong with you."

I snort a laugh. "I just mean, I fuck other people for a living. And I've been in and out of the hospital for the last few weeks. Oh, and not to mention, I'm an addict. That's a real attractive package right there, isn't it?"

"First of all, you won't be doing that job forever," she argues back, her voice hard and resolute. "Second, just because you have a heart condition doesn't mean you don't deserve love. And lastly, you've been clean for half a decade now."

"Right," I manage to respond, even as her words echo in my ears.

"You have been clean, haven't you?"

"Yes, Kai, I have been. And I'm certainly not gonna delve back into that world now, not when my heart's all fucked-up."

"And because you wouldn't do that to yourself, to me, to your family," she adds quietly.

"Yeah, that, too."

She chuckles, a soft, warm sound. "I'm really proud of you, you know?"

"Stop with the sappiness, Kai. I'll be okay."

"I know you will, despite everything going on right now. But I'm still allowed to tell you that I'm proud of you—for how hard you've been working, for taking care of your health, for making a new friend."

I chuckle at that, shaking my head. "*Making a new friend*? Jesus Christ, am I five years old?"

"Yeah, and I just dropped you off for kindergarten. So, be on your best behavior with Daisy, alright? Don't screw things up."

"I won't," I promise. And then my phone beeps loudly in my ear, indicating an incoming call. I pull the device back, squinting at the name displayed on the screen—*Daisy Grey*.

"Look, I gotta go," I tell Kaia. "But we'll talk later, okay?"

"Let me know how your appointment goes tomorrow."

"I will. See ya."

I don't wait for her goodbye before I end the call, answering Daisy with an apprehensive "Hello?"

"Hey, El," Daisy's voice filters through the line now, taut and strained. "How are you? Everything okay over there?"

"I'm fine. No issues." I run a hand through my hair, springing up from the bed and pacing the length of my room. "How are you?"

"Um, well, I really hate to bother you about this, but we tried Max, and he's not answering. I, uh, it's not urgent or anything, but I could use some help if you think you're up for it."

"What's wrong?"

"It's just Logan." She swallows audibly, the sound reverberating down the line and hitting me square in the chest. "We got into an argument, and now he won't leave."

"Won't leave? Are you still at your apartment?" My mind races, piecing together fragments of her hurried explanation.

"Yep, and he's outside . . . I locked myself in with Gracie." The quiver in her voice sends a rush of adrenaline flooding through my veins. "I just want to get in my car and come back to you, to Bentley, but I can't . . ."

I don't hesitate, don't ponder, don't question. It doesn't matter that I'm not supposed to leave my bed, that I'm not supposed to stress. That I'm one more fuckup from potential dire consequences.

"I'll be there as fast as I can," I tell her.

Because Daisy's in trouble. She's asking for my help. And already, I know I'd go to any lengths, push myself to any limits, just to be the one she leans on.

I PARK my Jeep in front of Daisy's apartment building, my hands steady on the steering wheel before I cut the engine. Silence fills the air, wrapping around me like a thick blanket. I take a few calming breaths before I step out and make my way toward her building.

But as I approach the front entrance, I instantly spot Logan, and it sets my nerves on edge. He's lingering there, his form outlined in the soft morning light. A rush of frustration washes over me, and I have to rub my temples to stay settled.

"Seriously, man?" I say as I approach him, working to steady my voice. "What are you still doing here? It's pretty obvious that Daisy wants you to leave."

Logan looks me up and down, his expression one of irritation and disbelief. "Oh, of course, it's you. This is just rich."

"You have some sort of problem with me?"

"No," he says, the sarcasm thick in his voice. "Just wondering how much she's paying you."

I pause, thrown off by his comment. "Paying . . . me? And what do you propose she's paying me for?"

"I think we both know well enough." He narrows his eyes, scrubs a hand over his chin. "I know what you do. I know who you are."

"Do you now?"

"Everett Rain ring any bells?"

I cross my arms over my chest, cocking one petulant brow. "Oh, are you a fan or something?"

"Hell no, but I asked around about you after our little run-in at the café. It wasn't until last week that a friend of mine put two and two together." He tugs at the hemline of his Dayton Baseball T-shirt, visibly uncomfortable. "That's why I was trying to call Daisy the other night, to warn her about you. I guess she already fucking knew about it, though, didn't she?"

"Okay, so you know that I'm a sex worker, and you think Daisy's paying me to . . . what exactly?"

"Paying you to fuck her, obviously."

His accusation barrels into me, and it's like the ground has been ripped from beneath my feet. I shake my head at him, fully incredulous. "If you seriously think that, then you've gone off the fucking deep end, man."

"So, you deny it?"

"Listen," I snap, my patience running thin. "I don't know what's gotten into that screwed-up head of yours, but you must be truly unhinged if you're the kind of guy who'd cheat on Daisy. So, let me just set the record straight for you. Daisy's not paying me for shit. I would get on my fucking knees in front of her, worship the ground she walked on, just for a chance to have a single taste."

He scoffs, something loud and heavy that grinds on my nerves. "Such fucking bullshit."

"You don't have to believe me," I say, standing my ground. "Daisy has nothing to prove to you. But you should know that she's one of the best things that's ever happened to me."

"The only reason she even gave you the time of day is because I fucked her off," he retorts. "And good on me because I had no idea she'd be the type to sleep with a fucking prostitute."

At this, I can't help but grit my teeth. But instead of losing my temper, I opt for a warning. "I strongly suggest you leave before I make you leave."

He huffs, turning on his heel. "Whatever. It's not worth it anymore."

"You have no right to stand out here and spew your bull-shit. No right to make Daisy feel like she's anything less than perfect," I say. "So, get the fuck out of here, and don't come back."

"Gladly," he mutters, heading for his car.

But before he can disappear entirely, I call out after him. "Oh, and Logan?" He turns, and I offer my parting shot. "Your team has really gone to the fucking gutters since Hayes graduated."

Logan swears at me, slamming his car door with enough force to echo through the quiet morning. And then, he peels out of the parking lot. His departure leaves a bitter taste in my mouth, but I shake it off, turning my attention back to the light in Daisy's window.

That glinting promise of peace.

# Chapter Twenty-Two

DAISY

A SOFT, rhythmic knock echoes through the apartment, jolting Gracie and me from our spot on the couch.

"It's just me," Elio calls, and a knot of tension finally uncoils from my chest.

Dragging in a shaky breath, I cross the room and pull open the door. Elio's dark eyes are filled with a quiet concern. His jaw is set, but his lips curve into a gentle smile.

"Hey," he says softly, slowly stepping across the threshold. He's cautious, wary of the fragile air surrounding me.

"Hey, stranger," I murmur, the words a hushed sigh of gratitude.

I lead him inside, and his eyes meet mine for a moment before skittering away, scanning the apartment. He gives a quick nod to Gracie, who's still sitting where I left her on the couch, and then makes a gesture down the hall.

"You want to go to my room?"

"Yeah," he says, voice still soft. "I think we should probably talk for a minute."

"Shouldn't we go back to your place first?" I ask, worrying over my bottom lip. "I feel like you should be in bed right now resting, away from all the chaos."

He gives me a long, disapproving look. "Daze, come on."

"Fine, we'll stay here. But just for a bit."

I blow out a breath and then guide him down the hallway

to my room. We sink onto the edge of my mattress together, the worn comforter bunching beneath us, the side of his thigh pressing into mine. I turn my head to meet his concerned gaze.

"So, talk to me," he says, smoothing his hands over his thighs. "Tell me what happened."

"Well, Logan was just standing out there when I first showed up. Pacing around the door like some sort of stalker," I tell him, my voice still shaky, fingers tapping against my knee. "It was weird—he tried to hug me as soon as I walked up, and when I didn't reciprocate, he instantly turned nasty. I've never seen him act that way before."

The words tumble out, a torrent of emotions. Elio snorts out a breath, but he remains quiet for the most part, letting me tell my side of the story.

"He asked me what happened to the 'sweet Daisy' he used to know. And I—I told him that girl was cheated on by someone she trusted." I let my shoulders slump. "He finally told me he was sorry for what he did. But it was so strange. It all felt like it came out of nowhere because it's not like he bothered to apologize when it first happened."

Elio keeps his eyes on me, but my gaze stays locked on my hands, fingers twiddling in my lap. He slides one palm over the back of mine, a silent show of support, a lifeline I'm eager to cling to.

"He'd been asking around about you," I continue. "He found out about Everett, about AfterDark. He said he wanted to warn me. That he heard you on the phone the other night and thought . . . Well, he obviously thought we were having sex."

Elio stiffens beside me, but he says nothing as his grip on my hand tightens.

"Logan accused me of hiring you," I say, embarrassment

creeping into my voice. "He said he's heard of this kind of thing before. I guess he thought . . . I wanted some sort of a 'spice coach' to . . . learn how to *please* someone. He thinks I'm doing all this just to get him back."

"*Jesus*, Daisy."

"He said that he loved me," I say, the words catching in my throat. "He said he realized that sex isn't *that* important to him anymore, and he just . . . He couldn't believe I would 'stoop so low.'"

A harsh stinging sensation pricks at the back of my nose, but I force the tears back. I refuse to cry over Logan. Not now, not ever again.

"When I told him to leave, he wouldn't," I finish, my voice shaking with pent-up emotion. "Gracie tried to reason with him. We called Max, but he didn't answer. With everything you have going on, I just didn't want to drag you back into this."

I look over at him then, his face a picture of quiet understanding. "You didn't drag me," he says. "I wanted to be here for you."

"Well, thank you. I'm really glad you came after all." I lean my head against his shoulder, and his hand moves to stroke my hair. "What did you say to get him to leave?"

"I just told him the truth."

"Which is?"

"That you're the best thing in my life right now. That he's out of his fucking mind if he thinks any of that bullshit is true. That I would . . . That I'd be lucky if you'd even so much as let me get on my knees in front of you."

I lift my head from his shoulder. "El . . ."

"I'm serious, Daisy. Anyone would be lucky to have you, and that includes me." He shifts on the bed, gaze meeting mine.

His hand moves to cup my face, his thumb tracing the curve of my cheek—softly, slowly. "Are you okay?"

I manage a small smile, leaning into his touch. "Yeah," I whisper. "Or I will be."

"I'm sorry this happened. I'm sorry he came here."

"It's okay. You lean on me, I lean on you?"

"Yeah, Daisy girl," he says softly. "That's the deal."

As I stare up at him, I get lost in the dark depths of his eyes, and the world slows down. We're close now, so close that I can feel his warm breath fan across my face. My heart throbs in my chest, my mind a flurry of emotions.

It's hard enough to think. All I know is that when I'm alone with him, I feel safe, calm, protected. Wanted, more than I ever have before.

And so, I lean in.

Our lips meet, and a million tiny sparks flutter around my head, like a beautiful, silent light show. The sensation is intense, all-consuming. It's a sweet kind of chaos, a perfect little whirlwind.

But then, he pulls back.

Gently, he grips my upper arms, his hands warm through the fabric of my shirt. His voice is low and deep, filled with an emotion I can't quite decipher. "*Fuck.*"

And just like that, my heart sinks. A hot blush creeps up my neck, my cheeks burning with embarrassment. I lower my gaze to my lap, blinking back the tears. "Sorry," I mumble, my voice hushed.

"Hey," he says gruffly. "Don't be sorry."

I feel his gaze on me, burning, but I can't bring myself to meet it. "I just—I thought you said . . ."

"I know what I said," he interrupts, and the intensity in his voice makes me look back up at him. His eyes are soft, full of conflict. "And I meant every word. But Daisy, is this really the best time to start something between us? You're in such a vulnerable spot right now, and so am I."

I swallow hard, my throat dry. "So, you don't want me to kiss you?"

"No," he groans, raking a hand through his hair. "I want you to fucking kiss me. That's not the problem."

"Then let me kiss you," I press, the words coming out as a soft plea.

"Daisy . . ."

"I promise to stop when your heart starts racing."

"Ship has sailed. It's already beating out of my fucking chest."

I deflate at his words, disappointment sinking in my stomach. "Oh," I mumble, dropping my gaze back to my lap. "Okay, then you're right. We shouldn't start this now. We'll table it?"

He sighs, but there's a hint of relief in his eyes. "Yeah, we'll table it. It's a rain check until I get this shit cleared up, until you're not reeling from the confrontation you just had with your ex."

"Okay."

"And Daisy," he starts again, his voice gentle. "Don't be embarrassed that you made the first move. I liked it."

"You did?"

He chuckles, the sound low and soothing. "A whole lot."

A relieved smile tugs at the corners of my lips, the first genuine one I've managed since this whole mess started. Despite the whiplash of emotions, despite the lingering awkwardness, a warm bubble of hope rises in my chest.

This isn't the end of the conversation between us, not even close.

. . .

Elio's sprawled out on my bed now, his eyes shut, the deep lines on his forehead relaxed for the first time in hours. I begged him to rest while I tidied up a few things in my room, and it didn't take long for him to pass out completely.

It's good for him, though. He'll be well rested for his appointment tomorrow, and we still have the rest of the night to spend at home.

So, I leave him there, tiptoeing out of the room, letting the door click shut behind me. In the living room, Gracie's curled up on the couch, her phone in her hand.

"How's he doing?" she asks, gaze darting from me to the closed bedroom door.

"He's okay, just resting," I say, tucking a loose strand of hair behind my ear. "Lord knows he needs it."

"And you?" She sets her phone down on the table, giving me her full attention. "How are you doing after everything with Logan?"

"I'm fine now, honestly. It's kind of weird, though. In a way, the whole thing already feels like ancient history." She nods, her eyes softening. The two of us sit in silence for a moment before a new idea crosses my mind. "What do you think about having a dinner tonight? A proper one, with Max and LJ, too."

"Yeah, I'd love that," she says. "And Max called while you were in there, said he got caught up with a study group earlier. He's sorry he missed your call."

"Okay, I'll just shoot him a text now."

I pull out my phone to message him, and the plans are set in motion. Gracie and I work together in the kitchen, a true picture of domestic bliss as we prep the meal. She chops the vegetables while I marinate some chicken for fajitas.

It's therapeutic, this semblance of normalcy. And as the sun finally sets, Max and LJ arrive, heralded by their joyous laughter and the sound of the front door slamming shut behind them.

"Hey, you two, we come bearing wine!" Max announces, brandishing some fancy-looking bottle.

"And Daisy's nasty strawberry shit," LJ adds, a teasing glint in her eyes.

Without missing a beat, I move closer and snatch the bottle from her hand. "Thank you very much," I retort, grinning as I set it in the middle of our dining table. Then, my attention strays to the closed bedroom door. "I'm gonna go wake up Sleeping Beauty."

I slip back into my room to find Elio still in the grip of sleep. And for a moment, I just look at him—at the peaceful expression on his face, at the frown lines that have finally relaxed. Hesitant, I brush the ruffled hair away from his forehead, and he stirs, eyes fluttering open.

"*Fuck.* I fell asleep again, didn't I?" he murmurs, pushing himself to a seated position.

"It's okay. I was actually hoping you would." I brush a hand over his shoulder. "Um, but Gracie and I cooked up some dinner, and it's ready to eat now. Max and LJ are here, too. We'd love it if you'd join us."

He clears his throat, glancing down at his lap. "I wouldn't want to intrude."

"You're not intruding at all," I assure him. "But if it makes you uncomfortable, you can take a plate back to your place, and I'll join you right after."

"Would it make you happy if I stayed?"

"Very much so," I say.

"Then I'll stay."

He offers me a small, quiet nod, and my heart clenches. I take his hand and lead him back to the living room, offering a formal introduction to the rest of my friends. Then we gather around the table, plates are passed, glasses clink, and the conversation moves right along.

Throughout the meal, Elio doesn't say much, his quiet demeanor a contrast to the lively chatter. He's clearly more of an introvert than I am, but we do have one other thing in common—preferring to listen.

Despite the fact that he's surrounded by new people, following an unexpected confrontation with my ex, he seems to be comfortable enough here. There's a certain softness in his eyes, a tiny half-smile playing on his lips as he watches us all.

As he watches *me*.

It makes me feel good inside, happy and content. Because deep down, I know that I've found exactly what I've been looking for here at Coastal—a sanctuary, a family, my true home away from home.

# Chapter Twenty-Three

ELIO

I'm in the waiting room at Harbor Point again, tapping my foot impatiently on the white-tiled floor. There's a soft murmur of nurses behind the reception counter, and the overhead lights are incessantly whirring, but the one sound I can't escape is the chaotic humming of the girl beside me.

Daisy's sitting there to my right, shuffling through a health magazine, probably one that's been collecting dust for the last five years. Her face is the picture of calm, but I can't shake the feeling of guilt that she's here. Missing her classes for this. For *me*.

"I still can't believe you skipped fisheries to be here," I say, voice low, trying to keep my frustration from showing.

She looks up, those warm brown eyes piercing into mine. "It's an easy class," she insists. "Besides, you need someone to be here with you. And I *want* to be here. So, stop feeling guilty and just accept it."

I groan inwardly. Daisy's stubbornness may be a force of nature, but her insistence, her desire to be here with me, warms something else deep inside. It's obvious that she cares more about me than she probably should.

The nurse calls us down to the exam room a few moments later and proceeds to take my vitals. Once she's finished, I take a seat on the edge of the table while Daisy claims the lone chair, placing her bag on the floor.

The nurse leaves, and we only have to wait a few short minutes until Dr. Foster walks in, clipboard in hand, a flat look on his face. "Good morning, Mr. Reynolds. How are we doing today?"

"Just fine, thanks," I mutter, hoping to move the conversation along. I came here for an official diagnosis, for a treatment plan, not to shoot the shit at eight o'clock in the morning.

"Well, after going through all your test results and your file from the ED, we do have some answers for you. It appears that you're experiencing ventricular tachycardia." He gives me a tight-lipped smile. "This is a serious condition, but with the right treatment and lifestyle adjustments, you can lead a normal life."

A weight lifts slightly. The confirmation is helpful, but it's quickly replaced by a dozen other concerns. "What kind of adjustments?"

"Firstly, you'll need to avoid long bouts of strenuous physical activity. No heavy lifting or high-intensity workouts. You'll also need to cut down on stimulants, particularly caffeine, as they can trigger an episode. Limit alcohol, of course."

"Right, no problem there," I mutter. "But what do you suggest instead of coffee?"

"Non caffeinated tea?"

"Oh, fucking hell."

He peers at me over the top of his glasses and clears his throat. "Right, well, stress management is also essential for you," he continues. "So, consider practicing relaxation techniques like deep breathing, meditation, or yoga. And, of course, regular check-ups and monitoring will be essential to track the condition."

He details the treatment, mentioning the name of a medication and potential side effects. As I work to digest the information, my head spins. But Daisy, God bless her, has pulled out a pen and notebook beside me, jotting down every word.

". . . and it's essential you monitor your body's reactions in the first week or so of treatment. Some side effects can be unpredictable, so it's a good idea not to be alone during this time period."

Daisy's gaze flicks to mine, and she gives me a warm, comforting smile. She asks a few more follow-up questions, and I just sit back and stew, overwhelmed with both confusion and gratitude for her.

As we exit the hospital together, the warmth of the morning sun feels especially nice, so calming and serene. Maybe it's the relief of finally having a solid treatment plan, or maybe it's just the fact that I have Daisy by my side now, caring about me, caring *for* me.

"It's a lot to process," she says quietly, threading her arm through mine.

"It is." I pull her closer, my side warming at her touch. "But thank you, Daze. Don't know how I would've gotten through that, through all of this, without you."

"You're welcome," she says. "Like I said, I'm happy to be here."

After picking up my prescription, we arrive back at the apartment about an hour later, and a thick sort of tension has grown between us. The memory of yesterday's kiss looms, as does the reason I pulled away in the first place. So, when we finally step inside, I wait for her to break it.

"You know, considering what Dr. Foster said about the side effects, I really should stick around till at least the end of next weekend. Maybe a bit longer."

I chuckle, a genuine smile playing on my lips. "Trying to find any excuse to stay, are we?"

Her cheeks flush. "I mean, I've grown accustomed to your extremely bitter morning coffee. I'm gonna need to stick around to watch you try out tea."

"And here I was thinking you'd stay just for my charm."

"Well, that, too." She gives a soft giggle, and my stomach fucking somersaults. "Um, I've got some afternoon classes that I should get ready for. Will you be okay here without me, just for a little while?"

"I've been managing alone for years now, you know."

"Just check in with me throughout the afternoon, will you?" She narrows her eyes. "For my peace of mind."

"Always the protector, huh?" I step forward, tugging at a loose strand of her hair. "Fine, just for you. But I'll be kicking back while you're on campus. Nothing's gonna go wrong."

"Maybe you could text me every half hour just to be sure?"

"How about I send you two texts while you're gone, and I also make you a promise that I won't run a marathon?"

"There's that ever-present sarcasm of yours." She gives me a humorless snort. "It's lethal, you know? One of these days, I'll—"

"Collapse from laughing too hard?"

Her jaw drops, and she swats me on the bicep. "Too soon."

I just chuckle in response, flopping onto the couch with Bentley as she bustles around the apartment. She collects her textbooks and then heads back to my bedroom—*her* temporary room. I can hear the shuffling of materials, the occasional rustle of clothing, and her soft hum as she picks out an outfit.

A few minutes later, she emerges dressed in a soft yellow sundress. Her hair is neatly pulled back into a half-up style, a few bright wisps framing her face. It's simple but striking, and I can't manage to take my eyes off her.

Of course, she catches my blatant staring and waves me off, though the tiny, lingering smile betrays her amusement. "Like what you see?"

"Always."

She muffles a grin and goes on her merry way. With a few last-minute checks in her bag, she's ready to head out. But for some reason, she lingers in the doorway, an uncertainty shadowing her expression.

"I really will be back soon," she says. "So, try not to miss me too much."

"Promise to try."

She draws her lips together, tugging them softly to one side, a hint of shyness in her gaze. "See you in a bit."

"See you, Daze."

With that, she turns and leaves, and the apartment already feels a whole lot emptier. I let out a sigh, the weight of this morning's appointment pressing down on me. But work beckons, and so I make my way back to my bedroom, hoping to distract myself from the silence.

I take a seat in my office chair and pull up my analytics on AfterDark. After a cursory glance, it's apparent how much my earnings have dipped. The inconsistency in content, combined with my unexpected hiatus, has made an obvious dent.

Rubbing my temples, I open a new document, drafting a post for my subscribers:

*Hey everyone, taking a small break from the usual webchat spots for the next couple of weeks due to health reasons. But don't worry, I'll still be uploading a few solo scenes. Any special requests? You can contribute to the fund, and I'll see what I can do. Thanks for understanding and staying supportive! - E*

Saving the post and setting it to upload, I recline back in my chair. My eyelids grow heavy, and before I know it, I drift into a light nap, comforted by the familiar sound of Bentley's snoring beneath my feet.

THE DISTANT SOUND of the apartment door closing stirs me from my sleep. Groggy and disheveled, I push myself up, leaving my room to find Daisy pulling a few books out of her bag.

She takes one look at me and flushes a soft pink, lips curving up in amusement.

"What?" I mumble, running a hand through my messy hair, trying to tame the unruly strands.

She bites her lip, failing to mask her full-on smile. "It's just . . . you always look so handsome when you've just woken up. The mussy hair, that hint of stubble . . . it's this perfect mix of rugged and soft."

I blink, surprised by the compliment, warmth flooding my chest. It's not often I'm caught off guard by comments about my appearance, especially in my line of work, but Daisy seems to have a particular knack for it.

Clearing my throat, I give her a petulant smirk. "Thank you for the ego boost. If I want to impress you, I'll just make sure to roll around in my bed first."

"Oh, shush." She flushes again. "You asked, and I answered."

"Yeah, you did." I scrub a hand down the side of my face,

rubbing the sleep from my eyes. "So, how was, uh, how were your afternoon classes?"

"Good. Boring," she mutters. "I mostly just wanted to get back here to check on you. You know, you only sent me one text when you promised two."

"I know, and I'm sorry for that," I say sincerely. "I fell asleep until just a few minutes ago."

"Ah, well, that's good, at least."

"Yeah, and I—well, I've been thinking. Before we get the rest of this week started, we should probably talk about us."

She nods, serious once more. "Right. *Us*."

"We're in agreement to . . . stay friends for now? Especially while you're still staying here?"

"Why would that matter?"

"With work, I've learned that boundaries are everything." I reach across my chest, rubbing my bicep. "I'm used to setting them, respecting them, maintaining them. With us living together, those lines are bound to get pretty blurry."

She nods, pursing her lips. "I suppose you're right. Boundaries are important, so . . ."

"So, until you're fully healed from your last relationship, until things stabilize with my health, and we figure out what *this is*—" I gesture between us and then slowly swipe a thumb across my lower lip. "—it's best if we keep things . . . friendly."

"Trust me, I'm so done with Logan. But yes, the rest holds true." She sighs, her gaze softening. "Just friends, it is."

I nod, not quite trusting my voice, so I let the words hang between us for a few long moments. Then, working to break the silence, I shift my focus toward the TV.

"You up for another one of Bentley's shows? I've got our guy David cued up, just waiting to narrate some wildlife cycles."

She gives a half-hearted chuckle. "I was hoping you might ask."

Bentley, ever the opportunist, jumps onto the couch, sprawling out across the middle. It forces Daisy and me to start off on opposite ends, which is probably for the best. But as the documentary plays out, we inch closer and closer together, as if drawn together by some invisible force.

It starts off with a light brush of our fingers while stroking Bentley's fur, an innocent enough graze, but it sends a jolt up my arm. We both pretend not to notice, focusing on the scene in front of us instead.

When Daisy shifts and Bentley jumps off the couch, she stretches her legs out and rests them lightly over mine. I struggle to swallow, acutely aware of the heat of her touch. My chest clenches, throat dries up, and I can't help but glance over at her.

She's absorbed in the documentary, her features soft and relaxed. But then her eyes drift to mine, and there's a question there, a hesitation. Slowly, as if in a trance, she moves closer, tucking herself in the small space between my legs.

My arms, unsure of where to go, eventually find a place circling her waist, one hand resting lightly on her stomach. The warmth of her back presses against me.

For a while, we simply watch in this newfound closeness, an electric charge passing between us. But instead of feeling heavy with tension, the moment feels soft, tender even. The gentle sweep of her fingers over the back of my hand is filled with promise, with understanding.

At some point in the next hour, I realize she's dozed off, her breathing deep and heavy, her head nestled perfectly under my chin. That signature strawberry scent fills my senses, grounding and intoxicating all at once.

Carefully, I slip one arm beneath her knees, the other supporting her back, and stand, cradling her against my chest. She stirs but doesn't wake as I make my way to our now-shared bedroom. Placing her gently onto the mattress, I settle in beside her, drawing her close.

Despite the boundaries I've tried to set, I'm not upset that we've already skirted our way around them. Sharing this space with her—feeling her warm and content wrapped up in my arms—it feels inevitable.

More importantly, it feels *right*.

# Chapter Twenty-Four

DAISY

THE WARM SCENT of Elio surrounds me, a mixture of spice and that earthy pine cologne he wears. The gentle flow of his breathing brushes the top of my head. I allow myself to sink into his embrace, the warmth of his chest pressed against my back.

But after five too-short minutes, it's time to dispel the magic.

Wriggling out of his arms without waking him, I slip from the cocoon we created on his bed. I'm still wearing the same sundress from yesterday, which means I most definitely fell asleep on the couch last night. And though Elio is supposed to avoid heavy lifting, he evidently carried me back to his bedroom.

When he wakes up, that'll earn him a slap on the wrist from me.

As I putz around, Bentley stirs from his spot at the foot of the bed, watching me with a sleepy gaze. I contemplate taking him downstairs for his morning potty break, but he seems content exactly where he is.

So, I grab the clothes I'd packed for the campus gym—a pair of compression shorts and a tank top with a built-in sports bra—and quickly pull them on. I'll just do some warm-ups, light calisthenic training inside the apartment. That way, Elio and I can still carpool to classes if he's feeling up for it.

With a soft click of the door behind me, I wander out of the bedroom and work up to a simple morning routine.

I start with a few poses to stretch, transitioning into dynamic exercises that will help strengthen my core for surfing. It's been a while since I focused on training these muscles outside of working my board.

Before college, my life was a strict regimen of drills and exercises. I don't like to brag, but I was a formidable force on the waves, particularly on the East Coast, even earning the title of Junior Champion at sixteen.

Underwater rock running, intensive paddle workouts, and countless hours on the board had been daily staples. My future seemed set on a path that could lead back to the pro circuit after college, a brief stint in the shimmering limelight before settling into my career.

But all those aspirations came to a head during my junior year of high school. A dislocated shoulder halted my training, I lost my sponsorship, and in that vulnerable moment, I realized how fleeting and fragile that dream really was.

Applying for colleges, I wanted distance from the world of surfing for a while, a fresh start.

Dayton was that escape for me, a place where my past felt more like a memory. And it helped that Logan was by my side through it all. But as time wore on, an undeniable emptiness crept in. I thought I was happy, content, but I was directionless, unanchored from my true passion.

And, in many ways, this realization is what prompted my transfer here to Coastal. Being closer to the water was essential, not just for the marine bio courses but to rediscover my connection with the ocean.

Now, I'm standing in the middle of Elio's living room, a

lifetime away from where I once was. But after everything, it just feels right.

From plank jacks to Russian twists, sweat beads on my forehead, my breathing becomes ragged, and every part of me burns with exertion. But it's not too much longer before the floor beneath me vibrates with footsteps. I know it must be Elio finally waking up, but I'm too lost in a bridge pose to greet him.

That is, until a soft, throaty chuckle breaks my concentration.

Lifting my head, I find the man in question leaning against the wall, sleep-tousled hair, shirtless, his eyes raking over me with a heat that makes my stomach flutter.

"Morning," he rasps, voice heavy with sleep and something else I can't quite name.

"Morning, stranger," I say as I roll to my feet, avoiding the urge to stare. I wasn't lying when I told him he looked handsome like this. In fact, I think this might just be his best look yet. "Enjoying the show?"

His lips twitch into a smirk. "Didn't know my living room doubled as a personal gym. But I'm not complaining."

"Well, now you know." I wipe a thin line of sweat from my forehead. "You should try it sometime. Dr. Foster said yoga would be good for you."

He cocks a petulant brow. "Oh, did he now? Must have missed that part."

"It's all in the notebook, El." I playfully narrow my eyes. "But you know what's also in the notebook? The fact that you're supposed to avoid heavy lifting."

"Think we're good there."

"You carried me into our—*your*—bed last night."

He huffs a laugh. "Right, and I could do that in my sleep."

"*Okay*, Mr. Tough Guy."

He gives me a humorless snort, and I return it with a roll of my eyes. Then, doing my best to ignore the charged atmosphere, I breeze past him toward the bathroom, the intensity of his gaze almost tangible on my back.

The shower is quick, steam and warm water helping to relax my muscles. But when I step back into the living room, the sight that greets me steals my breath away. Elio—still half-naked with his mop of messy hair—is lounging on the beige couch, legs spread apart, tattoos on full display.

But it's the mug in his hands that makes my stomach drop.

"Are you seriously drinking coffee right now?" I ask, jaw agape.

He tips the mug my way, giving me a little peek. The liquid inside is clear, steam swirling above it. "Just hot water," he says, his voice rich with amusement.

"Oh, why?"

He tilts his head, the playful glint in his eyes softening to something more introspective. "Miss the warmth. The routine, I guess. My mornings don't feel complete without a mug in hand."

"That makes sense." Drawing my bottom lip between my teeth, I contemplate a solution. "Are you—did you still want to carpool to classes today?"

"Yeah." He takes a thoughtful sip. "I think it should be fine."

"We could grab something else from the Seashell before we head in. You can try out some *super*-delicious herbal teas."

His lips twitch into a smirk at my enthusiasm, but his reply is a noncommittal grunt.

"Cheer up, buttercup," I tease, trying to lighten the mood. "We'll get some strawberry tea, and you can think of me while you drink it."

His chuckle is low, a rumble that sends warmth curling in my belly. "Alright, now *that* is an idea I can get behind."

A full-on blush creeps up my neck, heating my cheeks, but I simply wave off his attempt to get under my skin. Instead, I busy myself while he heads back to shower and change.

Bentley gives a little whimper, pawing at the front door, so I let him outside for a quick breath of fresh air. His tail wags, his eyes watchful as he takes in the morning scene. And once he's had his moment, I coax him back upstairs, ensuring he's settled with some of his special food and water.

A few minutes later, Elio's ready, and the two of us head back down to the parking lot together. He slides behind the wheel of his Jeep, and I settle into the passenger side. It's a calming drive as the familiar surroundings roll by, a blend of pastel storefronts and golden sunlit trees.

"You know," Elio says, the leather of the steering wheel creaking under his tight grip. "Until yesterday, I hadn't missed a single class this term."

"Really?" I glance over at him, taking in his tense jawline and the slight furrow in his brow. "I didn't take you for the type to care about perfect attendance."

"Yeah, it's just that last year was chaotic, to say the least. I was juggling too much. Late nights with AfterDark, my heart playing tricks on me . . . I missed more classes than I care to admit."

Reaching out, my fingers brush the warm skin of his forearm, and I can feel the coiled strength and tension beneath. "You had to make sacrifices, and that's okay. It's not a reflection of who you are but the situation you were in. Besides, one missed day now won't trip you up in the long run. And if it does, I'll help you get back on track."

His eyes, dark and soulful, find mine. "You know, Daze, at

the risk of sounding a little bit too sappy on a Tuesday morning —I just, I feel like you came into my life exactly when I needed you to."

"I feel the same way about you."

His gaze is skeptical, but he doesn't bother to argue.

He must realize that it's not just a blanket reciprocation. When I say the words, I mean them. Sure, I've done a lot for Elio in the few weeks we've known each other, but he's been a rock for me in ways he might never realize.

So, for now, he'll just have to trust that what I tell him is the truth—*my* truth.

The rest of the week breezes by, a nice mixture of sunrises at the beach, daytime lectures, and late-night reading sessions. Elio seems to be adjusting well enough to his medications, which has helped to smooth the transition for both of us.

He continues to put on a good front around me, as though the situation is barely weighing on him. But I can only imagine how hard this all must be—relying on medication to keep your heart steady, to keep you alive and well.

I'm worried for him, of course, but I've become a pro at maintaining an arm's length of distance during the day. To let him have his space and to keep my emotions, my growing feelings, on the back burner. At least for now.

Inevitably, once night comes and the sun dips low, we find solace in each other's arms again, cuddled up in the warmth of his bed.

We made the agreement not to complicate things further, not to cross certain boundaries while we're sharing this apartment. Though, it seems to be a threadbare promise at best. The pull between us is inescapable, an invisible string that hums with energy whenever our eyes meet or our fingers brush.

So, by the time Friday hits, all I can think about is spending the weekend together, poorly pretending that we're nothing more than friends.

Our classes are finally finished for the week, and as we head back to the apartment, Elio turns to me once again from the driver's side. "So, I got a call this morning from my brother," he says, rubbing at the back of his neck. "He and Harper asked me to babysit June tomorrow night."

My brow lifts. "For Halloween? That'll be so much fun."

"Yeah, Taylor's swamped with work. She's in charge of some big project at Raytheon, and my little sister Georgie has this huge sleepover thing at our parents' place," he explains, his fingers drumming against his thigh. "But there's a catch. They're kinda hesitant, given my . . . you know, with all my health shit going on lately."

I tilt my head, watching him closely. "So?"

He lets out a soft sigh, raking a hand through his hair. "So, they're wondering if you'd maybe come along. Walk the neighborhood with us, you know? Just in case."

He maintains his composure, but I can tell that this is hard for him—asking for help from me in light of the circumstances. From what I've gathered over the last month, Elio is fiercely independent, and he'd rather not bother me—or *anyone*—unless he absolutely needed to.

The fact that he's considering it now, yet again, shows just how much he cares for his niece. For his family, in general.

"Of course I'll come." I smile warmly. "Like I said, it sounds like fun. Besides, it's been ages since I went trick-or-treating."

His features light up. "Yeah?"

"Why not?" I shrug, stomach fluttering. "Besides, I bet they live in a really swanky neighborhood, don't they? It should be a good haul for June."

"They live about an hour or so from here. Just a little under halfway to the Bobcats home stadium." He gives me a soft, placating chuckle. "And yes, it's pretty upscale. According to my brother, kids walk out with bags heavier than they can carry."

"Then it's settled. But I do expect my fair share of the candy."

"You're gonna have to take that up with my girl Juney," he teases, his gaze softening with gratitude. "But thank you, Daze. Seriously. I owe you more than my life at this point."

I wave him off, though the warmth in my chest spreads further. "It's nothing, really. But I do have to warn you, if anyone's dressed as a clown, I'm running the other way. No holds barred."

"Duly noted," he says. "We'll protect June from the witches and goblins together. But I'm solidly on my own with the clowns."

We share a smile as he turns the wheel, rounding the last corner before his apartment complex. He flips his turn signal, and we pull back into the familiar parking stall. And there it is, our home sweet home, if only for a little while longer.

# Chapter Twenty-Five

ELIO

It's been a long, rough week adjusting to my new medications.

I've been even more tired than usual, light-headed, and a little bit queasy. And while I know it's nothing I can't handle in the long run, it's still been frustrating and exhausting to navigate. So, now that we've hit Friday night, I'm ready to sit back and unwind.

Daisy and I are both settled onto the couch, spicy popcorn bowl perched between us, and we're trying something new tonight. Much to Bentley's displeasure, we've swapped the nature docs for some true crime.

"Sooo, I was wondering . . ." Daisy starts, kicking her feet onto the coffee table in front of us. "What are we doing for costumes tomorrow?"

"I have no plans to dress up."

"It's Halloween! We have to. It's practically a law or something." She pauses and then, with a soft giggle, asks, "What's June going to be?"

"I have no idea," I say with a shrug.

She feigns desperation, holding her hands together in a faux prayer. "Please, for the love of candy corn, text Luca and find out. We have to match her. It'll be so cute!"

I chuckle, the idea amusing me more than I'd like to admit. But as she rambles on about our potential trip to the Spirit store in the morning, my demeanor changes. I've barely put a dent in my work this week as it is, and now we're planning on spending a full night away.

"Listen, Daze," I begin hesitantly, avoiding her gaze. "I actually need a little time tomorrow morning. Just, uh, time to myself to get some things done."

She tilts her head. "Oh, right. For . . . work?"

I'm not ashamed of talking about this with her, but it's something we haven't fully navigated yet. And now—with that kiss lingering between us, with our nights spent tangled up together—it's a tough subject to broach.

"I haven't had the steady income I'm used to, not with everything going on," I admit. "I just need to film a quick scene or two."

Her eyes widen a fraction. She's trying to hide it, but I can sense her discomfort simmering beneath the surface. "What kind of scene?"

"Solo," I reassure her. "Subscribers can donate and leave requests. Specific things they want to hear or see."

"Like what?"

I press my tongue to my cheek, searching for the right words. "Sometimes they want specific scenarios, or they want me to say certain things. It's all about fantasy, about giving them a worthwhile escape so they'll keep coming back for more."

She bites her lip, a clear sign that she's fighting with her own emotions. "Did you . . . I mean, when was the last time you . . ."

"Filmed a scene with a partner? It's been a while."

"A while," she echoes.

"Since before I met you." I swallow, thick and heavy.

"Why? You still a subscriber of mine? Looking to sample the goods?"

"No." She scoffs, trying her best to appear nonchalant. "I already told you I wouldn't look at your account. Besides, I haven't had the time to even open the site, let alone watch anything."

I raise a brow, the jealousy now biting at me, too. "So, who else did you subscribe to before?"

She hesitates, her gaze flicking away. "I don't remember their names."

"Oh, yeah? You want to pull up your account for me? I could help you go through the list, make sure you're not following any creeps."

"That seems unnecessary."

"I beg to differ."

"Fine." With a dramatic roll of her eyes, she pulls up the app and hands over her phone.

Immediately, her username jumps out of me from the top corner, and I can't help but chuckle at the irony. "*WildFlower*. A little too apt, don't you think?"

She glares, but there's no heat in it. "Okay, Mr. Everett *Rain*."

"No, you're right. I've got no room to judge," I say, snorting a laugh. "Besides, it's perfect for you."

I'm still smiling as I tap into her profile, but as I scroll through her subscriptions, my humor quickly evaporates. Each new profile feels like a sting, and my protective side rears its ugly head. So, naturally, I start deleting the subscriptions like a man possessed, one after the other.

"Hey! What are you doing?" she protests, lunging for the phone.

Laughing, I lift the device high above my head, challenging her. "Just trying to vet the competition."

Without so much as a word, she pushes off her side of the couch, climbing onto my lap. She's fully straddling me, one leg over each of my thighs, and I'm momentarily stunned. Our faces are inches apart, her panting breath coming in these quick, little huffs. The feeling of her weight, her warmth, it disarms me.

I may be stiff beneath her now, practically immobile, but she's clueless to the fact. She's still trying to grab for the phone, sliding and adjusting herself on top of me to get a better reach.

Our hips are perfectly aligned, the thin layers of clothing doing little to dampen the feeling.

My stomach dips, my body responding in a way I can't control. And when she finally realizes what's happening, I'm so fucking hard against her that it's embarrassing.

With a gasp, her wide brown eyes lock onto mine. "Elio . . ."

"Yeah?" I ask, voice rougher than intended, gaze fixed on her slightly parted lips.

"I didn't mean to, um, you know . . ." A faint blush creeps across her cheeks, but she doesn't look away. "I'm sorry."

I smirk. "Are you?"

Her fingers trace along my jawline, and a shiver racks down my spine. "Not really, I guess. You're the one who took my phone. But, um . . . would you like me to move?"

"Move?" I rasp the question, my head swirling. Every rational thought is lost, drowning in a heady pool of desire.

She swallows hard, her voice shaky. "I meant, like, to get off of you."

"I think"—I lean in so our foreheads touch, the phone forgotten on the cushion beside us—"that's the last thing I want right now."

Her face heats, thighs unconsciously squeezing around me. "Oh, is it now?"

"Yeah," I say, "sure is."

With her distinct combination of bold and shy, those movements switch from accidental to deliberate. I guide her gradually, ensuring that I take my time.

I'd rather savor this moment than rush it—her on top of me, brushing against my erection, finally acknowledging how much she turns me on.

She rests on my lap, my hands moving her hips in a slow dance of shifting, of sliding. Our breaths mingle, her soft moans urging me on, pleading with me to continue.

And so, I do.

Every small adjustment, every tiny gasp, only adds to the tension. I cup her face, drawing her in even closer. The space between us narrows, and every fiber of my being aches to close that distance—to drown in the warmth of her mouth, in the taste of those perfect lips.

But I resist. If we cross that line again, there's no coming back. And maybe, if I don't go there, we can still pretend we haven't torn down our self-imposed boundaries.

Her hands trail down my chest, fingers clenching the fabric of my shirt as she grinds down on me. The sensation has me gripping her hips tighter, guiding her, directing her in a way that maximizes the friction. It's torturous in its sweetness, each graze feeling like too much and never enough.

She tilts her head back, eyes shut tight, the column of her throat exposed to me. I can feel her heartbeat, fast and erratic, matching the thunderous beat of my own. And maybe that's not such a good thing, but I can't bring myself to be concerned at the moment.

Undeterred, I roll my hips directly against her warm center, and the sound she makes has me leaking precum like a teenager.

"Oh, God," she breathes, voice heavy with need. "El, I can't . . . I need . . ."

"Just let go, pretty girl," I whisper against her ear, her body quivering at the words. "Let go with me."

Her response is a whimper, her movements growing more erratic, more desperate. I can sense she's close, teetering on the edge. I trace my fingers up her spine, and she shivers under my touch.

"That's it," I murmur, "just a little more."

Her rhythm falters before she clutches onto me tightly, a shudder running through her entire frame. Her breathy moan fills my ear, and it's the sweetest sound I've ever heard.

Fully spent, she collapses against me, our hearts racing in tandem.

For a long moment, there's only silence, only the steady rise and fall of our chests. The aftermath leaves us both breathless, but the undercurrent of tension remains, reminding us that this is just the beginning of something, not the end.

"So," she pants, hiding her face in the crook of my neck, muttering the words against my skin. "Is that what '*just friends*' do?"

"No, Daze," I say with a gulp, holding her against me. "It's not."

Gently, she pulls back, her eyes searching mine for something. The playful glint they usually hold is now replaced with the weight of uncertainty.

"I should, uh . . ." She glances around, her gaze finally settling on the bathroom. "I need to freshen up."

"Daisy," I start, but nothing else follows. I have no fucking clue what to say right now, how to make her stay.

With a soft, almost inaudible sigh, she shifts off me and stands, clearly trying to hide the rosy shade coloring her cheeks. "I'll probably head to bed after," she says, her voice a soft murmur. "You can join whenever."

Then she quickly turns, heading to the bathroom and leaving me in a fog of thoughts, the warm imprint of her body still lingering on mine. I sit here, alone, and lose myself in the heady aftermath. The couch beneath me feels empty now, cold even.

*We should probably talk about this, shouldn't we?*

But it's obvious that she's looking for space. So, I'll give it to her, at least for tonight.

I WAKE up the next morning without Daisy by my side, Bentley curled up in the spot she's been occupying all week. With a disappointed groan, I roll over to grab my phone off the night-stand and come across a half-crumpled note:

> *Morning,*
>
> *Went for a workout and then hitting the beach for a surf. After that, I'm on a mission to pick out some costumes for us. You'll have some peace and quiet for work now. Text me if anything goes wrong. See you soon!*
>
> *Daisy*

My stomach dips as I notice the smiley face and a doodled pumpkin in the bottom right corner. After what happened last night, I half expected her to put up walls, to be distant. Instead, there's this small sign that she's not pulling away completely.

When I joined her in the bedroom late last night, she was already fast asleep, her breathing even and deep. It was the first night all week we hadn't curled up in each other's arms, and the change felt foreign, unwelcome.

*God*, it had been so fucking good to watch her come, moving on top of me the way she did, every inhibition gone. But if that equates to sacrificing our nights together—the closeness, the intimacy, the chance to forget everything for a little while—I'm not so sure I want the trade-off.

I set the note down and pull my laptop over, greeted by the AfterDark homepage. But I hesitate to get started—to sift through my requests and switch into work mode.

In the past, the line between Elio and Everett has always been so distinct yet so simple to transcend.

I could dissociate from my everyday life, assume a new character, and then focus fully on my work. Adopting a new personality was just standard procedure, and then I'd fade right back into my former self.

When I was Elio again, I didn't have to worry about sex, intimacy, attraction, or even the potential of romantic love. For the last three years, I've been worried about fielding these desires again, something real and natural, outside of work.

But with Daisy, she makes it all seem worthwhile.

That pull between us has been there from the start, from the first day she woke me up on the beachfront. And the more I've gotten to know her, the more she's become this magnetic force in my life.

I could've stopped what happened on the couch last night, but it felt inevitable between us. Actually, it felt fucking perfect.

She's assured me that she's moved on from Logan, but even I know that emotions aren't that straightforward.

As for me, I'm feeling things for her that I've never felt for anyone in my life. There's this flicker of hope inside of me, a flame that she continues to light whenever we're together.

But proximity is a tricky thing. I'm not physically or emotionally prepared to be a rebound. So, I still think it's wise to wait until she moves out to explore things further. If Daisy still wants me once she's settled back into her own life, then that'll be proof enough.

I should be able to make some adjustments with my work. For one, I could give up on those partner scenes for good. We could talk about the web chats, too, find alternatives to help maintain my income in the meantime.

New ideas, new compromises, are already taking shape in my mind. Solo content that could be sustainable, at least through the end of next term. And then, once I graduate, I'll be starting my career over in a new field, and I can leave that life behind me forever.

But I know I'm getting way ahead of myself here.

Once Daisy's back in her own apartment, once the weight of watching over me isn't there anymore, she could easily change her mind about all this. *About me*. She's got this expansive world of her own creation, with friends, hobbies, dreams.

As a partner, I don't have as much to offer her as she does me.

I never have, and I likely never will. Despite the fact that I'm clean now, I'll always be an addict, a former sex worker with a fucked-up digital footprint, and most of all, a man with a track record of disappointing those closest to him.

I don't want that life for Daisy, but if she chooses me, then I'll work to become at least a fraction of the person she deserves.

# Chapter Twenty-Six

DAISY

Bentley's heavy pants ring out in the Jeep's back seat, a quiet soundtrack as we merge onto the freeway. Elio's grasp on the wheel is firm, his profile focused and slightly tense. He's much quieter today than he's been with me in a long time.

Fingers brushing the fabrics of the costumes on my lap, I work to pierce the silence. "So, I ended up texting Harper this morning. Forgot she gave me her number at the game."

"What'd she have to say?"

"Just asked her about what June's wearing tonight," I tell him. "Apparently, she was gonna dress up as a puppy from some TV show she likes, but then she got really excited about the idea of matching."

"Oh, yeah?" The response is lackluster, and his gaze remains forward, a million miles away.

"Yep," I chirp, plunging ahead. "Want to know what we're gonna be?"

"Mhm."

"Wizard of Oz," I say, my cheery tone overcompensating for his distinct lack of interest. "June's gonna be Dorothy, of course. We thought Bentley could be the Cowardly Lion. I'll be Scarecrow because of my blonde hair. Um, and then, you'll obviously be the Tin Man."

He casts me a sideways glance. "Obviously?"

"You know, 'cause he's the one looking for a new heart."

He lets out a stifled chuckle, not quite reaching his eyes, and the space between us opens like a chasm. My back presses deeper into the seat, uncertainty pooling in my stomach. "Are you in a bad mood or something?"

"No, just a little distracted." He clears his throat, then, "As much I love talking about the lions, tigers, and bears, maybe we should focus on the elephant in the room first."

"Ah." I wince. "I'm guessing you're referring to . . . what happened between us last night."

A brow raises. "You mean the way you grinded on my lap until you came and how I practically begged you to do it?"

"El!" Heat rises to my cheeks, my words caught in my throat.

"My bad." He smirks, just a little. "Thought we were getting things out in the open."

"Yeah, okay, but it's . . . God, it's so embarrassing."

"Enlighten me. How could that possibly be embarrassing?"

"Because I . . . I mean, I literally orgasmed, fully clothed, just from . . . from—"

"Writhing around on my dick?" He runs his fingers through his hair. "Daze, that's not embarrassing. That's so fucking sexy. I've been thinking about it every minute since."

A strange sense of pride fills my chest. "You have?"

His smirk falters, sincerity replacing it. "Well, I would've, but you didn't let me hold you last night. My mind was a bit sidetracked."

"I thought it might be too much after . . . you know, what we did."

His expression is earnest, a hint of frustration bleeding through. "Too much?"

"Because of your boundaries."

"*Our* boundaries," he corrects, gaze darting between the

road and me. "Daze, you know why I drew the line, and it's not because I don't want you. Far from it, actually."

"So you've been saying," I murmur. He glances at me again out of his peripherals, sighing as he steers the car over, tires crunching on the gravel of the shoulder. "What are you doing? We're gonna be late now."

"We'll be fine. We left plenty of time to get there," he assures me, turning in his seat to face me fully. The gravity of his gaze pins me in place. "We've talked about this, but I don't think you realize just how much I want you."

He slides his hand over the center console between us, Adam's apple bobbing as he swallows. "It's . . . more than I've ever wanted anyone in my life. But the circumstances are what they are. We're leaning on each other constantly right now. I don't want proximity, the need for connection, to cloud the way you feel. And I certainly don't want to take advantage of that, either. I wouldn't do that to you."

I swallow, trying to find my voice, but he continues before I can get a word in.

"You're with me in the apartment for a few more days. But after that, if you still feel like you want me, want *this*, then I'm right there with you. We'll figure out the rest as it comes. But if you make it back home, settled into the routine you've just started to build, and you happen to change your mind . . . then I won't hold that against you, either."

It hits me then, like a slap of cold water, the depth of his vulnerability. Since our kiss, I had been thinking it was our shared circumstances, our proximity, that kept Elio on edge. But as he speaks, the truth unravels itself before me, and the realization is as humbling as it is heartbreaking.

It's fear. Pure, unadulterated fear.

Elio is scared, not just of our situation, but of me. Of the power I hold over the bond we're creating. He's terrified that these feelings between us might just be a fleeting fascination on my part, a product of our shared vulnerability.

That once I'm out of his proximity, back in my own world, the fire we've stoked might cool, leaving him with the ashes. That the promises we long to whisper in the dark might evaporate in the light of day.

For a man who has always seemed so unshakable despite his circumstances, so sure of himself in light of life's challenges, this glimpse into his insecurities rattles me. I realize now that what he's asking for isn't time or space.

It's a plea, a silent call for reassurance.

I clear my throat, my voice shaky. "Elio, I . . . I don't—"

He raises a hand, cutting me off gently. "Don't say anything now. Just think about what I said. If you choose me, we'll work it out. And if you don't . . . well, we'll cross that bridge when we come to it."

The weight of his words settles in my chest. "I won't change my mind about you."

He smiles gently, doubt touching the corners of his eyes. "Okay."

"I won't," I say firmly, honestly, and he lets it go for the rest of the drive.

A FEW HOURS LATER, Elio and I grip June's hands as we stroll down the tree-lined streets. She's practically skipping in her shiny red shoes, her gingham dress swishing with every step.

Twinkling fairy lights wind around columns of grand houses, and the sidewalks bustle with children all dolled up in their costumes.

"The big candy!" June's voice carries a note of pure joy,

pointing at a house up ahead. There are hordes of people walking from that direction, happily bragging at the size of the candy bars they've just scored.

Elio chuckles, adjusting her little wicker basket. "That's the plan, Junebug. Big candy for a big night. But we have a lot of houses to visit still."

Distracted, my gaze wanders. Mansion after mansion surrounds us, each with sprawling lawns and intricate Halloween displays. This isn't any ordinary neighborhood—it's suburban affluence personified.

Harper and Luca may seem down-to-earth, simple, and grounded, but their surroundings scream otherwise. I suppose it all makes sense, though. With Luca's near-celebrity status, this gated community affords them at least a semblance of normalcy.

From what little I know about them, and despite their hectic schedules, it's obvious they crave a quiet family life. When we arrived at their place earlier, they were both in a rush but didn't hesitate to shower their daughter with love—endless hugs and kisses, spooky stories, and costume pictures—before they slipped out for the night.

"I want that one!" June's voice, filled with that charming toddler tenacity, brings me back to the present. I look to see her pointing at a house that's turned its entire yard into a mini haunted maze, practically dragging us behind her.

"Alright, alright," I laugh, matching her steps. "Let's speed it up."

"Hey, do you think there'll be any clowns in there?" Elio asks with a mischievous gleam, nodding at the maze entrance.

I squint, assessing the situation for myself. "This is a kids' maze. I seriously doubt they'd traumatize them like that."

He smirks. "You never know. Some of these rich people might have a twisted sense of fun."

We drop June's hands as he swings her on top of his shoulders, making her giggle with glee. Then his free hand reaches out to me, an unspoken invitation. Our thumbs brush, and there's a slow, deliberate curling of his fingers over mine.

"There better not be any surprises in there," I mock warn, squeezing his hand.

He laughs, the sound warm and inviting. "If there are, just hang on to me, and I'll protect you from the super-scary balloon animals."

We move closer to the entrance, Bentley in tow, and an older woman slows her pace to look down at June. "Oh, what a perfect little Dorothy you are!"

June beams. "And Toto, too!" Her hand, so small, gestures down to Bentley, trailing beside her with utmost dignity.

"He's the lion tonight, June," I correct gently.

"No, he's Toto," she says, nose wrinkled, as if stating the most obvious fact in the world.

Elio lifts a hand up to her level, ruffling her hair affectionately. "Alright, tonight he can be whoever you want him to be. Toto or the lion."

June giggles, her laughter infectious, causing both Elio and me to join in. Moments like this—so intimate, so domestic—feel like stolen fragments of what could be. A glimpse of a picture-perfect future.

"Think Toto wants to hop in your basket, Junebug?" Elio asks.

"Only if he fits," June says, her tone so gravely serious it makes us all snort with laughter.

"Right, well, I think we're out of luck there." He taps the

tops of her ruby-red slippers. "So, you think you're ready to head inside?"

"Yup!" she all but shouts. "Go, go, go!"

Together, we venture into the entrance of the makeshift maze. It's well done, filled with glowing ghosts that bob in the air, cackling witches that stir cauldrons, and goblins lurking behind faux gravestones. But the spooky creatures are more delightful than dreadful, every turn revealing something new and surprising.

Before long, there's a gentle tug of Elio's hand on mine, pulling me closer when June gets excited, kicking her little feet against his chest. I want to ask him to put her down, to take it easy on his mending heart, but I have to trust that he knows his own limits.

And that he can remember to enforce them while honed in on his favorite niece.

As we move away from the maze and continue our quest, I can't help but notice the quiet moments between us—a lingering touch, a knowing smile, our shared laughter when June does something endearing.

At one house, a gangly teenager kneels before her, offering the candy bowl. "Pick your favorite, Dorothy."

June's eyes, wide and innocent, dart between the candy and her uncle. "Ello, what should I pick?"

He squats down to her level, bringing his face close as if they were about to discuss a grave secret. "Get the peanut butter cups. Your dad doesn't like them, so you won't have to share."

Her eyes light up, and she eagerly snatches the bright orange package, offering a whispered "Thank you" to the Jedi.

We continue along as the night fades, passing gaggles of trick-or-treaters. Our bags grow impossibly heavy with treats, and June's energy finally wanes. One final stop stands between us and our return back to Luca and Harper's home. This place is grander than most, its entrance guarded by a duo of flaming torches.

June hesitates, gazing up with trepidation. But Elio, ever the protector, nudges her forward. "Last one, Junebug. So, let's make it count."

With newfound determination, she marches up to the door, the rest of us trailing closely behind. The door opens to reveal a kindly old woman with silver hair, her eyes crinkling into a smile. "My, what a sweet Dorothy we have here."

"Thank you," June chirps as she accepts a few handfuls of candy, and the woman offers a friendly smile to the rest of us.

"Such a perfect little family," she says, gaze flitting over the group. "Would you like me to take a picture?"

The woman clearly believes that we're June's parents, and my cheeks heat at her assumption. Memories of my own family drift into my thoughts: the distance with my sister that's grown over time, not just physical but emotional, the fading phone calls with my parents that were never really frequent to begin with.

I love them all, of course I do, but it's a love tethered by blood and old memories, not by regular heart-to-heart conversations or shared laughter over dinner tables.

Here, however, with Elio, June, and my new friends at Coastal, I feel a burgeoning sense of home. Not just the place where you sleep but where you're loved, where you belong, where you're needed.

I open my mouth, ready to correct her, but Elio steps forward instead.

"Thank you," he says, reaching into his pocket and pulling out his phone. "We'd love a photo."

For a moment, I'm struck by the ease with which he embraces the idea. But as we gather closer together, with June's little arms wrapped around both of our waists and Bentley sitting proudly at our feet, it feels like the most perfect moment to capture for eternity.

Because no matter what happens between us in the future, I know it's one I'm not likely to forget.

# Chapter Twenty-Seven

ELIO

THE MOOD in the apartment is heavy, punctuated by the sounds of zippers closing and soft sighs. It's Tuesday morning, and the reality that Daisy's finally leaving brings a bitter taste.

I run my fingers through my hair, glancing around the familiar space. The morning sun pours in, but it feels empty, hollow now. It's the same sunlight, the same apartment, but without Daisy here, it's bound to feel different.

She stands near the window, taking in the view one last time.

"You sure you've got everything?" I ask, my voice hushed, subdued.

"Yeah, got it all."

She turns to face me, and a quiet, unmistakable tear wells in the corner of her eye.

"Hey." My brow furrows as I step toward her, thumb swiping along her cheekbone. "Don't do that, not now. This is going to be a good thing for both of us."

"Good, how?"

"For you, it means being able to put yourself first again," I say, pulling her closer. "And for me, it means I'm well enough to be able to take care of myself now. To trust that my new medication will keep me steady enough to be on my own."

According to my one-week follow-up appointment, Dr.

Foster says that I'm doing well. That I'm adjusting appropriately to the medications. That I've had no abnormal heart rate spikes or arrhythmias for the last week.

That, from now on, our follow-ups will be regular monthly visits. And then, I'll work up to a point where he's comfortable with me coming in every three to six months, and then eventually, just once per year.

These are short, measurable goals for me to work up to. A visible, achievable light at the end of a long tunnel. And, I have to admit, it's been more than a relief to finally have these concrete answers.

"I know," she murmurs, that single tear welling over and spilling onto her cheek. "I'm so happy for you. But if it's such a great thing, then why does it feel like the end of something and not the beginning?"

"You know, you're really pretty when you cry." I tilt her chin up, slanting a smile at her outraged expression. "And endings aren't always a bad thing."

She gulps. "But won't you miss me at all?"

"Daze—" I clear my throat, softly rubbing the tear away. "I don't often say the right thing. In fact, I rarely do. But you should know that I'll miss you so fucking much. Everything about you living here. I won't forget what it's been like—to have you taking care of me, watching out for me, just . . . being here with me. I don't know what I did to deserve you, but I'm not taking it for granted. Not for a second."

"See." She sniffles, practically melting in my arms. "That was such a nice thing to say."

I snort a laugh. "Yeah. For you, I try."

"I really like it when you try."

"Me too." I reluctantly pull away from her and blow out a

heavy, centering breath. “Well, we should get you back to your apartment now. We’ve both got classes.”

“I don’t want to go.”

“Don’t act like I’ll never see you again.”

“We should go to the Seashell first, shouldn’t we?” she asks, turning on her heel, blatantly ignoring my words. “Bring Bentley along. Get us some nice, warm tea?”

“Prolonging this won’t help.”

She visibly deflates. “Fine. Push me out of here, why don’t you?”

“Come on.” I sling a few of her bags over my shoulder, patting Bentley on the head before I move to the door. “I’ll get this stuff out to your car. You can say your goodbyes without me watching over you. Just meet me down there in a few minutes, okay?”

I swing the door open, kicking her suitcase over the threshold. Before it closes behind me, she calls out one last argument, one last parting word. I ignore the sound, carrying on down to the parking lot alone.

The truth is, I’m a bit miserable that she’s leaving me. I’m putting on a good show because I don’t want this to feel like the end of the road. I want her to feel good about the change. I want her to feel relieved, content that she can go back to her own place and start building on her new life.

A life where she can pursue her passions without Logan, without anyone, standing in the way.

She takes about ten minutes to meet me down by her car, and by that time, I have everything packed up in her trunk. Her eyes are red-rimmed and puffy, and the fact that she was crying up there breaks my heart a little bit more.

“Hope you didn’t get those tears all over my dog,” I say in a low voice. “He’s sensitive.”

She hiccups a laugh and swats me on the shoulder. "Don't be so mean to me in my time of crisis."

"Why not? It earned me my favorite smile."

Her cheeks tighten, and a red-hot blush creeps up her neck. She glances past me to the driver's side of her car, gulps low in her throat, and says, "I better go now."

"Oh, you in a rush?" I mean, I haven't even hugged her yet.

"It's just, the longer I stand here, the more likely I am to burst into tears. *Again.*" She rubs at her temples, pinches her eyes closed. "And honestly, I don't know why I'm even acting this way. We go to the same school; we live ten minutes away from one another. I wasn't nearly this upset when I . . . when . . ."

"When you left Dayton?"

"Yeah," she mumbles. "When I moved away from my ex."

I can't help it, but I fucking beam at the thought. I may not like that she's upset, but it warms me up to know that all this emotion is just for me.

"Would you look at that," she says. "I earned *my* favorite smile, too."

I breathe deep, run a hand through my hair, and move to open the car door. "Get outta here, will you?"

"Yeah, okay."

The moment seems to stretch out before us, two points converging in a world that, for the briefest of moments, stops turning. When I pull her in, her body fits perfectly against mine—familiar and warm. Her soft curves nestle against the solid plane of my chest.

My arms snake around her, one arm at her lower back, the other just beneath her shoulders, anchoring her to me. I tuck my face into the crook of her neck, inhaling deeply, letting her scent—strawberries and a hint of citrus—wash over me.

It's a scent that's become synonymous with mornings waking up beside her, late evenings curled up on the couch, and nights spent wrapped in each other's arms. It's a hard pill to swallow—the thought that I'll no longer be enveloped by that smell.

As her arms wind around my waist, I can feel the faint tremors in her frame, the thud of her heart against my chest. Each second that passes with her in my arms, the grip of the impending separation feels tighter. I cling to the moment—we both do—trying to memorize the feel of it.

Her fingers splay against my back, tracing lines as if trying to remember the layout of my spine, the contours of my shoulder blades. I feel her take another shaky breath against my collarbone, the warmth of it seeping through my shirt.

"I'll see you when I see you?" I murmur the question against her neck, and she stiffens.

"Not a chance," she says. "I'll see you when we make a concrete plan to meet up. Multiple times a week, at the very least."

Pulling back slightly, I cradle her face with my hands, our foreheads touching, our eyes locked. There's nothing I want more than to tilt her chin, press my lips to hers, and never come up for air. But I don't, because there's still that nagging part of me that's uncertain about how she feels.

"Anything you want," I say instead. And then, with a reluctant sigh, I release her, the crisp fall air rushing in to fill the void she leaves. She climbs into her car, our fingers lingering for just one more second before she pulls away.

I watch her go, her car making the final turn out of the lot, silent and alone. Then I head back up to my apartment and break down like a fucking baby.

. . .

As NIGHT FALLS, restlessness takes over. Despite the chaotic expanse of the apartment, every corner seems to echo with Daisy's absence. I make an attempt to engage with my work, to dive into filming for AfterDark, or even just muster the focus to respond to a few lingering messages, but it's futile.

I give up, abandoning my workspace to slump onto the couch, its cushions no longer as welcoming without her presence. Just as I'm about to drown the silence with some random TV show—anything to avoid the ones we used to watch together—my phone buzzes.

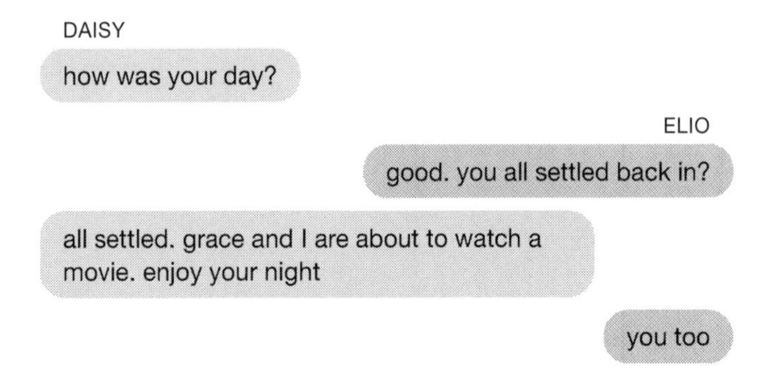


*Fucking hell.* That exchange felt hollow, empty, a far cry from the comfortable conversations we've shared over the last few weeks. I can't bring myself to pass pleasantries over text when I'm feeling this way—so lost and unanchored.

I flick on something random, letting the noise fill the void. But my mind is elsewhere, trapped in how it felt to have someone here beside me. To have *Daisy* here beside me. It was more than just easy companionship between us.

I've always prided myself on being sort of a lone wolf. Of course, I have my family, I have Kaia, but at the end of the day, I'd come home and spend the majority of my time alone. I enjoyed the solitude, the silence.

For the longest time, it's how I filled my cup.

But when Daisy entered my world, I realized that perhaps I wasn't meant to be so alone. That despite the comfort Bentley's provided, this apartment started to feel repressive, empty, long before she came along.

She had this way of sliding seamlessly into the gaps of my life, gaps I didn't even know existed until she filled them.

As a distraction, I should drive over to Amber Isle and take Bentley for a walk. He'd appreciate it, and I could get myself out of the apartment. But I doubt that would help ease my mind even a fraction.

Just like my home, Amber Isle seems to belong to Daisy now.

As I'm about to switch off the TV, a knock breaks the silence. Brow furrowed, I head to the door. Opening it reveals the girl that won't escape my mind, her soft brown eyes shimmering with determination.

"Forget something?" I ask, my voice wavering.

"You wanted me to settle back into the apartment. To readjust to my old life and then revisit my feelings for you." She shifts her weight, biting the corner of her lower lip. "Well, I'm settled."

My pulse thunders in my ears, and I battle the urge to slide a palm over my chest. "You didn't give it much time, did you?"

"El, if you truly want me, then stop making excuses."

The distance between us narrows in a heartbeat. My breath ragged, I curve a hand around the base of her neck, inching us closer. But she pulls back one last time, gaze flitting across my face.

"If you kiss me now," she murmurs, her voice a soft challenge, "there's no changing your mind. There's no going back.

You can't wake up tomorrow and tell me that we need more time. You're either all in, or you're out."

"I'm all in on you," I say, my throat tight. "Now and always."

And then I pull her in for a kiss.

# Chapter Twenty-Eight

DAISY

Elio's lips crash onto mine, softer than I remember but with a hunger I didn't see coming. Heat races through me as he yanks me closer, his grip on my waist firm enough to leave a mark. I hitch my legs around him without thinking, relishing the solid feel of him against me.

He kisses me like he's trying to prove something—like he's been waiting for this just as long as I have. He's nipping at my lips and tangling his tongue with mine, messy but so fucking perfect. Our breathing is erratic, heads spinning from the rapid rush of desire.

"God, Daisy," he groans, pulling back just enough to look at me, voice rough with want.

His grip on me is firm as he walks us back through the open door, our bodies flush against each other. But the spell breaks when Bentley bounds up to us, tail wagging wildly.

As Elio shifts his weight, trying to avoid the excited dog, he stumbles. I let out a short laugh, our faces inches apart, and we narrowly avoid disaster.

"Damn dog," Elio mutters, a grin tilting his lips, the comment more playful than annoyed.

Once we navigate past the living room, the bedroom comes into view. He strides inside, releasing me just enough to shut the door behind us. My body's craving his touch, craving the feel of him against me.

He gently lays me onto his bed, the cool sheets offering a brief respite from the fiery need coursing through me. For a long moment, he simply looks at me, not daring to speak a word.

My chest heaves, my breaths short and shallow, desire pooling low in my belly.

"This is what you want?" The question rumbles deep in his throat, and I blow out a hot breath at the sound of it.

"Yes."

With that affirmation, he closes the space between us, his body blanketing mine. Our lips meet again, but this kiss is deeper, more exploratory. His fingers slide into my hair, caressing and pulling, sending waves of pleasure cascading down my spine.

The slow, deliberate grind of his hips is torturous, and I arch up, seeking more contact, more friction.

His solid length presses into me, and I'm aching with a desperate need to be filled by him. But there's still a part of me that's stuck inside my own head. I haven't been with anyone since—or before—Logan, and he was less than satisfied with what I had to offer.

Noticing the change in my demeanor, Elio gently withdraws, his eyes clouded with concern. "Why'd you stop?" I ask, fingers unconsciously reaching for his.

"You left me there alone for a minute."

"I know," I murmur. "I'm sorry."

"What's wrong?"

"You've had . . . a lot of partners, right?"

He lets out a sigh, tension rippling across his face. Lying down with his arm draped over his eyes, he says, "I'm clean, Daisy. I get checked religiously. My scene partners always come with a clean bill of health. Not to mention, I haven't been with anyone in months."

"No, no, no. That's not—" I place a hand on his cheek, fingertips guiding his gaze back to me. "I know you wouldn't put my health at risk. I just—I don't have a lot of experience. And before this all started, I was on my way to figuring out more about myself in that . . . arena. But certain things got in the way, and I just never had time to focus on it."

He frowns, processing my words. "So, you're worried I won't enjoy myself?"

"It's just that I'm not . . . I mean, I'm no porn star, that's for sure."

"All I want is you. Just as you are," he says. "No pretense. This—kissing you like this, holding you, just fucking looking at you—is better, hotter, than any sex I've ever had. Trust me on that."

"El . . ."

"Seriously, Daze. Being with you like this? It feels more real than anything I've ever known. In a lot of ways, this is kind of like my first time."

"I believe you. And I want this, want you," I whisper, my voice a quiet tremor. "I just want it to be good for both of us."

A mischievous glint appears in his eyes. "Then how about we start slow?"

"Slow?"

"You could touch yourself for me."

My breath catches in my throat. "Oh."

"Or I could touch myself, and you could watch."

"No, I'll, um, I can do it. How should we—I mean, should we both lie here on the bed, or—"

"Come here," he murmurs, pulling me closer, chuckling softly at my nervousness. The sound of it—so raw and genuine

—somehow makes me feel better, relieves a bit of the tension in the room.

I nestle in beside him, our bodies aligned but not touching, a thin layer of space between us. The bedsheets are soft beneath me, but all I can focus on is his intense gaze, studying me with warmth and curiosity.

"Just do what feels natural," he encourages, his voice husky. "There's no right or wrong way. And remember, it's just you and me here."

A nervous laugh escapes my lips. "You make it sound so easy."

The corner of his mouth lifts. "It can be. Just lie back."

Obediently, I recline against the soft pillows. He leans over, wraps a hand around the back of my head, and presses his lips to my forehead. Then he slides off the bed and situates himself on the desk chair, placing himself directly in my line of sight.

He tilts back, thighs spread apart, and raises an expectant brow. "This is about exploring," he says gently. "For both of us."

His encouragement eases the nervous knot in my stomach. The moment feels surreal, vulnerable, but his presence is an anchor. "Okay, I think I'm ready."

"You know, you're so fucking beautiful," he whispers, drinking me in.

I pause, taking a deep breath before meeting his gaze head-on. For a moment, the weight of our shared anticipation fills the room. Elio has always been the one in the spotlight, constantly on display, every move a sensual dance for an eager audience.

But now, it's my turn.

It's a thrilling and daunting idea. The thought of him watching, of him wanting, fuels a kind of courage I didn't know I possessed.

With my eyes fixed on his, I take a deep, steadying breath

and sit up slowly. My fingers move to the hem of my shirt, pulling it over my head with deliberate care. The cool air of the room makes my skin prickle, but it's Elio's unwavering gaze that sends shivers down my spine.

Reaching back, I unclasp my bra and let it fall away. His sharp intake of breath isn't the only sign that he's affected. It's his eyes, darker and hungrier, that tell a different story.

My fingers slide down to the button of my jeans, the zipper's sound loud in the thick silence. Shifting, I slide the denim down my legs, leaving me in just my panties. Elio's gaze is burning, but there's a restraint there, a quiet respect as he allows me to dictate the pace.

Taking one last deep breath, I hook my fingers into the sides of my underwear, slowly pulling them down. As I bare myself completely to him, I'm met with a reverence in his eyes that makes everything else fade away.

"Flawless," he whispers, voice raspy and filled with awe. If I didn't know any better, I'd assume he's never seen a woman naked before.

His focus on me feels like a physical touch, electric and tingling, heating my skin and pooling warmth deep inside me. Slowly, I let my fingers wander, exploring, teasing, taking my time as he watches with rapt attention.

His eyes follow every movement, darkening shades further as my fingers trace a path down my abdomen, skimming the sensitive skin there. Hesitantly, I let my fingertips dance over the most intimate part of me, the sensation sending jolts of pleasure through my body.

Elio's grip tightens on the arms of the chair, his knuckles white from the strain. As I continue my slow exploration, pressing and circling my clit, a low whimper escapes from the depths of his throat.

The sound sends a rush of excitement through me, spurring me on.

My pace gradually increases, the rhythm of my fingers and my breathing syncing. At the same time, Elio's jaw tightens, eyes flashing with barely restrained lust. His chest rises and falls with rapid breaths, mirroring my own.

There's something incredibly erotic about being watched this intimately, especially by someone who looks at you with such a raw, undeniable hunger.

His voice, thick with desire, breaks the silence. "You have no idea how much I want to touch you right now."

My eyes flutter closed as my fingers continue their dance, drawing out the pleasure. "Then come here," I challenge breathlessly, granting him the permission he so clearly craves.

He's off the chair in an instant, joining me on the bed. I welcome him with open arms, and his fingers quickly work to replace mine, thick and insistent.

"We're gonna learn together, aren't we?" he groans, an index finger filling me, pumping against my walls. "What we both like, what we want?"

"Mhm."

I gasp as he adjusts the angle, pressing into that spot that makes my vision blur. His free hand cradles the back of my head, pulling me into another searing kiss. I can feel every ounce of his want, his need, in the way his lips move against mine.

Drawing back, Elio moves his lips to my ear, whispering, "Can I taste you?" His voice is ragged, filled with anticipation.

"Please."

With infinite patience, he kisses a path down my body, pausing to nip and tease at my sensitive skin. When his mouth finally reaches my core, the anticipation has me trembling. His tongue moves in languid strokes, finally tasting me.

He starts with the delicate crease where my thigh meets my body, lapping at the sensitive skin there. His tongue trails a wet path up and down, teasingly close to where I crave his touch the most.

Spurred on by the sounds of my moans, it doesn't take long for him to shift his focus directly to my center.

He starts on the outside, circling my entrance with the tip of his tongue. Each swipe is frustratingly slow, building the anticipation until I'm writhing beneath him. He moves upward, parting my folds with expert precision, lavishing his attention on my swollen clit.

As his tongue flicks over it, my hips buck off the bed, desperate for more pressure, more contact.

His hands grip my hips, holding me in place as he continues his assault, alternating between long, slow licks and quick, tantalizing flicks. Every stroke of his tongue brings me closer to the edge, and the sound of his deep, appreciative groans only intensifies the sensations.

I gasp, clutching at the sheets, as he delves deeper. The flickering movements of his tongue have me writhing on the mattress. My mind goes blank, thoughts consumed by the sheer ecstasy of his touch.

"Oh, God, El," I moan, the sound torn from me as I move closer and closer to the edge.

He doesn't let up, fingers and tongue working in perfect harmony, pushing me higher and higher. He grips my thighs with both hands, spreading me open, and slides his tongue as deep inside of me as he can. I clench around him, unable to stop myself from bucking my hips.

"Yeah, just like that," he mumbles when he pulls out. "That's how you fuck my tongue."

The tension coils tight, ready to snap. With one last push, I shatter, pleasure washing over me in a tidal wave. The world fades away, replaced by the aftershocks and Elio's soft murmurs against my skin.

"That's it, baby," he rasps. "Watch how you come for me."

As the intensity of the moment wanes, I'm acutely aware of the weight of his body. I want to see him, touch him, explore every inch. My fingers fumble with the buttons of his shirt, desperate to reveal the skin beneath.

As the fabric falls away, I trace the dips and ridges of his muscles, the heat of his skin pouring into me.

My eyes fall on the ink that adorns parts of his arms—a collection of stories in the form of tattoos. I touch each one gently, making a mental note to ask him more about them later. But for now, I want to give back, to show him the same pleasure he's shown me.

I meet his gaze, thick lashes fluttering as I blink up at him. "El"—my voice is breathy, filled with need—"I want you in my mouth."

The desire that flashes in his eyes is unmistakable. He swallows hard, throat bobbing. "You sure?" The vulnerability in his voice hits me. This isn't just about physical need. This is about trust, intimacy.

Nodding, I move lower, trailing kisses along his chest and down his abdomen. He shivers under my touch, a low groan escaping his lips as my fingers find the waistband of his jeans. I make quick work of the button and zipper, pushing them down to reveal the length of him.

"Take my cock out, Daisy," he tells me, and I do exactly as he says.

His erection stands loud and proud, its velvety skin a deep shade of flushed pink. The head is thick, swollen and glistening with a bead of precum at the very tip. I've never really thought much of dicks before, but the sight of his makes my mouth water.

His breath catches as I wrap my fingers around him, stroking gently. He threads his fingers through my hair and guides me even closer. I glance up at him, seeking approval, and the raw need I see there is all the encouragement I could ask for.

My lips wrap around the tip, teasing him with soft flicks of my tongue. His response is immediate, a sharp intake of breath followed by a low growl.

"Fuck, yes," he breathes out.

Slowly, I take more of him into my mouth, setting a rhythm that has him writhing beneath me. The weight of him, the heat, the subtle taste—it's all-consuming.

"That's it, Daze," he murmurs. "Take all of me just like I know you can."

He's lost in the sensation, his hips bucking gently, seeking more. The grip on my hair tightens, guiding me, urging me on. The needy sounds he makes—the tiny whimpers, the heady groans—are a testament to how close he is, and I double my efforts, wanting to see him come undone.

Without warning, he pulls me off him, eyes wild with passion. "I'm close," he warns. "Where do you want me to come?"

Not breaking eye contact, I take him in again, hollowing my cheeks and increasing the suction. His response is swift and sudden, his body tensing as he reaches his climax. He spills into my mouth just like I wanted, and I take all he offers, unwilling to waste a single drop.

Breathing heavily, he gently pulls me up to meet him. His face is flushed, eyes half-lidded with satisfaction. We lie there for a moment, simply staring at each other. And then he tucks a loose strand of hair behind my ear.

"Hey," he whispers, his voice hoarse. "That was . . . perfect. By far the best I've ever had."

"For me, too," I murmur, leaning in for a tender kiss.

Our lips move slowly, languidly, both of us reveling in the taste of one another. Eventually, we shift apart, breathing a little harder than before. Elio pulls me into his embrace. The warmth of his skin, the steady rise and fall of his chest . . . it's comforting, familiar now.

"It's supposed to be your first night back at home," he mumbles into my hair, planting a soft kiss on my forehead.

I nod in agreement, snuggling deeper into his embrace. "I know. And I'll go home in a bit. But first, promise me something."

He raises a curious brow. "Anything."

"Promise me there's more to come?"

"Yeah, I promise." He smiles, eyes shining with emotion. "I'm not nearly done making you mine."

# Chapter Twenty-Nine

ELIO

When I pull up to Daisy's apartment on Friday, Bentley's restless energy mirrors my own. This night is the culmination of our long week: a mix of Daisy's early morning surfs, followed by lazy strolls along the shoreline.

It's been a good, stable routine—one that gives us a chance to connect before our classes.

But we've also been tiptoeing around more pertinent topics. Namely, my work as Everett. Daisy wanted to keep things simple, carefree, at least for a few days while we adjusted to being together. And I have no issues following her lead.

Tonight, though, it may finally be time to stop pushing the subject aside.

The door swings open before I even knock, and Daisy appears, the golden highlights in her hair catching the evening sun. She's as stunning as ever.

"There she is," I say, swooping in to press my lips to hers. My hand brackets her waist, the other cradling the back of her neck while I deepen the kiss. As I pull away, my fingers brush over her sternum and strum lightly along the column of her throat.

She sucks in a sharp breath, the corners of her eyes crinkling. "Hi," she whispers, cheeks stained a rosy hue.

"Hi," I echo, a grin etched on my lips. One of my hands finds a loose strand of her hair, tucking it behind her ear while I lean down, burying my face into the crook of her neck. "Strawberries, again."

She giggles softly. "I had a glass of wine before you came."

"I always love the way you smell."

She bites her lip as I pull back, cheeks flushing, eyes sparkling. "Mm, thank you."

"You're really fuckin' pretty, you know that?"

"Same goes for you," she murmurs. And then, bending down to give Bentley a loving rub, she adds, "And you too, buddy." I interlace our fingers as she beckons us both inside. "Come on, I have dinner on the stove. Gracie's here, too. And, um, another new friend of ours."

Before I can ask who she means, the scent hits me—earthy mushrooms, the tang of garlic, and a faint hint of simmering wine. I stop in my tracks. Memories surge forward, of Ma's kitchen, of laughter and shared stories around the dining table, of a time far less complicated than now. "Is that—"

"Your mom's risotto?" she interrupts, a touch of mischief in her gaze. "Yeah, it is."

"How did you even . . .?"

"Well, I texted Harper for the recipe. We've been talking here and there since last weekend. Anyway, she got the details from your older sister a long time ago, and so, here we are."

A genuine smile tugs at my lips. "You know this is one of Bentley's favorites, too, right? He used to sit under the family table, waiting for our youngest to hand over the mushrooms."

She chuckles. "I did hear something about that, actually."

Emotion tightens my throat. "This is really fucking cool of you, Daze."

As we move further into the room, a familiar face greets me, and I'm floored by the sight. It's my sister Taylor, standing right there in the middle of Daisy's living room.

Bentley, not much for biding his time, immediately gravitates toward her, wagging his tail in sheer joy. Taylor kneels to embrace him, eyes shimmering with a fresh set of happy tears.

"I missed you so much," she murmurs to him, voice thick. Her gaze shifts to me then, a hesitance in her eyes. "Sorry, El. I didn't want to intrude, but Daisy insisted."

Over the past week, I've been sharing a little bit more about my family with Daisy. I told her that Taylor and I had always been the closest of my siblings. That she was soft with me growing up—caring and nurturing—whereas our brother played more of a stern role.

I told her that Taylor raised Bentley from just eight weeks old but had to part ways with him last year due to her partner's allergies. How she asked me of all people for help, and how it was one of the best damn things to ever happen to me.

And despite me feeling like Bentley is mine and I'm his, there will always be a part of him that belongs with my sister.

I know that she's been busy lately, but I also know that the transition has been rough on her. She hasn't been able to see Bentley as much as she'd like. The fact that Daisy picked up on that and carried through with this sneaky plan to reunite them . . . well, it's a fucking gift in and of itself.

"Don't be sorry. I'm glad you're here," I tell Taylor. "It's been a while."

"Too long," she says with a smile.

"So, Daze, did you make the risotto, or was it actually my sister?"

"It was a group effort," she says, nodding to the kitchen. "Gracie helped, too."

Gracie offers a cheery wave from across the island counter, and I nod in greeting, offering a quick thanks. My sister, regaining her composure, adds in, "I'm only staying for dinner, though. I promised Noah I'd take her out tonight."

"So, Luc isn't hiding around the corner, waiting to surprise me, too?"

Taylor laughs. "Nope, just me tonight."

She steps forward, wrapping me in a quick hug before rejoining Gracie in front of the stove. Once she's out of earshot, Daisy takes a moment to pull me aside, her voice a hushed whisper. "I really hope this is okay? I know you don't like a lot of fanfare, but you mentioned missing her, and I—"

Before she can finish, I cut her off with a kiss, lips pressing a soft trail across her neck and back. "It's more than okay," I mumble against her skin. "You're just so fucking good to me."

"You're good to me, too."

Once dinner's over and Taylor's said her thousandth goodbye to my dog, Daisy and I make our way back to her bedroom. The door closes behind us, Bentley finds his quiet home in a corner of the room, and there's a static charge that flares between us.

It's a quiet kind of intensity, slow and simmering, and it makes my skin prickle.

Daisy pauses by the foot of her bed, turning to me with a shy smile, her eyes searching mine before they drop to my lips. There's a vulnerability there, a raw openness that pulls at something deep inside of me.

Slowly, she steps into my space, her fingers brushing over the material of my shirt, guiding me closer. As if in a trance, I follow, every nerve ending alive, every sensation magnified.

She tilts her head up, the faint fragrance of that damn strawberry wine still lingering on her skin, beckoning me to lean down. Our lips meet in a kiss that starts out gentle, a mere brush of mouth against mouth.

It's sweet and soft, a fleeting touch at first.

Then I pull her closer, hands settling on her hips, the curve of her body pressing into mine. Her fingers grip the fabric at the back of my shirt, holding me to her. The kiss deepens, growing hungrier, aching in its intensity.

I let one hand drift upward, gliding over the fabric of her top until I'm pressing it flat against her chest. The steady thrum of her heartbeat pulses beneath my palm, syncing with the rapid rhythm of mine.

Daisy's mouth opens, inviting me in, and I accept the invitation eagerly. Our tongues meet, dancing and tasting, exploring and teasing. There's no rush, no urgency. Just the two of us, getting lost in the sensations, in the intoxicating feel of one another.

She breaks away for a breath, eyes dark with desire, and whispers my name against my lips. Her voice is thick, husky, stirring something primal in me.

Guiding her back, we tumble gently onto her bed. I'm hovering over her, supporting my weight on my elbows, ensuring I don't crush her beneath me.

We continue to kiss, deeply, slowly, every slide of lip against lip, every brush of tongue against tongue, drawing soft moans and sighs from both of us. My palm finds its way back to her heart, and she stiffens beneath me, nose crinkling as her eyes pop open.

"Something wrong?" I rasp the question, searching for answers in her gaze.

"No," she breathes out. "Just wondering . . . why do you put your hand there when we kiss?"

"I like to feel the way your heart beats for me."

She gulps low in her throat. "For *you*, huh?"

"Yeah." I nudge her nose with mine. "It picks up speed when I do something you really like—when I brush the tip of your tongue, when I nip at your lower lip. I'm learning you, Daisy. And it's my new favorite subject."

She huffs a laugh. "Shouldn't I be the one monitoring *your* heart? Making sure it doesn't go haywire."

"Nah, that's what the meds are for."

"Cheeky boy." She grips the fabric of my shirt, pulling me in for another quick kiss before she says, "I do have another question for you, though."

I raise a playful brow. "Is this one about the way I move my tongue, because—"

"It's about your work, El."

"Ah." I roll off her, propping myself up on one elbow, giving her my full attention. "I was wondering when we'd talk about this."

"As much I enjoy kissing you," she starts, her voice wavering, "I just—I can't help but worry about . . . you doing these things with someone else. How do you feel about it?"

My brows skyrocket. "Being with someone else? Not too fucking great, if I'm being honest."

"I mean, I know it's different because it's for your job, and it's not personal. But considering what happened with my ex, and just in general, there isn't a part of me that wants to share you."

"You're talking about me filming partner scenes?"

"Mhm." She nods, her gaze dropping. "And, um, maybe the web chats, too. Just because they're with real people, and it feels . . ."

"No, I know what you mean."

Her eyes reflect a storm of emotions—guilt, affection, insecurity. "I feel terrible even bringing this up. I was more than aware of your job before we started all this, and so if it's a deal breaker, then—"

"It's not," I gently interrupt. "Of course it's not. And you have every right to bring this up. You're my girlfriend. Your opinion matters."

"Your girlfriend?"

I chuckle softly, cupping her face. "Yeah, aren't you? That's what *all in* means to me, at least."

"Oh." She nibbles at her lower lip, eyes lighting up. "Good we're on the same page, then."

"Yeah, good." I give her a knowing smirk. "So, as my *girlfriend*, your opinion means a lot to me. Besides, now that I've felt what it's like to be with you, I can't picture doing that with anyone else. Job or not."

"I just hate asking you to give up on your work," she says, "I know you rely on that income."

"There are compromises. Other ways I can make money. I've been looking into this audio-only app called Echo. It's contract-based, so I'd know my earnings up front. No video, no real interaction. Just upload and be done."

Her brow furrows. "And you're okay with that? That's what you want?"

"I've been having a hard time separating the two parts of my life—me and Everett—for a long time, even before I met you," I confess. "And now we're together, the line is even more fragmented."

"So, you're absolutely sure about this?"

"I'm sure," I reiterate, tracing a finger along her jawline. "And you shouldn't feel bad asking for what you want, not when it comes to me. I like it when you're greedy." I pull her closer, our foreheads touching. "Besides, this will be a good step. I was gonna fade out once I graduate next term, anyway."

She breathes out, low and slow, the tension in her shoulders easing. "Well, that was much easier than I thought it'd be."

"Glad I could be of service."

"Mm, do you think we can go back to kissing now?"

One hand pressed to her heart, I murmur against her lips, "Your wish is my command."

# Chapter Thirty

DAISY

My bed is such a cozy little haven first thing in the morning. Today, the sound of chirping birds, running water, and Bentley's soft snores slowly stirs me awake. But my peace is interrupted by the repetitive chime of a phone.

I turn over, expecting it to be mine, but as my eyes adjust to the room's dim light, I spot Elio's phone lighting up on my nightstand. Bentley wakes with me, pacing around the room, ears pricked as his pants grow heavier.

Squinting, I lean in to inspect the onslaught of notifications. An unknown number floods the screen, and my heart thuds as I take in the last few messages.

UNKNOWN

why have you been ignoring me?

where did you go???

A muffled sound of water echoes from my en suite bathroom, reminding me that Elio's in the shower. A pang of guilt tinges me as I realize I've invaded his privacy, even if it was mostly unintentional.

*But honestly, who could be so desperate to reach my boyfriend this early in the morning?*

Wrapping a tiny throw blanket around my shoulders, I get out of bed, clutching his phone to my chest. Bentley follows as I patter toward the door, his nails clicking on the hardwood. A whiff of Elio's scent envelops me, the hem of his oversized T-shirt brushing against my thighs—the only barrier between the morning chill and the bare skin of my legs.

As I near the bathroom, steam slips through the edges of the closed door. The muffled hum of water and the scent of shampoo fill the air. Swallowing hard, I knock lightly, hesitating for a split second. The water stops.

The door eases open, revealing a shirtless, dripping Elio. His skin glows, water droplets tracing the path of every well-defined muscle. And his face, so handsome and rugged, lights up with the same breathtaking smile I've come to adore.

"Somebody's blowing you up," I manage to say, stomach fluttering as I extend his phone.

His brows draw together, and he takes a moment to process my words. He pulls the phone from my hand, eyes scanning the screen rapidly, the warmth in his eyes replaced with dread.

"Fuck, fuck, fuck," he mutters.

My worry deepens. "What? Who is it?"

He rubs the back of his neck, looking torn. "I think it might be this subscriber of mine, Sapphire something."

"She has your personal number?"

He scrubs a hand down the side of his face. "I swear, I don't know how the hell she got it. Should I text her back or just block?"

I ponder for a moment. "Maybe ask how she got it first?"

He nods, texting quickly. Then, with a huff of frustration, he slams his phone on the counter. Water drips from his sopping hair down his naked chest, pooling on the tile.

"This is a whole new level of fucked-up," he says, voice near shaking.

I frown, pressing further, "What makes you think it's her?"

His face pales, and he gives me a resigned sigh. "She'd asked me over a month ago to try out two-way video chats. I decided not to do it, but apparently, she didn't like my answer."

"And what do you mean by that, exactly?"

"She went kinda overboard—messaging me constantly, creating new accounts, getting her friends involved. It felt weird—creepy, to say the least—so I blocked her and any accounts she created. I haven't heard from her in a while, so I assumed she just went away. But I also haven't been checking my messages that often anymore."

"And somehow she got your phone number?" My eyes go wide. "That's kind of scary, El."

"Believe me, I'm well aware."

"We'll handle it, though," I say, trying my best to be reassuring. "Let's just see if she responds, and we can take it from there."

He turns away, gripping the counter's edge, his posture taut. His knuckles whiten, and the muscles of his neck tense, belying his effort to stay in control. "Just when everything was going so well, too."

I move toward him, gently sliding my arms around his waist from behind. My cheek presses against the hard planes of his back, still slick and warm from the shower. I breathe him in—soap, spice, and a lingering touch of steam.

"Things are still going well," I whisper against his skin, hoping to pull him back from the ledge. "For us, at the very least. Speaking of, why didn't you wake me before?"

He flips around, and my arms drop to my sides. "You didn't want the extra sleep?"

"No, that was nice," I say shyly, a blush warming my face. "I just thought . . . I mean, maybe we could have . . ."

"Showered together?"

"Mhm."

He regards me for a moment, the corner of his mouth lifting in a smirk, a flicker of amusement in his eyes. "Don't be shy. I told you, pretty girl—" He tilts my chin, leaning in for a quick kiss. "—I like it when you're greedy."

Gulping down my growing nerves, I say, "I know, but we still haven't . . . gone all the way yet."

"Oh, we're getting there." He smiles, a lopsided, boyish grin that robs me of air. "But we're taking it slow, remember? Figuring out what you like, what you need?"

"Same goes for you, right?"

"Exactly."

"Well, I think what I *need* is to have sex with you," I confess, the heat of embarrassment coloring my face. "I mean, God, just look at you right now."

A storm brews in his eyes, darkening them. His gaze slides to my lips, and he unconsciously wets his own with a slow swipe of his tongue. "Gracie's still here, isn't she?"

I arch a brow, feigning indifference. "Yeah, so?"

"So, let's maybe wait until we're completely alone. We can make a whole night of it over at my place."

"Oh, a whole night of it, huh? Ambitious."

"Only time you can call me an overachiever."

"So, tonight, then?"

With a predatory swiftness, he draws me closer, eliminating the space between us. His arousal, hard and insistent, presses into me through the thin terry cloth of his towel. "Eager, aren't you?"

Drawing in a shaky breath, I manage to mumble some sort of affirmation. My fingers graze his lower back, seeking more of him. He leans closer, lips peppering kisses against my neck as every inch of him presses against me.

"You want me to fill you up, Daisy?"

"Yes," I nearly moan.

"Pump inside of you until you're so fucking full that you can't stand it?"

"Jesus, El."

He chuckles, deep and low. "You like that, don't you? When I talk to you like that?"

"I really do."

"Good to know."

I tilt my head, genuinely curious. "Where do words like that even come from?"

"At this point, it just comes naturally."

"I'd like to say I know what you mean, but I think my mind just goes blank during sex. I feel like if I tried to come up with something, whatever I said would make me sound silly."

His brow furrows, a shadow of concern crossing his features. "Sorry, back up—your mind goes *blank* during sex?"

"I mean, sometimes?" I shrug a tad defensively. "Is that not . . . normal?"

"I mean, there are variations of normal. But . . . I don't know, that doesn't sound all that great." He hesitates, searching for the right words. "I mean, if we're talking about the same kind of blank here, then I can relate to the feeling. I dissociate a lot while I'm working, disconnect from my real self to get the scenes done. Though, I'd imagine you wouldn't want to when it's someone you care about."

I take a moment, digesting the depth of what he's saying and finding it surprisingly hard to swallow. "Oh, I see."

"I'm sorry." He moves a hand to caress my cheek, thumb gently stroking my jawline. "I shouldn't cast judgment on whatever your sex life was before me. God knows I don't like thinking about it."

"Me too." Drawing a deep breath, I muster a smile. "Ancient history, right?"

"Right, let's just leave it in the past." The tension in the room lifts a fraction. "Instead, we can focus on you and me. Tonight, at my apartment."

"Ah, my favorite topics."

"Should we break apart for the day, get our shit done, and then regroup later?"

My lips turn down in a faux pout. "You want to leave already?"

"I've seen you pretty much daily for the past several weeks. I spent the night in your bed last night." He gives me that familiar exasperated-yet-fond look. "Is that not enough for you?"

"Never enough."

His hand trails over my hip, curving around the swell of my ass and yanking me against him. "See? I knew you were insatiable."

"I am," I say, my smile brightening. "Only when it comes to you."

Another smirk. "And I love that about you."

"Fine, fine." Resigning myself to his point—for now—I pull back, lingering in the doorway for an extra few seconds. My gaze sweeps across his tall frame, and I do my best to drink in the sight of him, still dripping wet and half-hard in my bathroom. "Get yourself dressed, and then get out of here."

"Sounds like a plan." He slides his phone off the counter and gives me a tight-lipped smile. "Oh, and Daze, I'll let you know if I get a text back."

"Right, I almost forgot."

His gaze softens. "Wish I could say the same."

. . .

When I step into Elio's apartment later that night, there's an immediate sense of spaciousness that catches me off guard. His couch has been pushed against the wall, and the entirety of the living room stands bare, cleared of all its usual clutter.

The space is bathed in a soft glow, with candles lining the windowsills, their flames casting gentle, flickering shadows. My eyes dart to the vast open area, and I can't help but let out a small chuckle, wondering if he really thinks we need this much space for whatever he's planning.

Against this transformed backdrop, his silhouette appears—tall and lean with that mess of dark hair. He looks up as I walk in, his deep brown eyes searching mine. There's a tension there, an apprehension that makes me wonder if everything's okay.

The gentle hum of Noah Kahan plays out in the background, contrasting with his sudden, slightly frantic demeanor.

"Daisy," he starts, voice a touch shaky, "I . . . I think I fucked up." Raising a brow, I tilt my head, urging him to continue. With a sigh, he runs a hand through his thick hair. "I invited you over for sex before we even had our first official date."

"I invited myself. And I think we're beyond that point by now," I say, taking a step closer, attempting to stifle my laughter. "Besides, I don't want you to spend your money on me."

His eyes, previously filled with worry, now sparkle with a hint of mischief. "What if I tell you I only spent a few bucks on this."

He pulls a wrapped package off the coffee table beside him, thrusting it into my waiting hands. I take a cursory glance at the back of it, immediately noticing that it's some sort of video game, a round disc in a clear, used case.

My laughter dies down, replaced with disbelief. "You want us to play video games for our first date?"

"Thought you said we were past that point?"

I give him an incredulous scoff. "Well, now that you mention it—"

"Would you just look at the writing on the top, please?"

I flip the case right side up, gaze tracing over the scribbled letters. "Surf Pro Live? El, what is this?"

"Virtual surfing." His face lights up with excitement. "The cool thing about it is it syncs real-time data about weather and wave conditions. And, er, I already checked—they have your actual board on here and everything."

A lump forms in my throat, my emotions threatening to spill over. "Elio—"

"I know it's a shoddy excuse for the real thing." He gives me a sheepish grin. "But I'm supposed to avoid strenuous exercise, and I thought this could be the next best option."

I remember the moment distinctly, that day at the beach when we first met. I asked him a million questions then, not knowing where I was going but just hoping to crack his shell. My heart races now, palms clammy. "You once told me you've never surfed, and you never will."

"Yeah, well, I guess I'm a changed man." His lips quirk into a half-smile. "Though, I'm not sure that virtual surfing really counts."

I step closer, my fingers lightly touching his cheek. "Oh, it counts. It more than counts."

"So, you don't think it's, like, really fucking corny?"

"It's a bit corny," I concede with a grin. "But it's so sweet and so . . . you. If I had any doubts about having sex with you tonight, which I didn't, this would've sealed the deal for sure."

His laughter is rich and warm, echoing through the room. "Well, damn, I guess I did something right."

"Thank you, El. Seriously." I pull him into a gentle hug. "I love it."

His fingers trace circles on my back, sending shivers down my spine. "You want to try it out?"

Pulling back, I meet his eyes. "I do. I really do. But . . . after."

He blinks, a grin slowly stretches across his face. "*After*," he repeats, low and husky. "Right, well, you're the one in charge here."

# Chapter Thirty-One

## ELIO

Daisy's tongue darts out to wet her bottom lip, eyes shining as she meets my gaze.

My breathing slows as I take her in. Her soft, blonde hair, her full lips, and all the perfect curves of her body. I know she may not see it, but she's the sexiest woman I've ever laid eyes on.

She takes a step toward me, her hips swaying with each movement. The sight of her—so confident, so brazenly determined—is mesmerizing.

I swallow, my mouth going dry.

"Elio," she murmurs, the sound of my name on her lips setting my blood to simmer. My gut clenches, and liquid heat pulses through my veins, my desire for her growing with each passing second. "Take me to your room."

I swallow a deep, shuddery breath, trying to steady myself. "You don't have to ask me twice," I say, my voice barely more than a hoarse croak.

My palm slides into hers, and I pull her behind me down the hallway, a sense of urgency pounding in my chest. I'm burning with anticipation, my mind racing with thoughts of all the lovely, wicked things I want to do to her, *with* her.

My room is already dimly lit, hazy shadows dancing along the walls. The soft sounds of "Everywhere, Everything" filter in from the living room. Daisy's eager eyes linger on my bed, her lips parted in anticipation.

And I'm determined, with every last shred of decency inside of me, to make this experience unforgettable. For her, for me, for two people who've been bruised and jaded by love before.

Without a single word, I take her hand, and we slide into the bed together, the blankets wrapping around our bodies. I pull her close, savoring the warmth of her skin against mine. Slowly, I capture her mouth, my tongue flicking against the tip of hers just the way she likes.

My hands work to explore her body, tracing the dip in her waist, the swell of her full hips. I press my lips to her cheek, then to her neck, kissing her hungrily as she melts into a whimpering mess.

She slides her hands into my hair, and I move on top of her. The two of us slowly work together to remove every last shred of clothing from our bodies. It's not the first time I've seen her naked, but it sure as hell feels like it—like every little perfect piece of her is meant just for me.

My hand patiently works its way between us. I swipe my fingers along her slit until I reach that little bundle of nerves, touching and teasing her until she's so wet, so fucking ready for me. Her hips involuntarily writhe against my thigh.

She looks up, blinking at me through thick lashes, her deepest desires, her insecurities, all laid bare. "Take care of me, will you?"

"Only if you take care of me," I say. And then, with one solid, earth-defying thrust, I'm finally inside of her.

Nothing else exists. There's just us, and this bed, and this fucking perfect, unending moment between us. I move slowly, savoring each breath, trying to be aware of her every reaction.

I want this to be good for her, so good that it erases every single experience she's had before. And God, do I want this moment to last.

My movements gradually become more urgent, our bodies working in harmony as I sink deeper and deeper inside of her.

"You feel so fucking perfect, baby," I tell her, panting into the crook of her neck. "So *mine.*"

"Yes, yes," she whispers in a chant.

My grip on her tightens, my arms trembling as I drive myself deeper inside of her. She holds on to me, her nails digging into my back, and pleasure radiates through every inch of our intertwined bodies.

I brush her hair away from her forehead, curve one hand behind her shoulder, and fuck her like I mean it, like I was made for it. As the intensity builds between us, one hand inevitably presses against her heart—exactly where it belongs.

"Fuck," I whisper, taking in a sharp breath. "Want you so much."

She lets out a moan that I capture with my mouth. Her left hand clutches at my wrist as her right circles around my bicep, and I keep thrusting inside of her. Her lips are flushed and swollen, her golden hair fanned out across the pillow behind her head.

And God, it's an image that's seared into my brain for a lifetime.

This girl—my Daisy, my wildflower—she's fucking everything to me.

For once, I'm not thinking about anything else but how much I want this, want her. I'm not consumed by the pressure to perform, to please a waiting audience. I'm not mentally checking out, counting down the seconds until I can inevitably finish.

Instead, I feel liberated. I feel at home.

"Wait, El," she says, her hand moving from my wrist to caress my jawline. "I want to feel what it's like to ride you."

*Oh, fucking hell.*

She gasps when I flip her over on top of me, unwilling to sever our connection, if even for a second. As she adjusts to the new position, I slowly thrust up inside of her, groaning as I hit the perfect angle.

It's a tighter fit this way, snug and secure, but God does it feel good. So good that she nearly collapses on top of me, head sunk forward like she's never felt such pleasure in her life.

"You like that, baby?"

"Yes," she murmurs. "Just like that."

Without question, I grab her hips, guiding her up and down along my shaft, grinding into her from below. She clenches around my cock, her arousal spilling out and leaking onto my thighs.

"Oh, God, El," she cries with a strangled breath. "So good."

I trail my thumb along the seam that separates us, teasing her clit as I go. Her breath catches, and a deep moan shudders out of her. I know she's close now, and I can't fucking wait to watch her come undone, to fall apart on top of me.

"Wait, wait. I'm doing it wrong," she says, her voice a low whine. "I'm supposed to be the one in control."

"You can't do it wrong, pretty girl. Everything you do is so fucking good, so perfect." Another deep, heady groan forces its way out of me. "Don't question it."

I cover her lips with mine, not giving her a chance to protest further. My movements grow wild as I bury myself in her warmth. She trembles around me, and the strength of my thrusts from below force her to cry out my name.

It's heaven, I think, this moment between us. And like a

man who's been roaming the desert for days, I greedily drink up every sound she makes.

It's just one more short gasp of breath, another strained whimper, until I'm falling apart with her, drowning in how fucking good she feels.

We stay there for a long while—our breath mingling together in perfect unison—until eventually, everything comes back into focus. When I pull out of her, I'm nearly dizzy, but my heartbeat is steady now, unshaken. So, I wrap her up in my arms, careful to keep her close.

"What the fuck did I ever do to deserve you?"

She smiles and snuggles deeper into my embrace. "You didn't have to do anything," she says softly. "I'm here because I'm meant to be."

She turns toward me, pressing a gentle kiss to my lips, and I can't help but smile. She's mine, and I'm hers, and nothing in my life has ever felt so right.

AFTER MAKING Daisy come three more times—with my fingers, my mouth, and then once more with my cock—we somehow force ourselves to crawl out of bed. It's obligatory that we let Bentley out, no matter how much our bodies are screaming for us not to.

As we stand near the grass patch together, waiting patiently for my dog to do his business, Daisy kicks at a lone pebble on the pathway. "So . . ."

I lift a curious brow. "*So?*"

"So, I've been thinking about going to Cape Casserat for Thanksgiving," she says softly, giving me a shy smile. "I need to see my family. Get the yearly visit out of the way."

My brow furrows. "You're not going home for Christmas, too?"

"I'd rather just stick around here over winter break. I told you that my sister and I aren't all that close. Well, it's the same with my parents."

"You don't have a good relationship?"

"It's not that, really." She sighs, searching for the right words. "It's just that we're not, like, the warm and fuzzy family you see in the movies. I might want that, but it's not reality."

A pang of sympathy hits me. "I'm sorry, Daze."

"Don't be. It's not like they're particularly cold or anything, and they weren't bad to me growing up." She glances at her feet, kicking at the pebble once more. "It's just, I don't know, they weren't all that interested in the baby, or the toddler, or the school-aged stages. When I was a bit older, they seemed invested in my potential surfing career. But then, after that went out the window, I felt like I was kicked out of the nest."

A protective sort of outrage grips my chest. "That sounds pretty fucking cold to me."

"Yeah, I suppose it's a *little* frigid."

I step closer, sliding her hand into mine. "I didn't know you wanted to go pro."

"I thought I might." She gives me a placating smile. "I placed in the Under-18 Girls competition in El Salvador. But then I got injured, and I lost my sponsorship, and I just kind of let go of the dream altogether. I always intended to go to college first, anyway. So, when I hit my senior year of high school and still couldn't surf, I ended up applying for a university further away from the coast. That's how I ended up accepting a spot at Dayton."

"And now that you're back here, have you changed your mind?"

"No, I think it's better to keep it as a hobby, a passion, rather than a job. It's just too much pressure. I think, though, that giving up on the idea so quickly forced me to cling to something else in its absence."

I give her hand a gentle squeeze. "And what was that?"

"You probably don't want to hear about it right now." A hint of a blush colors her cheeks. "Not after what we just did."

I bump her hip. "Humor me."

"Um, that last year of high school is when I first met Logan." She hesitates, a war of emotions playing out in her eyes. "We'd gone to the same schools all our lives, but we never really crossed paths until senior year. He was laser focused on baseball, and I ran with a different crowd. When we both found out we were going to Dayton, it's like our fate was sealed."

A sting of jealousy surfaces, but I tamp it down with a joke. "So, a matter of convenience, then?"

"I guess so." She chuckles, tilting her head. "At the time, I think I was looking for something that I didn't have. A family tie of some sort to help keep me grounded. We didn't start officially dating until right before college, and then all of our friends melded into one."

I bring our clasped hands to my mouth, pressing a gentle kiss to the back of hers. "You know, you don't really talk about your other friends from Dayton."

"I haven't kept in touch with them, to be honest."

"Why not?"

"I wanted distance from everything that reminded me of Logan. And then, I've sort of realized that I don't miss them all that much." She traces an imaginary line on the ground. "Since I cut ties, I don't even feel their absence. It's like nothing is missing from my life at all. In fact, if anything, life feels a whole lot fuller now."

"Hm, I see."

She winces, glancing up at me. "I know . . . that probably makes me sound like an awful friend."

"It doesn't," I say, "not in the slightest."

"But, um, well, my point is . . . I think some of them are gonna be around during Thanksgiving break. And I'm not really looking forward to seeing them."

"Did you—I mean, would you want me to come with you?" I ask, the offer tumbling out of my mouth before I can stop it. "I could ward them off for you."

Her eyes light up. "You'd do that?"

"Of course I would."

"Then yeah, I think that'd be really nice." Her smile finally returns, tentative but genuine. "You'd have to meet my parents, though."

I chuckle. "That's okay. Parents love me."

"Really?"

"Not at all."

She releases my hand, giving me a playful shove. "Aw, come on, El."

"For you, though?" I throw an arm around her shoulder, pulling her back against me. "I'll be on my best behavior."

# Chapter Thirty-Two

## DAISY

Elio's arm is draped across my shoulders, his chest steadily rising and falling beneath my head. A wave of warmth washes over me, and I'm blanketed by a profound sense of belonging.

I take a deep breath, blinking back the emotion that threatens to surface. We slept together for the first time last night, and now I'm waking up in his arms, ready to burst into tears.

It's such a silly thing . . . that I would be so moved by a normal night of sex with my boyfriend. But I felt so sexy, so wanted. Revered and adored by him in the way I always hoped for.

It was more than just sex for me, though. It was fucking magic, and all I can think about now is how much I want—*need*—more of it.

It's strange how quickly things can change. In the past few weeks, I've seen so many unexpected sides to Elio, all the lovely little secrets he keeps locked away. He's funny, kind, and supportive. And he has the biggest heart, despite his arguments to the contrary.

And now he's offered to come along with me for Thanksgiving break, to act as a safeguard between me and my old friends, my family—a gesture that lights me up all over.

I snuggle closer, the corners of my lips turning up in a

contented smile. Elio stirs, shifting on the bed to peer over at me.

"Good morning, pretty girl," he murmurs, pressing a kiss to the top of my head.

I smile, loving the sound of his sleep-filled voice. "Good morning."

"Sleep well?"

"Much better than I expected."

"Me too."

His fingers move to my face, thumb tracing the outline of my cheekbone before sifting through my hair. His touch is so gentle, like he's scared I'll break if he presses too hard.

"Gorgeous," he says before leaning in and capturing my lips in a slow, sensual kiss.

It's the type of kiss that's long and lingering, full of tenderness that only intensifies as the seconds tick by. His other hand smooths across my collarbone before pinning both of my arms above my head.

I gasp as his teeth nip at my swollen bottom lip, murmuring words against his mouth. "I think you're the one who's insatiable."

"Maybe you're right," he murmurs, and he gives me a devilish grin before his mouth finds mine again.

We kiss, and kiss, and kiss until neither of us is able to concentrate on anything else. My head spins, and desire builds up in my core. I'm squirming beneath him in need and want of something—anything—to ease the fire raging inside of me.

And then, he pulls away like nothing happened, grinning down at me. "So, what does one do the morning after he's slept with the girl of his dreams?"

My cheeks flush. "Do it again?"

He chuckles, warm and full, gently stroking my hair. "Let's take a break, baby. We should eat."

I nod, my stomach rumbling at the thought of food. Elio climbs off the bed, offering me a hand to help me up. I take it gratefully, a little unsteady on my feet. He supports me with his hands on my hips, the heat of his skin seeping in through my silk nightgown.

I smile up at him, feeling lighter than I have in months. "You're very good at this," I say.

He raises a questioning brow. "At what?"

"At this," I say, gesturing between us. "At making me feel happy."

His expression softens, and he brushes a strand of hair from my face. "You make it easy."

We make our way to the kitchen, Elio leading me by the hand. He sets me down at the small table, quickly lets Bentley out, and then sets about making our breakfast, humming as he does.

I've never seen him act quite like this, so at ease and content with life.

I watch him move around the kitchen, his muscular, tattooed arms flexing as he reaches for ingredients. A sense of awe fills me, a pinch of disbelief that he's all mine.

Once he's done cooking, he catches me staring and gives me a light chuckle, shaking his head. "What?" he asks, as if he doesn't already know.

I wave a hand dismissively. "Nothing. Just thinking."

He flashes me another grin, sliding a plate of pancakes in front of me. "You're always thinking."

"That's just because I have a big brain," I say, taking a bite of the fluffy pancakes.

They're topped with strawberries and whipped cream,

warm and fresh from the stove. I'm touched by the thoughtfulness of the gesture; he must have gone out and bought the ingredients specifically for this moment.

He laughs, pouring us both a cup of chamomile tea. "Well, let's put that big brain to use, then. What are you thinking about, Daisy?" he asks, settling into the seat beside me.

I chew thoughtfully for a moment, swallowing before I reply. "I'm just thinking about how lucky I am to have you," I finally say, my gaze meeting his. "And how . . . good last night was."

He hums in agreement, a hint of mischief sparkling in his eyes. "Best night of my life."

"Yeah?"

"Of course. I didn't know that sex could be like that." He leans over, swiping at a dollop of whipped cream from the corner of my mouth. "I mean, being with you . . . it was the first time I felt that true connection. The all-encompassing need to just exist in the moment."

I reach over the table, my fingers curling around his. "It was pretty special, huh?"

He smiles, squeezing my hand. "Yeah."

"And we should do it again. Right now."

He snorts a laugh. "Daisy, we're leaving the house today whether you like it or not."

"Oh, God, who have I become?"

"Someone who's mesmerized by my dick, I guess."

"Hey!" I laugh, swatting his arm with the back of my hand. "You be nice to me."

"I will." He sets down his fork, running a hand through his hair, pausing as if to collect his thoughts. "Not to ruin the mood, but there's something else we should talk about before the day gets ahead of us."

"Which is?"

"I still haven't heard back from Sapphire."

"Seriously." I stop eating, frustration gnawing at my insides. "All that urgent texting, and for what?"

"I know." He swallows hard. "I think she's trying to play mind games or something."

"I'm sorry, El. That's so stressful."

"Like you said, we'll figure it out." He takes a sip of his tea and holds back a wince. Evidently, he's still not used to mornings without his black coffee. "I think I'm just gonna block the number. I'm sure if she wants to get ahold of me again, she'll find some other way."

"This is bordering on criminal, you know? It's stalking."

"I know." He gives me a helpless shrug. "And if it gets to a point where I don't feel like I can handle it, then I'll escalate things."

"Okay, well, thank you for keeping me in the loop."

"Of course."

I shovel the last little bite of food into my mouth, chewing happily until a realization hits me. "Wait a minute, where did that topic come from?"

He raises a petulant brow. "What do you mean?"

"You said *someone who's mesmerized by my dick* and then immediately brought up Sapphire. Thank you very much for the comparison."

His laughter is heavy. "Daze, that is so not the case here."

My lips curve into a mischievous smile. I shove our empty plates away and crawl onto his lap, one leg over each thigh, narrowly avoiding disaster.

"It better not be," I joke, raining kisses along his neck.

"Oh, and is this my punishment?"

"Yes," I say, nipping at the soft skin.

We both chuckle, and he wraps his arms fully around my waist, drawing me closer. I'm straddling him now, our bodies molded together, every inch of him pressing against me.

"Hey, Daze?" he murmurs, holding me tight.

"Yeah?"

"You should know . . . that being with you? I think it's the closest thing to heaven I'll ever get."

My heart skips, and I fight back the urge to cry again. I rest my head against his shoulder, taking a moment to savor this newfound closeness. "Let's get ready and go," I say. "Before I melt into a puddle in your lap."

He grins against my hair, a low rumble of laughter vibrating through his chest. Then he stands up and sets me on my feet. "Yeah, alright. Come on, then."

"Do you think when we get back, we can finally play Surf Pro?"

"Yeah." He smiles, shaking his head. "Anything you want."

Elio and I have spent the majority of November living in our little bubble of bliss. Swapping apartments, waking up beside one another, strolling on the beach with Bentley, and spending dinner dates with Gracie, Max, and LJ.

I'm hit with a twinge of gratitude for Bentley's quick adjustment to our new dynamic, but it's also strange not having his familiar weight at my feet. Luca and Harper generously offered to look after him for the break, sending us off with a chorus of teasing comments and promises of spoiling him with treats.

Although, I'm fairly certain that it's no sweat off Luca's back. His team isn't playing this weekend, and I know that he used to live with Bentley, so he must be missing him.

As for Elio and me, we're stuck inside this giddy stage where everything's still a mix of heart-fluttering looks and lingering touches. But it's not just our nights that have me on a high—it's the mornings, the afternoons, every stolen moment where we find another secret, another quirk, another whisper of vulnerability between us.

As I look out the window of his Jeep, the trees streak past in a blur of autumnal colors, making me realize just how much has changed this month. We've explored each other in every way possible, both in whispered conversations in the dim light of morning and in the passion that sparks between us at night.

Elio's hand reaches over, his fingers lacing with mine, and I'm drawn out of my thoughts. I turn to him, taking in the way the sunlight catches on his dark hair, the slight scruff on his chin.

"Everything okay?" he asks, his thumb drawing small circles over the back of my hand.

My lips curl into a soft smile, and my gaze momentarily drops. "Just thinking."

"Surprising."

"About us." I playfully roll my eyes. "But also, about my parents, my sister, my old friends."

"Still feeling nervous?"

"Yeah, a bit," I admit, the corner of my lip tugging upward. "Better, though, knowing I have you with me."

"I'm glad." A spark of pride lights up his eyes. "Speaking of old friends, Kaia's been blowing up my phone this week. Apparently, she's just *so* proud of me for meeting your family."

I arch an amused brow. "Big step, huh?"

"Yeah, the first of its kind."

Curiosity prods. "And Kaia knows *your* family really well, right?"

"Yeah, she's been around forever."

"You two have known each other since you were little kids. And yet, you never . . ."

"Never what?"

Fidgeting with our entwined fingers, I push on. "Had feelings for her?"

"Absolutely not." He lets out a dry laugh. "She's always been more of a sister to me. Actually, that's how we met in the first place. Her sister, Sofia, dated Luc for three years."

"No way!"

"Yeah, hard to believe he existed before Harper came into his life, huh?"

"Totally." Grinning, I nudge him with my elbow. "But you and Kaia made it through the breakup okay?"

"Yeah, it didn't affect our friendship. There were . . . other things that got in the way of it, though. At least, for a little while."

"Like what?" I ask, trying to decipher his cryptic words.

He hesitates for a brief moment, and I know he's treading on delicate ground. "It's kind of a heavy topic, actually." His voice lowers, his throat clears, and he offers me a tight-lipped smile before glancing at the open road. "Do you mind if we save it for after the break?"

My heart sinks at the question. Despite everything we've shared, there are aspects of his past—some secret dark corners—he's still reluctant to divulge. But it seems like he might open up eventually, and that's all I can ask for.

"Yeah, of course," I say, aiming for an understanding tone. My fingers gently squeeze his, a silent promise of support.

He releases a deep sigh of gratitude, his shoulders visibly relaxing. "This is gonna be good, you know? I've never been to Cape Casserat before."

"You'll like it." As our fingers continue to play, I tap my thumb against his. "I can show you my favorite spot in town. It's overlooking this little harbor where these massive cruises dock up."

There's a tiny spark in his eyes, a grin that spreads at my enthusiasm. "Sounds like a plan, Daisy girl."

"Yeah," I say. "It's a plan."

# Chapter Thirty-Three

## ELIO

Daisy's family home is far from what I expected.

Something about the way she is—so soft, so sweet, so genuine—suggested a cozy, relaxed atmosphere. Some sort of cottage or maybe a little cabin in the woods. Instead, I find something very different here: a grand estate nestled in the hills of Cape Casserat, with a sprawling garden and a gated drive.

It's a strange kind of intimidation—seeing the wealth and power of her family up close. I wasn't prepared for it, other than knowing I'd need to be the perfect gentleman in front of her parents. A polished, proper version of myself.

While that still holds true, I also need to act like the whole prospect—extravagant wealth, estranged family members—doesn't nag at my insides. I'm not used to it, and I'm not so sure that I want to be.

But then Daisy takes my arm, squeezing it ever so slightly, and I'm reminded of why I'm here in the first place. To support her, to be her shelter.

We enter through the grand double doors, and Daisy's father is the first to greet us. He's a stately-looking man with salt-and-pepper hair and a strong jaw. I notice that he and Daisy share the same soft, brown eyes, but that's where their similarities seem to end.

His expression is unreadable, his voice tight as he shakes my hand in greeting.

But Daisy doesn't seem to notice. She's made it clear that she isn't close with her family, but still, her face lights up at the sight of him.

"Hi, Dad," she says softly, sweetly. "It's so nice to be home!"

Her father responds with a simple nod. "Nice to see you, too. You can show your guest to his room."

Daisy's eyes, normally full of light, seem a little dimmed as she shoots him a half-hearted smile. "Come on," she murmurs, guiding me deeper into their home.

Every step on the marble floor echoes like a reminder of its grandeur. The sweeping staircases are lined with portraits of stern-looking ancestors, probably the same ones who'd designed this posh prison.

She leads me up to what's to be my room for the weekend, and the opulence doesn't stop—marble-tiled bathroom, plush bedding, and gold-encrusted furniture. But it's the view that captures my attention: the sprawling, manicured estate stretches out as far as the eye can see.

She gestures grandly, an attempt at lightness. "Everything the light touches is yours . . . until Sunday."

"Ah, I suppose I can't sneak into your room?"

A sound between a snort and a chuckle escapes her. "You'd have to scale down the tree outside this window, make your way through the garden maze, and then climb up my trellis."

"Really?"

"I'm kidding. It's just across the hall." She tugs on my hand, pulling me behind her. "Come on, I'll show you."

I follow her lead, mesmerized by every step. When we reach her room, I'm met with an explosion of colors. She has a massive window lined with a pale blue valance, allowing light to pour in and illuminate the room. There's a bright white bedspread with yellow polka dot pillows, her nightstand covered in trinkets and books.

I can't help but grin at the sight. It's the first place in this house that actually feels like *her*. I let out a low whistle, eyes roaming around the room. "I like it."

"Thanks. I like it, too," she says, soaking up the nostalgia. "My little home for the first eighteen years."

The pause between us grows heavy, my mind racing with questions. "You know, before, when you mentioned a surfing sponsorship, I just assumed . . ."

"That I needed the money for comps?"

"Well, yeah, isn't that the point?"

"I did need it, actually. My parents wouldn't pay for anything to do with surfing. They were interested in my success, sure, but they've always wanted me to pave my own way. If I wanted to surf, I needed to find a way to cover the expenses, the travel, on my own. It was hard enough to convince them to cover my tuition."

I give her an incredulous look. "Seems like they can spare the money."

"Yeah, but they wanted me to go to an Ivy. And, well, something like that isn't really up my alley."

"Yeah, I can see that." I wrap a gentle hand around her, pulling her toward me. "You fit in perfectly at Coastal, anyway."

"Thanks, baby."

"Mhm." I lift her arm, pressing a kiss to the inside of her wrist. "So . . . you still doin' okay?"

She sighs, her smile not quite reaching her eyes. "I mean, I guess so. Dad didn't have much to say earlier, did he?"

Treading carefully, I shake my head. "And your mom, did she tell you she'd be gone when we got here?"

She gives me a sad little shrug. "Not a word."

"That's frustrating," I say with a gentle squeeze of her hand. "But you know, we don't have to spend much time here if you don't want to. We'll do the obligatory dinner tomorrow. Other than that, why don't we just explore on our own?"

"Yeah, I like that idea." Her eyes light up with gratitude, and she squeezes my hand back. "But I should probably go check in with my sister, Summer. Say hi before we break free."

"You want me to come?"

"Maybe you could just meet her later?" she suggests. "Who knows what kind of mood she'll be in."

"Yeah, do what you need to do. I'll be here when you get back."

She leaves, and I'm alone with my spinning thoughts. The chill of the house, the distance of her parents—it doesn't make sense. The contrast between them and their vibrant daughter feels like night and day. I wonder, not for the first time, how Daisy came to be who she is amidst such coldness.

And I know, at least for the rest of this trip, that I'm resolved to be her warmth.

By the time Daisy finishes up greeting her sister and we've unpacked the car, both of us are famished. So, we decide to take a walk around downtown, planning to stop at one of her favorite places for a late lunch.

As we stroll down the cobblestone street, she gives me the low-down on all the shops and restaurants that line our path. She recalls stories of how her family used to hit up the tiny cinema on Christmas Eve, one of her favorite and only holiday traditions.

It's so nice to see her spirited again, talking a mile a minute as she wanders around town with me. I can tell that this place is special to her, filled with fond memories despite the lack of care from her family.

We eventually come across a small café tucked in between two buildings, its outside walls adorned with bright potted flowers. We take a seat on the wooden patio outside and order hearty sandwiches and some warm tea.

In between sips of her drink, she leans in and asks, "You know what I was just thinking?"

"Tell me."

"I feel like Bentley should be here."

"Fuck, I know. Sorta feels like he's our missing piece." I glance down at our feet, staring at the spot where he'd usually be nestled, and it feels profoundly empty. "We haven't been apart more than a day since he moved in with me."

"I'm sorry you couldn't bring him."

"It's not your fault that Summer's allergic."

"Yeah, she's so annoying," she says, glancing down at her lap, nearly mumbling the words under her breath.

I cock my head to the side, assessing her disappointed frown. "Did she say something else before we left?"

She gives me an apologetic look. "Just something silly about Logan."

A muscle in my jaw ticks. "What about him?"

"Just that he's here. That he *texted* her."

I rear back. "What, why? Were they close?"

She shakes her head, her expression troubled. "I don't think so. But you know those friends I told you about? They don't know the real reason we broke things off. I'm sure he made it sound like it was all my fault. I mean, for God's sake, he cheated on me, and somehow, my little sister still took his side."

"That's bullshit," I say, placing a comforting hand on her arm. "You deserve to be supported by your family."

She leans into my touch, looking up at me with big, sad eyes. "Thank you," she says softly. "It's just harder than I thought. Being here. I want to leave the past in the past, but I think it always has a way of coming back to haunt you."

"I can agree with that." I stroke my thumb along the side of her forearm. "You want me to straighten Summer out when we get back?"

"No." She gives me a full-body laugh. "God, no. That would just give her more ammunition to be annoyed by me. I don't know why she has to act like this, like I'm her competition or something. We used to be so close when we were little."

"Well, people change," I say softly. "Sometimes they grow apart."

She nods, her eyes downcast. "Yeah, I guess so."

We finish up our lunch and continue our walk around town, stopping by the harbor that Daisy loves so much. The two of us make our way to a bench that overlooks the water, the huge cruises docked up in the distance.

"It's nice here," I say, taking in the salty air.

"I know," she murmurs beside me. "Do you see why it's my favorite?"

"Yeah, I do."

We sit in silence for a few minutes, wrapped up in each other, her head resting on my shoulder. The wind ruffles the water and shakes the branches of the trees lining the shoreline. Seagulls fly low over the water, and boats of all shapes and sizes bob up and down in the harbor.

After a while, a loud voice interrupts us, calling out Daisy's name. I turn toward the direction of the sound, and there's a group of people walking toward us from further up the road.

One girl in particular stands out, and she's coming toward us at a fast trot.

"Daisy!" she calls as she approaches. "Oh my gosh, I haven't seen you in months! I didn't realize you'd be coming home."

Daisy stands to greet her, stammering out something about visiting her parents before introducing us. The girl, Hailey—one of Daisy's old high school friends, now a Dayton coed—is clearly surprised by my presence.

She gives me a tight-lipped smile before stretching out a hand in greeting. I return the shake, grinning when Daisy tacks on the fact that I'm her boyfriend.

"Your boyfriend, really?" Hailey's eyes visibly widen. "Already?"

"It's still new," Daisy adds softly.

"Hmm, right." Hailey glances back to the group of people, now just a few yards away. "Well, we're all headed to my family's place tonight for a bonfire. Would you want to come? It'll be just like old times."

Daisy looks at me uncertainly, and I can sense that she's conflicted. That maybe she wants to say yes, to bridge that gap and enjoy the night, but is hesitant because of me. I gently squeeze her hand in reassurance, turning back to Hailey with a smile.

"Sure," I tell her. "We'll be there."

"Oh, uh, great," she says quickly. "We'll see you later. Oh, and um, just a heads-up . . . Logan will be there tonight, too."

The moment his name is mentioned, a subtle tension fills the air. I notice Hailey's expression change, a hint of reproach—or is it guilt?—flashing in her eyes, but she quickly regains her composure.

Daisy tries to hide her discomfort, but her voice wavers slightly. "Okay, no worries."

I observe closely as Hailey rejoins her group. They share a brief, whispered conversation before they leave, a strained silence following their exit. I glance over at Daisy, and her gaze is downcast, her fingers nervously tapping together.

"I'm sorry." She lifts her eyes to meet mine, a shadow of guilt in them. "We don't actually have to go."

I step closer and gently shake my head, wanting to erase her uncertainties. Drawing her into a comforting embrace, I place a gentle kiss on her temple. "Oh, we're going," I say with a grin.

She pulls back, searching my eyes, amusement bubbling in her voice. "Why? You trying to cause trouble?"

"Only if there's trouble to be found."

She swats at my chest, brows raised in mock reprimand. "El . . ."

"I'm kidding." I wink at her. "I'll be a good boy."

"Will you now?"

I snake a hand around the nape of her neck, pulling her closer, and my voice drops to a husky whisper. "And if I'm really good, maybe I can earn a prize."

Her cheeks flush, but she plays right along. "What kind of prize?"

"Oh, I think you can come up with a few creative ideas."

She pulls away, tapping her finger thoughtfully against her chin. "Hmm, nope. Fresh out."

"Your loss."

With a teasing eye roll, she pushes me aside and heads straight back for her favorite bench. I join her there, wrap an arm around her shoulders, and we watch together as the ships keep on sailing by, reveling in the endless horizon.

# Chapter Thirty-Four

## DAISY

As we walk up the path to Hailey's family home, Elio's hand envelops mine, his warmth and strength seeping in, providing me with the sense of comfort I need.

It's been months since I've been around these people, and the idea of seeing them all again is making me uneasy. But I wanted to come here tonight to prove something to myself, to give my past one last chance.

Not Logan, of course, but the rest of them.

Maybe when we ended things, I wrote everyone else off too quickly. Filled the gaps and spaces in my life with new places and new friends, with Elio and Bentley, who've filled up my cup until it's overflowing. But that doesn't mean I can't hold space for anyone else.

As we step into the backyard, an all-too-familiar sensation grips my insides, twisting and turning them like a cloth wrung dry. I'm engulfed in a sea of memories. Each familiar face serves as a reminder of a past I've tried to put behind me, and each unfamiliar one a sign of how much has changed in my absence.

I grip Elio's hand tighter.

Hailey immediately greets us both, pulling me into a hug that feels a little too tight, and I wonder if she's trying to make amends for something. Then she turns to Elio and gives him a barely there nod.

"Oh, Daisy!" She shifts her attention back to me and points to a group of people I recognize in the corner. "The Dayton group's just over there. We're all so excited you're here!"

"Really?" I try to keep the shock out of my voice. I haven't returned any of their texts in months or even bothered to acknowledge their existence elsewhere. "That's . . . nice."

I glance at Elio nervously, but he just gives me an encouraging smile.

"Come say hi to everyone," she pleads, bouncing on her heels. "Elio, you can go get a drink while we all catch up."

She waves a dismissive hand in his direction, and before I have a chance to protest, she takes my wrist, pulling me toward the group. I reluctantly follow, shooting an apologetic glance over my shoulder, feeling like a sheep being herded to the slaughter.

But as we near the group, I can sense the excitement oozing from their pores. They all greet me with open arms, and before I know it, I'm surrounded by people wanting to catch up. Everyone is asking me about my life, about Coastal, about where the hell I've been for the last two months.

I don't know what to say, so I just deflect with a smile, telling them how busy I've been, how much I love my new school.

"Yeah, I'm sure you do." The words, followed by a heavy scoff, come from a girl named Nessa, arms crossed tightly over her chest. "So much that you've forgotten about the rest of us. And why show up now? Just to rub your new boyfriend in Logan's face?"

"Ness," Hailey scolds, eyes narrowing in reprimand.

"What? It's true, isn't it?" Nessa shoots back, her eyes coldly fixed on me. "It's what everyone was saying before you got here."

My face flushes with embarrassment and shame. It's not just anger I see in Nessa's eyes; there's something deeper, something more personal between us.

Memories of her laughing at Logan's jokes—the lingering touches and the stolen glances—they all flood back to me. It always bothered me, but I would brush it off, convincing myself I was just imagining things.

Maybe, during my absence, she and Logan grew closer. Maybe she was the shoulder he cried on, the one who helped mend his broken heart.

*Did she hope, even for a moment, that she'd finally have a chance with him now?*

The hurt in her eyes suddenly makes sense, as does the sharp edge to her words. And I can't fault her for wishing I'd never shown up here again.

Before I can formulate a proper response, Elio appears at my side, red Solo cup in hand. He passes the drink over, and I stare down at the contents for a quick beat. It's something pink, and it smells fruity and sweet.

He once told me he's off booze, and I've certainly never seen him drink, so I have no idea what this could be. Regardless, it's something to hold—a way to keep my hands busy—grounding me in the midst of chaos.

"Hey, guys," he says, his voice smooth and confident. "I'm Elio, Daisy's boyfriend."

The group grows silent for a long moment, caught off guard by his presence. There are a few blatant stares, some of the guys awkwardly sizing him up before they even bother to acknowledge his greeting.

Nessa, on the other hand, shoots me a sly look before she asks, "So, how long have you and Daisy been together? A few months now?"

I'm not sure if she wants to catch me in a lie or if she just wants to make me more uncomfortable than I already am. But whatever her game plan is, I think it might be working.

Elio's dark eyes flicker to mine for a moment. "No, not long," he says with a shrug, slipping an arm around my shoulders.

I'm grateful for his casual response, for his ability to swoop in and know exactly what I need, but I'm upset that I put him in this position in the first place—one where he feels the need to defend our relationship.

Before I can get a word in, another one of my old friends speaks up, trying to apologize for Nessa. He says that they just haven't heard from me, and it's hard to know what to even say. He argues that they're all used to seeing me with Logan, despite how much that might sting to hear.

"Well, she is her own fucking person," Elio cuts in, his voice carrying an air of authority I didn't know he possessed. It's like he's daring them to challenge him, to say another negative word against me.

The atmosphere grows tense, and I take a timid sip of the mystery liquid to distract myself. *Strawberry wine*. Because of course it is.

"Um, anyway, it was good to see you guys," I carefully interrupt. "We're gonna go grab another drink."

As we walk away, the weight of curious eyes follows us, likely wondering about our relationship, questioning my every decision. Yet for me, a silent realization takes root: our dynamic has irrevocably changed, and there's nothing I can do about it.

At least now I have the answers I've been looking for, and I know that leaving them all behind wasn't the wrong choice.

We step into the kitchen together, and I sink against the

countertop. The cool touch of the granite countertop presses into my skin, anchoring me back to the present.

"You okay?" Elio asks, gaze tracing over my pinched features.

I nod, taking another slow sip of my drink. "Yeah, just . . . I wasn't expecting all of that, I guess."

"I can tell," he says as he wraps his arms around me. "But you handled it well."

"I'm sorry for how they treated you."

He waves off my concern. "Don't be. You can always lean on me, remember?"

"Yeah, I remember."

We stand there together, the noise from the gathering a quiet murmur in the background. As much as I disliked this whole experience, facing my past head-on was the closure I needed. And having Elio by my side made it all the more bearable.

"Do you think we could sneak out of here without anyone noticing?" I ask, my voice a hushed whisper.

"Yeah, but first—"

Before he can finish, the door to the kitchen swings open, revealing the person I least want to see at this moment. Logan's face is a mixture of surprise, anger, and something else entirely unreadable. Our gazes lock, and for a moment, a strange sense of fear strikes me.

Despite our past—all the good, happy memories that we've shared—all I can picture now is how he acted the last time I saw him. The way he yelled at me outside of my apartment, the way he refused to leave, and all the nasty things he accused me of doing.

"Daisy." Logan's voice is a rough whisper, laden with a mix of nostalgia and yearning. "I didn't think you'd really come."

A pause hangs in the air, the weight of our shared history pressing down. But before I can find the right words, Elio steps in, physically placing himself between our past and our present. His posture is protective, ready, a silent guardian shielding me from the emotional minefield Logan represents.

I finally muster up the courage to speak. "I just wanted to come and see everyone. To, um, formally close this chapter of my life. You know?"

"Right, of course." Logan's eyes darken, and he takes a step forward. "And you don't give a shit about *my* closure, right?"

Elio's grip on me tightens, but I gently disengage. "This isn't the time or place to have this discussion," I say. "I've moved on, and you should, too."

"Yeah, bud," Elio cuts in. "I think you found '*your closure*' when you slipped between somebody else's legs."

Logan's face contorts into a mask of rage, and he lunges forward. Elio reacts quickly, grabbing his arm and twisting it behind his back. Logan grunts in pain, struggling against his quick strength.

"You don't have to be with this piece of shit," Logan nearly spits. "I still want you, Daisy. I always have."

"You have a real funny way of showing it," I mutter.

"Seriously?" Logan scoffs a laugh. "You think *this* guy, some loser who fucks other people for a few bucks, is the better choice?"

I step forward, my heart pounding with anger. He can insult me all he wants, but when it comes to Elio, I have to draw the line. "Just give it up already," I say, my voice a pleading whisper. "This isn't what I came here for."

Logan's features soften slightly as he looks at me, but his tone remains harsh. "Fine," he says, "I'll leave you alone. But don't come crawling back to me when he breaks your heart."

"Don't worry," I say. "There's not a chance of that happening."

Elio loosens his grip on Logan, giving him a shove toward the door. "Go before I do something I'll regret."

Logan shoots him a venomous look, but behind his anger, there's a hint of brokenness. A realization that he truly lost something precious. He hesitates for a second, as though contemplating whether to apologize or at least explain. But instead, he turns on his heel and storms right out of the kitchen.

As the door slams shut behind him, murmurs arise from the living room, evidence that everyone's been eavesdropping. The weight of the confrontation pushes down on me, and I lean back against the countertop, my hands shaking with adrenaline.

"I'm so sorry, Daze," Elio says, his voice low and sincere. "I didn't want to cause a scene."

I shake my head, tears pricking at the corners of my eyes. "It's not your fault. And trust me, I'm not crying over Logan hurting me. I'm just overwhelmed by this whole night. God, I've never seen him act so unhinged before."

"He just can't handle how jealous he is, how badly he fucked up when he lost you." He steps closer and brushes his thumb across my cheek, wiping away a stray tear. "He'll spend the rest of his life regretting what he did. Missing you, wishing he had you back. I know I would."

The genuine warmth in his words gives me a surge of hope. After the deep pain of a broken heart, I didn't know if I could ever feel like this again. Yet, with him, I feel more alive, more at home, than I ever have before.

And as much as Logan's words sting, I know deep down that they're not true. Elio won't break my heart. I trust him with it, despite my past, fully and without restraint.

"Well, he's just gonna have to live with that," I say, leaning into his touch. "Because for me, there's nothing left to miss."

"Good," he says. "Because I'm here, and I'm not going anywhere."

"I know you aren't."

He tilts his head, brushing his lips tenderly against mine, lingering as if he's savoring every second. And all the mistakes, the heartache, the pain of my past seems worthwhile now.

After all, it's what led me back to him.

He draws back, eyes locked on mine. "Ready to get out of here, pretty girl?"

"More than ready."

# Chapter Thirty-Five

## ELIO

THANKSGIVING DAY CAME and went with Daisy's family. It was a quiet, reserved night, with her parents acting as though they had little to no interest in what she's been up to.

Meeting her mom was inconsequential, much like I expected, and her sister, Summer, was no better. In fact, she mostly glared in Daisy's direction the whole two hours we spent together, painfully silent at their family table.

And then, their mother asked their personal chef to slice up a pumpkin pie. Once the pieces were doled out, she had the audacity to suggest we eat it upstairs.

I watched, helpless, as my girlfriend held in a wince, clearly disappointed by the outcome. But in true Daisy fashion, she found a way to smile through it all.

When we ate our pie later that night, alone together in her childhood bedroom, I did my best to cheer her up, to make her feel a little bit more like herself.

All in all, it was a far cry from the holidays I'm used to spending with my own family. The six of us siblings would parade around the table, laughing and eating until we couldn't move, sharing stories and memories from the past year. But this was just . . . lonely.

Daisy's family seemed to be more comfortable in their own silence, and I found it difficult to connect with them on any level.

And now, the morning after, Daisy's finally decided she wants to cut her visit short.

I'm all for it since this trip has been nothing but draining for both of us. It's been heartbreaking to see the light sapped out of my favorite person's eyes, and I'd rather not spend another three days suffering through it.

Once we're all packed up, Daisy says goodbye to her parents, reminding them she won't be home for Christmas. Of course, they don't seem disconcerted about her absence.

So, we grab a bite to eat by ourselves and then take a long detour home to pick up Bentley. Once he's safe and secure in the back seat, the hour-long drive back to campus is nothing but a soothing blur, filled with the comforting hum of the road and the soft music Daisy picks out.

There's an unspoken sense of relief brewing between us now, a mutual understanding that we're heading back to friendly territory. Back to our own little world. And by the time the familiar campus buildings come into view, the tension from the past few days is like a distant memory.

LATER THAT EVENING, the lifelike sound effects of Surf Pro fill my apartment. Daisy's fingers dance over the console, a glee-filled smile plastered on her face. She's completely at home here, and it's good to see her like this again—so happy and full of life.

She told me she doesn't want to talk about what happened anymore, so we're finding new ways to occupy our time. We've been playing this game for the last half hour now, riding digital waves and consistently wiping out.

Well, at least that's true on my account.

Every now and then, she glances over at me, eyes twinkling

with mischief. "Lean into the wave more," she advises with a grin, executing a perfect spin on her board.

Trying to mimic her, my character bails into the water for the tenth fucking time in a row. I chuckle, setting the controller down. "Okay, I officially need a break. My guy has drowned too many times."

Her laughter fills the room. "Sorry you can't keep up."

I smile, making my way to the couch and sinking down into my seat. My heart rate's been kicking up anyway, and I need to rest before I trigger something catastrophic.

*Wouldn't that just be the icing on the cake?*

Local man life flighted due to excessive video game play. The perfect ending to this shitty week.

I grab my phone and quickly scroll through my emails, relieved to find the message I've been waiting for. The subject line reads: "Further Submission Required—Echo."

"Hey, Daze?" I start, slightly hesitant. "You remember that audio gig I told you about? They've finally replied to my application."

She pauses the game and turns toward me, eyes shining with curiosity. "Oh? What did they say?"

I show her the email, gnawing at my bottom lip. "They want a few more clips. Audio only. I think I need to show more versatility. Most of my AfterDark content is . . . visually centric. This needs more vocalizing, maybe even a bit more scripting."

Raising a brow, she says, "Well, I'm sure you can manage that."

"Look, I know this was supposed to be our weekend. And after everything with your family, your old friends . . . I don't want to ruin it. But I was hoping to get these clips done soon. Secure this job, and then start the transition from AfterDark."

"No, I totally understand. How much time do you need, exactly?"

Relief washes over me. "I promise it'll just be a few hours. You can keep playing or just chill here. I'll . . . retreat to my room, get into the zone."

"Can I help?"

"*Help*, how?"

She drops the controller and moves closer, her voice dipping to a soft whisper. "Maybe I can . . . inspire you."

My pulse jumps in my throat. "Inspire me, huh?"

She gives me a shy look, tracing a finger over my chest. "Think of it as immersive role-play."

A grin stretches across my face. "Well, can't argue with that."

I stand from the couch, setting Bentley up with a few toys and a fresh bowl of water. Then I grip Daisy's hand, immediately leading her back to my room.

In some ways, this all feels strange—the idea of finally inviting someone else behind the curtain. Yet, the thrill rushing through me pushes past any reservations I might hold. Because Daisy's not just anyone.

She's my person.

And maybe this is exactly what I need to bridge that gap. To prevent the dissociation from creeping in while I switch over to Echo. Someone who understands me, who's willing to support me in whatever way she can.

As soon as we step inside my room, she turns to me, curious and shy. "So, where do we start?"

"Well, I have a few different scripts I've been toying with . . ."

Her smile grows. "Lead the way."

I pull out my laptop and open up a dedicated folder, scanning through my list of rough ideas. One in particular catches my eye, entitled *Late Night Call*.

"What do you think about this one?"

She reads over my shoulder, lips pursed. "Mm, I like it."

"Alright, then."

I gulp low in my throat, moving toward my recording equipment, adjusting the settings to capture the perfect sound. While I set up, Daisy takes a seat on my bed, crossing her legs in front of her. It's an innocent act in and of itself, but considering the circumstances, it sets my mind on fire.

"You ready?" I ask. And when Daisy nods her confirmation, I clear my throat, settling into character. "Hi, baby," I say into the microphone, affecting a sultry tone. "I was hoping you'd answer my call."

Daisy watches me intently, her eyes roaming over my body as I deliver the lines.

"Did you miss me?" I ask, speaking to my imaginary audience. My voice is raspy, a faux deepness carrying through. But Daisy easily plays along, nodding as if the question was meant just for her.

"Are you in bed, baby? Wishing I was there with you?"

Daisy swallows thickly and pulls her plump bottom lip between her teeth, nibbling on it until it's nice and swollen. She silently moves back on my bed, adjusting the pillows into their perfect place. And once she's propped up, she removes her scrunchie, golden hair fanning out behind her.

"I miss you, too," I say roughly, nostrils flaring as Daisy shimmies out of her pants, dropping them onto the floor by my nightstand. "What are you wearing right now?"

Daisy removes her shirt next, followed by her lace bra, and I have to bite down on my fist to keep from groaning out loud. Her perfect tits spill out, those pert, rosy nipples staring straight at me. My eyes travel up and down her flawless form, my chest throbbing.

"Ah, you took your clothes off for me?" I ask, finally releasing a needy whimper. "Fuck, I really need to see you."

Daisy slides out of her panties and kicks them aside, still watching me hungrily. I can barely get the words out now, gasping into the microphone.

"Touch yourself for me," I say, praying to God that Daisy will continue following my lead. "Tell me how fucking wet you are. Tell me how your pussy's dripping for me."

She swipes a finger through her folds, her gaze burning into mine. She parts her lip, sucking the finger into her mouth, and my cock strains to break free. "You're so wet, aren't you? Been soaking your panties all day, just thinking about me."

A low growl rumbles in my chest as Daisy nods, plunging a finger into her tight heat. God, do I want that to be me—my fingers, my tongue, my cock, any part of me she'll allow.

"I'm sorry I couldn't be there with you," I say, choosing my words carefully. "But I can help you feel better. Just do what I say, okay?"

Daisy swipes a finger over her clit, spreading her legs for me, the wetness seeping onto her inner thighs. I groan into the microphone, blowing out a strained breath, and say, "Take two fingers and push them inside of you. Pretend they belong to me."

Daisy follows my command, her head falling back onto the pillows. I can tell she wants to make a sound, struggling through the pleasure, but she's doing her best to stay quiet for me.

"Does that feel good?" I ask, the question rumbling out. "Mm, I bet it does. But not as good as my cock. Only I know how to fill you up, how to please your needy little cunt."

And I guess that fucking does it because Daisy cries out, a desperate moan finally ripping from her throat.

*Well, fuck me.*

I'm gonna have to cut that out later, but I can't even bring myself to care. I want her way too badly now. I cut the recording, barely able to contain myself, and crawl onto the bed beside her.

I waste no time as I devour her neck, too overwhelmed to worry about anything else.

"El, wait," she whimpers as my fingers take over, sliding inside of her with ease. "You need to finish."

"Oh, I'm gonna finish. Don't you worry about that."

She laughs. "I mean the audio."

"There are more important things to take care of, don't you think?"

"Mm," she moans as my fingers hit the front of her walls, curling against her favorite spot. "Like what?"

"Like taking care of my girlfriend and her needy little cunt." I punctuate each word with another curl of my fingers, pulling and pushing against her until she explodes around me, her body trembling with pleasure. "You like those words, don't you?"

"Yes."

"Good girl."

She makes quick work of removing my pants, and then I'm finally inside of her, my cock sliding through her wetness. We moan together, our movements synchronizing. She's tight around me, squeezing me in just the right ways as I thrust into her.

"That's my pretty girl," I murmur. "You stayed so fucking quiet for me, but now I need to hear you."

She moans, high-pitched and uncontrolled, murmuring

something about how much she likes my cock, how perfect the fit is. It's mostly gibberish, but it still makes me feel good to know she's enjoying herself.

She tilts her hips, grinding against me with every stroke, and suddenly, I'm right there with her. I yell out her name as I come, plunging deep inside of her. And once we're done, we just lie there for a while, tangled in the sheets, spent and breathless.

Finally, she breaks the silence, her hand tracing patterns along my chest. "So, did I fully ruin your take, then?"

"Not at all." I laugh softly, planting a sweet kiss on her forehead. "I'm sure I can fix it up in editing. They just needed a quick clip."

"Good," she whispers, breath heavy. "Because I don't think I could sit through that again."

"Ah, but you did so good."

"Really?" she asks incredulously. "I don't think they want to hear my desperate, heavy breathing in the background."

I press a kiss to her lips, the smile clear in my voice. "Well, I, for one, love it when you're desperate."

"Of course you do," she says with a playful huff, nestling closer.

I tighten my grip around her, and we lie together like that—limbs twisted, hands intertwined—until my heart steadies beneath her, until we can't manage to stay awake another second longer.

# Chapter Thirty-Six

DAISY

THE MORNING SUN, the sizzle of bacon, and the sweet scent of fresh strawberry muffins—it's the perfect recipe for a lazy Sunday morning.

Gracie meticulously cracks one of the muffins open, steam pouring out. She spreads butter on one side, and then smashes the two halves back together, her nose scrunched in concentration.

Next to her, Elio flips the bacon with the expertise of a seasoned chef. I can't help but smile at the picture of domestic bliss we make, the three of us gathered around the kitchen cooking breakfast.

"So," Gracie begins, taking her first bite. "I'm assuming you two aren't heading back to Cape Casserat for Christmas?"

"Hell fucking no, we aren't," Elio mutters, not bothering to turn from his post.

"*No, Gracie, we're not*," I correct in a mocking voice, lobbing an oven mitt at my boyfriend's back. "But thank you for asking."

"Right, what she said." Elio snorts a laugh. "What are your plans, Gracie?"

"I'm heading back to Virginia," she says, seemingly lost in the thought of home. "Mom's already pestering me about the tree. We always go out to the woods to cut our own."

"That's a sweet tradition." I stir my tea, pushing around the frothy cream on top before taking a sip. "I'm just staying here on campus, I think."

Elio looks up from the bacon he's plating, brow raised in question. "Same here," he says with a grin. "But I'll spend Christmas with the family. You should come with me, Daisy."

The invitation surprises me. The thought of meeting his parents is both exciting and nerve-racking all at once. I know he just met mine, but I can already tell that the experience will pale in comparison.

"Really?" I ask, hesitant. "Are you sure your parents won't mind? I know you already have a full house."

"Trust me, my mom will be over the fucking moon to have you there. I'll call her right now, and you'll see."

The look in his eyes is so sincere, so full of warmth, that it's hard not to believe him. I feel Gracie's gaze on me, and when I glance over, she's smirking. "Look at you two," she teases. "Already planning all your holidays together."

Elio simply rolls his eyes, pulling out his phone from the pocket of his sweats. He quickly dials a number, waiting for the person on the other end to pick up. As he talks, his face lights up.

"Ma," he says in an affectionate tone. "I was wondering how you felt about me bringing my girlfriend home for Christmas?"

I strain my ears to catch bits of the conversation, curious about her response. Elio's smile widens, confirming my suspicion that his mother is indeed thrilled. But then, something shifts. His brow furrows, his posture changes, and his relaxed demeanor fades.

"No, wait, what are you talking about?" Elio's voice rises, laced with confusion and frustration. "*High school friend*? Ma, I haven't spoken to him in ages. You told him where I *live*?"

Gracie and I exchange a concerned look, both of us trying to piece together the puzzle. Without another word, he abruptly stands and heads for the door, leaving us alone in the apartment.

Silence settles between Gracie and me, our earlier happy mood completely shattered. "What do you think that was about?" Gracie asks, her voice a hushed whisper.

"Not a clue," I say, mind racing with possibilities.

It feels like an eternity before the front door finally opens, revealing a visibly shaken Elio. He looks worn, as if he's aged years in mere minutes. He runs a hand through his tousled hair, taking a deep, shaky breath.

"Hey," he starts, eyes meeting mine, filled with an emotion I can't quite place. "I'm sorry, I think I need to go."

I stand from the table, slowly moving toward him. "What, why? What happened?"

He swallows thickly, looking away for a second. "It's, uh, nothing too serious. I think. Just something I need to take care of."

I nod slowly, allowing him to take me into his arms, our faces close together. He plants a tender kiss against my temple, a goodbye for the time being. Then he steps away, strides determinedly out of the kitchen, and just like that, he's gone.

Gracie and I look at each other, but neither of us can say a word. It's obvious he's downplaying the severity of whatever just happened.

Dread bubbles up inside of me, fueled by uncertainty. *Why didn't he want to confide in me*? I know he has a habit of shouldering burdens alone, but I thought we'd moved beyond that. That we'd become partners, facing our challenges side by side.

But if he needs his space, I suppose I should grant it. I just have to trust that he'll come to me when the moment's right, when he's ready for it.

Aside from a quick "talk later" on Sunday night, Elio leaves the rest of my messages on Read for two long days. My attempts to reach him are fruitless, and I'm left to fret over the mystery of that phone call on my own. Finally, late Wednesday night, he finally picks up.

"Hey, Daze," he says, his voice somber.

"Where have you been? I've been worried. I didn't know if it was your heart, or your family, or—"

"I know, and I'm sorry for that." He sighs heavily into the receiver. "I just needed to take some time to think things through. Figure out if dredging up the past was a good idea or not."

"What do you mean?"

He lets out a long breath. "There are things about my life that we haven't talked about yet. Things I haven't told you. And it's not because I'm hiding them or because I'm too ashamed, but it's just heavy stuff. Stuff I'd rather not think about."

"Are you . . . ready to talk about it now?"

He pauses, and I wait with bated breath. "Yeah, I think so. Can you come over?"

"I'll be there in fifteen."

The drive to Elio's apartment feels both agonizingly long and far too short. I pull up outside and take a moment, steeling myself for whatever he's about to share.

Once I'm out of the car, I climb the stairs two at a time, knocking softly on his door. It swings open almost immediately, revealing Elio in the dim light, his face a canvas of raw emotions.

"Hey," he murmurs, stepping aside to let me in.

I enter the cozy apartment, and as per usual, Bentley rushes over, his tail wagging in delight. He circles my legs, nuzzling my hand for a quick scratch before retreating to his spot on the couch.

Elio closes the door behind us, the latch clicking into place with an air of finality. We stand in silence for a beat, neither of us quite sure how to begin. Eventually, he motions for me to sit down, taking his spot beside me.

Bentley curls up next to us, his soft whines and gentle nudges begging for attention.

Wordlessly, Elio brushes a stray strand of hair behind my ear. My skin tingles at his touch. Despite the knot of anxiety in my stomach, I lean into it, letting the warmth of his fingers soothe me.

He notices the tension in my posture, his face scrunching up in a pained expression. "I shouldn't have ghosted you like that," he admits, his voice raspy. "It was a fucked-up thing to do."

"Yeah," I whisper, gaze dropping to my hands. "It was. And I'm not too happy with you about it."

He swallows hard. "It's a bad habit," he confesses. "I used to do it all the time to Kaia when things got heavy. It pissed her off, and rightfully so. But I can't be like that with you . . . I won't allow myself to."

"Do you promise?"

"Yeah, I'll do better, baby."

I let out a sigh, some of the tension releasing from my shoulders. "Okay, then I'll let it slide just this once."

He offers me a small, thankful smile. "Thanks for coming over, even though I've been acting like a piece of shit."

"I'm here for you," I say simply, placing a gentle hand on his cheek.

He leans into my touch, his eyes closing momentarily. "I know."

"You gonna tell me what's going on now?" I prod gently. "These secrets from your past that you've been keeping?"

"It's . . . complicated, but I feel like you should know," he says, taking a shuddering breath. "When I was younger, I was involved with a group of people who . . . who weren't exactly upstanding citizens.

"We did some things that weren't legal, and I don't just mean smoking some pot here and there. It was a wild time, and eventually, things escalated too far. I was caught up in the middle of it all, and I didn't know how to get out."

My stomach drops, and I pull his hand into my lap. "What are you saying? You didn't—"

"I didn't hurt anyone, if that's what you're asking," he says quickly, his grip tightening. "But things got bad. Kaia and I grew apart, and I clung to this one guy, Jackson. He was . . . a little more than a friend, at least on my end.

"He and his older brother introduced me to coke, and I was hooked almost immediately. Turns out he was just using me to skim money off my parents, off my siblings, to feed our little habit."

"Wow, that's awful," I say, my hand still tightly clutching his. "And a lot for a teenager to handle on his own."

"I know," he says, hanging his head. "I'm far from perfect, and I've made countless mistakes in my life. There were times when I thought I was invincible, but I realized eventually that I was just a kid who was in over his head."

"And somehow, you found your way through?"

"Eventually, yeah. After a few wake-up calls from my

family, I got clean, and I distanced myself from that life. But it's always been looming over me, and the guilt has never really gone away." He hesitates, pain flashing in his eyes. "When I was on the phone with my mom the other day, she brought up Jacks, and everything came flooding back."

"When was the last time you saw him?"

"When I was eighteen." His expression darkens. "He overdosed and ended up in the hospital. I was there with him, but he checked out AMA and didn't bother to say goodbye. Just fucking vanished on me."

"I'm so sorry."

He laughs, but there's not an ounce of joy in the sound. "It was for the best, anyway."

"So why is your mom bringing him up now?"

"I guess he came to our fucking house. Talked with her, asked her about me. She told him I was up at school. Gave him my phone number and everything."

A tight knot twists in my stomach. "Oh no."

"Yeah, I don't think she realized the damage she was doing, but I can't really blame her. She doesn't know all the context, all the history there is between us."

"Was this just last week when we were gone?"

"No, apparently, it was weeks ago now. I've barely spoken to my mom since the two of us got together, and I guess she *forgot to mention* it somehow."

"And he hasn't shown up again since? Hasn't reached out to you at all?"

"Not that I'm aware of."

I play with our linked hands, absorbing the weight of his revelations. I was partially aware of his sobriety but hadn't grasped its full scope until now. His willingness to share his past struggles means a lot to me, and it doesn't change my feelings for him in the slightest.

If anything, it proves just how strong he's always been.

"So, what are you going to do now?" I ask. "Are you going to respond if he reaches out?"

"I don't know," he says, averting his gaze. "For now, I'm trying to ignore it. Part of me wants to tell him to fuck off and never come back. But another part of me wonders if maybe there's a reason he tracked me down after all these years."

"Well, whatever you decide, I support it."

"Thank you," he says. "And thank you for just listening, for not judging."

"Of course. Thank you for telling me." I give him a small smile, trying to lighten the mood. "Though, it's kinda weird, all these shady people vying for your phone number lately. Does your mom know Sapphire, too?"

He snorts, shaking his head in disbelief. "Oh God, don't even joke about that. Knowing Ma, she'd probably give that woman my social security number and my childhood teddy bear if she asked."

"You're telling me you have a *teddy bear* that I don't know about?"

"Figure of speech, Daze."

"Mm, I don't believe you," I tease, tapping him on the nose. "I'm searching your bedroom over Christmas."

"Go right ahead," he says with a smirk. "I've got nothing else to hide."

# Chapter Thirty-Seven

ELIO

An unsettled feeling sits heavy in my gut as we make our way to my family's house, Bentley sprawled out in the back seat.

Finals had been brutal on us. Nights spent hunched over textbooks, brain fried and herbal tea gone cold, the stress stretching Daisy and me thin. But we rallied around each other.

We both buried the unpleasant memories of Thanksgiving and the gnawing dread of Jacks' visit. But now, with the pressure of exams gone, the suppressed emotions and memories are surging back.

As we near my family's neighborhood, Daisy's voice cuts through my spiraling thoughts. "I hope you're not nervous about me meeting your family," she says. "I've already met two of your siblings, and it can't be any worse than my own."

I try to match her levity, but it's a half-hearted attempt at best. "Yeah, I know."

When we finally arrive, the living room is filled with warmth and laughter. My younger sisters and niece are seated around the coffee table with Harper, stringing popcorn garlands for the tree. Bentley immediately weaves between their legs, stealing stray pieces that fall to the floor.

After a quick introduction, Daisy rushes to join them, and I stand off to the side with my brother. There's a weight in my chest that feels both warm and suffocating. The familiar laughter, the cozy closeness of my family, should feel welcoming. Instead, a cold, nagging feeling has sunk deep inside.

"I'm really glad you found Daisy," Luca says. "Bentley brought light back into your life, sure, but I've never seen you this happy before."

We share a rare, genuine smile, the truth behind his words shaking me out of my haze. But before I can formulate a proper response, an insistent knock on the front door steals our attention.

Luca sighs, grumbling under his breath, "How many more people can fit in this goddamn house?"

June hops up from her spot at the table, racing to answer it, but her mother is quick to intercept. "Junebug, you can't open the door for strangers," she says, gently nudging her back. "Finish the popcorn, okay? We'll let your Uncle El answer."

I shoot her a half-assed glare as I move toward the door, chuckling when she sticks her tongue out in return. But when I finally pull it open, a ghost from my past is standing on the other side, eyes bloodshot and posture unsteady.

My stomach churns, haunted by the familiar sight. Of course, Jacks has chosen the perfect time to show up here again, and he's clearly high as a fucking kite.

"What the hell are you doing here?" I hiss, glancing back at the joyful scene behind me. With a heavy sigh, I shut the door until it clicks, the noise sealing off the warmth from the chilly outside.

"I just needed to see you," he says, scrubbing a hand across the side of his face. He looks strung out, worn down, worse for wear than I've ever seen him before.

"Are you fucking serious?" I snap, trying to keep my voice even. "Why now? After all this time?"

"Like I had any other choice," he spits back, eyes narrowing. "I've been trying to get ahold of you for weeks, and you've been ignoring me."

"I don't know what you're talking about," I say, clenching my fists to prevent them from shaking, gaze flitting to the door behind me. "But you need to leave. Now."

His laughter is bitter. "Fine, go ahead. Go back inside with your perfect fucking family. Abandon me just like you did when we were kids."

"Abandon *you*?" I echo, incredulous. I take a step closer, the heat of my anger bubbling up inside. "You're fucking delusional, man. I was there! I was there on what became one of the darkest days of my life, and you were the one who left. You disappeared, changed your number, and I spiraled. I never abandoned you. I cared about you when you sure as shit didn't deserve it."

He shoves me, pushing me back against the door. I stumble but regain my footing.

"I didn't want to leave you like that," he snarls, voice strained. "But I had to. Cops were outside, ready to nab me. So, I ran. But a month later? They caught up with me, anyway. Possession with intent to sell. And where were you? Rehab? College? While I rotted away alone?"

I shake my head, disbelief muddling my thoughts. "How can you possibly blame me for that? You cut ties first, long before I pulled myself out of that hell."

He smirks, a twisted curve of his lips. "So, what's your problem? I helped you, didn't I? Now you've got money, a family who cares about you, a little girlfriend."

"You don't know anything about my life. Not anymore."

He leans in, his voice a whisper of menace. "But I do, E.

I've seen all your fucking videos. You and whoever you can get, making money hand over fist."

A cold, creeping realization snakes its way through my veins. The pieces fall into place feel like shards of glass embedding themselves into my brain. My vision narrows, focusing only on him.

*Those comments. That familiarity.*

"It's you, isn't it?" I ask, choking back the dread, the feelings of violation. "You're Sapphire?"

"Yeah, it's me." His chuckle is dark, twisted. "And I've got so much dirt on you that you wouldn't believe. You need to let me in on this. Split the fucking profits, or I'll show everyone in there exactly what kind of man you are."

I square my shoulders. "I'm not giving you anything."

He juts his chin out defiantly. "You *owe* me."

"Owe you?" I ask, tugging at my hair in disbelief. "Yeah, maybe you're right. Because if you weren't such a waste of space, if you didn't wake me up all those years ago, I wouldn't have the life I do now. And it's a damn good one."

His eyes gleam. "You think your girlfriend would be happy knowing about your side gig? How you played into my hands, *over and over*?"

"You're sick." I shake my head, trying to clear the fog of memories. "This isn't just about blackmail. It's about some twisted obsession, some infatuation you have with me, just like in high school. You spent money to watch me fuck myself on camera, and you think I'm the one who has something to be ashamed of? You're so far gone that you can't even admit it to yourself."

His face contorts in a mask of rage. "This has always been about the money for me. You're just easy prey, and that's not my fault."

"You're wrong." I grit my teeth. "I'm not that same kid anymore, the one who let you take advantage of him time and again."

"Really? Because when I got out of jail, I came looking for you, and you were easy as shit to find. Your little game as Everett? You opened up to me without a second thought, let me in so damn easily."

"What do you want for that, Jacks? A medal?"

His response is a hiss. "Shut up! Shut the fuck up, or you'll see just how fast I can ruin you."

I straighten up, refusing to be cowed. "It doesn't matter. You have nothing on me. Everett? AfterDark? My past with you? Everyone already fucking knows. My girlfriend knows, and like the goddamn angel she is, she supports me. It's just a fucking job, man, and I'm not hiding it."

The door behind me swings open. Luca steps out, his face a mask of cool rage. "Step away from my house and my family, Jackson. I know where you've been, and trust me, blackmail, extortion? That violates your parole."

His defiance finally wavers, the threats sobering him up. "I'm not scared of you."

"You should be." Luca stands tall, his voice colder than I've ever heard, and it chills me down to the bones. "You get one warning, Jacks. This is it. I have the money, the resources, to make sure you disappear for good."

"Fuck you," Jacks shouts, eyes red and wild. "Fuck your whole family. I don't need you. I never did."

Jacks turns, and before he can get away, Luca's hand snakes out, gripping the back of his collar like a vise. He pulls him back forcefully, the rage in his eyes undisguised. "E, you have any last parting words for your old friend here?"

I step forward, my face inches from Jacks', my voice low

and dangerous. "If you come near my family again, my brother will send you back to jail, no question about that. As for me, I'll knock your fucking teeth to the back of your throat first. Got it?"

Jacks' bluster finally dissipates, and he looks genuinely terrified. He scrambles off the porch, tripping over his own feet in his haste to get away from us.

Once he's gone, I smooth a hand over my chest, working to steady my heart.

Luca moves closer, eyes soft. "You okay?"

I shake my head, releasing a strained breath. "You knew? You knew he's been in jail all this time, and you didn't mention it?"

"I just wanted you to have a chance at healing without any distractions. I kept tabs on him for a few years after you got clean. I know that he caused you a lot of pain, and I wanted to protect you."

I nod, the anger evaporating into a strange mix of liberation and exhaustion.

I remember the nights lost to darkness, the mornings I wished I wouldn't wake up. The drugs, the pain, the betrayal. All those nights with Jacks, trying to drown out reality. But with the help of my family, and despite it all, I found my way back to the light.

I meet my brother's gaze, his exasperation forcing a half-smile to my face. He's worried that I'll be angry with him for hiding the truth, that I'll resort to the harsh words I used to sling at him. But all I can feel is an overwhelming sense of peace.

A sort of closure I didn't realize I needed.

"Well, thank you," I finally tell him.

"*Thank you*? That's it?"

I push off the door, standing a bit taller. "Yeah. For everything. Not just now but for always looking out for me. You saved my life back then, and I don't think I'll ever stop feeling indebted."

"You don't owe me a goddamn thing, E. You're family, and I can't imagine losing you."

We've never been the type to express emotions openly, always keeping our feelings behind fortified walls. We deal in actions, not words, at least when it comes to each other. It's just how we've always been. So, hearing such raw sentiment from him is . . . unexpected, to say the least.

"Same goes," I say, because it's about the only thing I can manage at the moment.

"But if you're okay now, we should get back inside," he says, briefly checking the time. "I don't know about Daisy, but Harper's gonna storm out here if we don't go in soon."

"Yeah," I say, "my girl's the exact same."

He gives me a knowing smile. "Figured she might be."

THE DEEP BLUE walls of my childhood bedroom, a shade I'd chosen in the midst of teenage angst, had long ago been my safety net. A place where I could isolate myself and deal with my issues alone. But now, I don't have to.

Now, I'm lying on my bed, tucked in between Daisy's legs, her warmth encasing me, her fingers gently playing with my hair. It feels right to have her here, to help me unwind after the roller coaster this day has turned out to be.

I gave her a quick explanation of what happened earlier, and we'd done our best to salvage the rest of the evening—

laughing with my sisters, crafting makeshift decorations, and ordering an obscene amount of takeout.

Moments of genuine joy sprinkled through the hours. But it's late now, and Daisy and I are finally alone. We have to continue the conversation one way or another.

"How are you feeling?" she asks in a soft murmur.

"I'm really fucking tired, Daze," I say, leaning into her touch. "Sorry it's always like this."

She strokes my hair, loosely curling an end around her finger. "Like what?"

"Like . . . I'm constantly the broken one, and you're perfect."

"I'm not perfect, El. You know that."

"Yeah, sorry, but I fail to see your faults."

"Stop that." She gently tugs at my roots, a pointless reprimand. "Do you want to talk more about what happened now or rest first?"

I dip my chin, blow out a heated breath. "Let's just do it now."

"Go ahead, then. I'm here."

"You know, at first, I felt . . . violated. Disgusted that he would do something like that, and that I was so oblivious to it this whole time." I pause, trying to find the right words to explain my feelings now. "But I took a step back, and I've realized now there's just . . . calm."

I tilt my head up to meet her gaze, an understanding smile tugging at her lips. She brushes a few strands of hair back from my face. "Like . . . you've found clarity?"

"Yeah, like the fog's been lifted after all these years."

She studies me, trying to see if I'm merely putting up a brave front, and the genuine care in her eyes nearly undoes me.

"I'm so proud of you," she finally whispers. "You've been really strong through this whole thing."

"Thank you." Pulling away slightly, I reach over to my nightstand and grab my phone, bringing up an email. "And look at this."

I hand it over, and she squints at the screen, reading carefully. "Oh, my God! It's a formal contract offer!"

"Yeah, the notification came in while we were having dinner. I wanted to wait until we were alone to tell you." My thumb swipes over the email. "It's not just an offer, though—it's a way out. Saying goodbye to Jacks, to Sapphire . . . it also means saying goodbye to AfterDark for good. Echo's my fresh start."

"I'm so glad." Her fingers leave my hair, softly tracing my jawline. "You deserve it."

*Goddammit.*

She may think otherwise, but I swear, she's as close to perfect as it gets—the sweetest and most compassionate person I've ever met. And the fact that she knows about every dark corner of my past and still wants to be with me?

It's like finally being told that I'm good enough and actually believing it.

"You're a light in my life, Daze," I tell her. "I think I might have forgotten how to be happy until I met you."

"God, I'm so, *so* glad we met and beyond sorry for everything you've had to go through."

"I'm not," I say, choking back the gravel in my throat. "Meeting Jacks? Falling down that path with him? Maybe it was the start of a ripple effect, a cascade of events that all led me back to you. Right where I belong."

"Is this your way of saying that you love me?"

"No, but this is—" I push up from the space I'm lying in, press one hand to her chest, and cup the other around her cheek. "I love you, Daisy. And I don't think I'll ever stop."

"I love you, too," she says, eyes shining. "And I *know* I won't stop."

# Chapter Thirty-Eight

DAISY

It's New Year's Eve, and we're cocooned in the lazy warmth of Elio's bed.

He's lying on his side facing me, and I have my head nuzzled against his chest, one thigh slotted between both of his, curling into him like a large, sleepy cat.

My fingers trace over a collection of small symbols on his forearm, like constellations on the canvas of his skin. I tap each one lightly, tracing over them as he stirs beneath me.

"Do these mean something?" I ask, my voice still husky from sleep. "Or are they just drawings you like?"

He chuckles softly, opening one eye to peek up at me. "Curious Daisy," he murmurs with a grin.

I poke him lightly. "Always."

"Well, Mia and Vivia, my two younger sisters, they're the stars. The Gemini twins." His fingers guide mine over the tiny cluster, their lines delicate but distinct.

"The clover?" I ask, hovering my finger above it.

"That's Luca. Georgie coined him 'Lucky' a long time ago. She uses the same symbol on her communication device."

I hum in response, moved by his dedication to his family. As I lightly trace the horseshoe, I arch a curious brow. "And this?"

"Taylor," he says softly. "She and Luca, they've always

stood together. The eldest siblings. Our lucky charms. Our protectors."

A small crescent, beautifully detailed, catches my eyes next. "Little Georgie's the moon," he says. "Our wild child."

I smirk, pressing my finger on the last symbol—a radiant sun. "And you? Let me guess . . . the sunshine of the family?"

He chuckles, pulling me closer. "No, the name Elio comes from a word that means sun. Kind of ironic, considering."

"I don't think that's ironic," I murmur, placing a soft kiss on his chest, right above his heart. "They say the sun represents hope and renewal. And that's what you did for me. Renewed my faith in love, in family."

He gulps low in his throat. "Hmm, suppose you might be onto something there."

"I usually am." My thumb runs along the collection of tattoos before reality nudges. I glance at the clock on his nightstand. "You've still got that appointment in an hour, you know."

He groans, throwing an arm over his eyes. "Dr. Foster can wait. I want to keep lying in bed with you. Listen to you say more sappy things for the rest of the morning."

"El!" I swat him on the arm. "You know, Dr. Foster is the reason you're healthy right now. The reason we're even together in the first place."

"So, you wouldn't have weaseled your way into my life if it weren't for the doctor's orders?"

"Mm, no, I don't weasel," I say defiantly. "Actually, now that I think about it, we should probably get him a present."

He shifts into a seated position, and I topple off him. "Daze, you can't give doctors gifts. I've heard that it's illegal or something."

"It's not *illegal*. They just say not to because of fair service provision."

"Yeah, exactly what I said."

"I meant, like, a gift of strawberry muffins or something. Not a Rolex watch." I roll my eyes at him, and he grins, reaching over to pull me back into his lap. "Ridiculous boy."

We stay like that for a few moments, wrapped up together, until Elio finally groans and rouses himself from bed. I follow behind, playing with Bentley on the floor as he rifles through his clothing.

"You know," I begin, shifting on my knees to face him. "I'm excited to finally meet Kaia."

I can already picture the four of us together, watching the sky light up over Amber Isle as we ring in the New Year.

"Yeah, she won't shut up about it, either," he says, giving me a sideways smile. "Too bad Beck's tagging along with her."

I tilt my head. "What's your deal with him, anyway?"

"Nothing really," he admits. "We used to rag on him before they started dating. He's just rich, perfect, a silver-spoon sort of guy. It's more so just a running joke at this point. I think he's actually a decent person."

I lift a brow in mock surprise. "*Decent*? Wow, high praise."

"He's good, I mean," he amends, and I can't help but notice the slight grimace, as if admitting such a thing costs him dearly. "Good for Kaia, anyway. I'm glad they're together now, actually. He's helped her work through a lot this past year."

I nod, a teasing smile playing on my lips. "Much better. Let's keep that attitude when we see them tonight."

"Yeah, yeah," he says with a mock groan. "For you? Always on my best behavior."

"That's what I like to hear."

. . .

THE EVENING CHILL of the beach sweeps over us, tendrils of cold wind gently tugging at the hem of my sweater. But the bonfire fights back, radiating heat against the backdrop of the vast, dark ocean.

Kaia and I are seated on logs around the fire, roasting marshmallows. There's an art to it, one that I've never quite mastered. They always end up too charred or too raw.

Kaia, on the other hand, roasts hers to a golden-brown perfection.

As we carefully sandwich them between graham crackers and chocolate, I glance over to where our boyfriends are tossing a football. Their movements are fluid, easy, and their laughter reaches us over the sound of crackling wood and the distant murmur of the sea.

"I have to admit," Kaia starts, watching them with an amused glint in her eyes, "I never imagined those two doing something so . . . what's the word? *Bro-y*?"

I chuckle, biting into my too-charred s'more. "Right? I didn't even know Elio knew how to throw a football, to be honest."

She laughs, her silver bangles jingling, the lighthouse charm glinting in the firelight. "Yeah, he definitely doesn't take after his brother in that department." She sighs, her gaze drifting toward the gentle waves. "But it's really good to see him like this. So carefree."

"Yeah, he's come a long way this semester," I agree, licking melted chocolate from my fingers. I lean back, the grit of the sand pushing through the blanket beneath me.

"He has a lot of good things going for him now," she says. "You being one of the most important."

I give her a warm smile and cast a fleeting look in Elio's

direction. He meets my gaze, a lopsided grin in place, and all I can feel is butterflies.

"Fresh starts," I muse, turning back to Kaia. "That's what the new year's all about, isn't it?"

She nods, her dark curls catching the firelight. "Second chances, new beginnings. Maybe some resolutions we'll pretend to keep for a week or two."

I nudge her with my elbow. "Cynic."

She laughs. "Yeah, I get that a lot."

The night darkens around us, and as the hour draws nearer, we layer up with blankets, huddling close to the fire. Holden leans against his girlfriend, and I catch a glimpse of their sweet intimacy.

"Baby, you make every year better than the last," he whispers, and I can't help but smile at the tenderness in his words.

And then, someone produces a speaker from somewhere, and the air is filled with a countdown broadcast. It's the final ten minutes of the year.

Elio sits beside me, his warmth seeping through our multiple layers. "Ready to say goodbye?" he murmurs, his breath warm against the shell of my ear.

I nestle closer. "More than ready."

The horizon lights up, fireworks waiting in the wings. As the seconds tick by, the anticipation grows, everyone on the beachfront holding their collective breath.

Kaia and Holden, wrapped in each other's arms, are a mirror image of Elio and me. There's a unity, a togetherness in this moment that wraps around me like the calm after an eastern hurricane.

"Ten," the man's voice carries through the speaker, and we all join in.

"Nine."

"Eight."

Each second feels drawn out, suspended in time. My grip on Elio's hand tightens.

"Three, two, *one*."

The world erupts in color. Fireworks shoot up, painting the sky. The noise is ear-splitting, yet all I can focus on is the man by my side. He turns to me, his face illuminated by the brilliant flashes of light.

Without a word, he leans in, and our lips meet—a tender kiss that holds the promise of everything to come. A new year has finally begun.

THE END

# Epilogue

ELIO

I STAND ON THE SAND, my feet sinking slightly with every restless shift, Gracie on one side of me, Max and LJ on the other. My eyes are trained on the water, searching for one figure in particular.

And there she is—my Daisy girl, poised and ready, her silhouette cutting through the glimmering ocean surface. She's biding her time, waiting patiently for the perfect wave.

My stomach's in knots, a curious mix of pride and nerves. It's funny how even after witnessing her in action countless times, the sight never ceases to amaze me. The way she moves, the ease with which she rides the waves—it's art in motion.

"She's looking good out there," Gracie says, her voice tinged with a touch of awe.

Max nods, arm wrapped tightly around his girl. "Definitely got a chance at placing in this heat. Our little Junior Champ is making a comeback."

And that's when it happens.

A massive wave builds behind Daisy. With a burst of speed, she's riding it, weaving and twisting with a grace that enraptures the crowd. The performance is unparalleled, and when she finally rides back to the shore, there's a sense of victory on her face.

She knows she's done it.

Minutes later, when the results are announced, it's

confirmed that Daisy placed first in her heat. She was right to wait. My chest swells with pride, and I can't wait to wrap her up in my arms, to tell her how fucking phenomenal she was.

As she approaches, her face glowing and suit dripping, I pull her close, the coolness of her skin seeping into mine.

"You were incredible," I whisper into her hair. "Can I take a picture with your trophy later?"

She laughs, pulling back and flashing that infectious smile. "No, you can't."

"Ah, come on, I've never won anything before."

"You beat me at Surf Pro just last week."

"That's true. And they can never take that away from me."

She gives me a humorless snort. "No, babe, that one's all yours."

Her friends join in with their praises, each one taking their turn to hug her and snap a few pictures. But soon enough, we sneak away on our own.

First, we head to the house to pick up Bentley and shower, and then we drive to the Seashell together. Daisy steps inside to order some iced tea and muffins, and Bentley and I secure our favorite outdoor spot.

As we all settle in, Daisy kicks off her sandals and sticks her feet up on my lap. She takes a long sip from her drink, already talking about what competitions she plans on entering next year.

There are endless amounts of details when it comes to different locales, different waves, different heat systems. Daisy can recite them all.

As for me? I'm still lost when it comes to surfing, but I listen intently because I love hearing the passion in her voice.

When she tells me about her favorite surfer turning up at a

local comp, she runs her fingers over my forearm, searching for my hand. I wince, a jolt of pain running through me.

"Careful, it's still a bit tender," I say.

She frowns. "What happened?"

Rolling up my sleeve, I reveal the fresh ink—a delicate daisy resting right beside the sun, nestled amongst the symbols of my family. The lines are crisp and refined. But the tattoo is still on its way to healing, and it's a little sore to the touch.

"It's new," I say, taking in the way her face lights up. "Got it while you were prepping for the comp this week."

"You got a tattoo for me?"

"Nah, pretty sure it's for me."

"Elio."

"I wanted you to be here, too. You're part of my family now. My home. Bentley already has his spot." I point to the little broken dog bone near my wrist. "It's only right that you're properly represented."

Her eyes are misty, and she leans in to place a soft kiss on my cheek. "Thank you," she says, practically beaming with excitement. "I love it."

I grin at her. "Anything for you."

"When we get home," she murmurs, looking up at me with those big brown eyes, "I can show you just how much I love it."

I raise a brow, a smirk curling my lips. "Oh? You have a specific reward in mind?"

She tilts her head, nibbling on her lower lip. "Maybe . . ." she says, and I'm all for it. But keeping her on her toes is one of my favorite pastimes.

"Sorry, pretty girl," I say, drawing out the words, savoring the faux disappointment on her face. "I have some . . . work I need to get done."

"Work?" Her lips pucker into a pout. But before I can tease

her any further, her eyes spark with recognition. "Oh! You mean *work* that I can help with?"

She gives me an over-the-top wink, and I chuckle. "I mean, if you insist."

"Mm, what's the scene you have in mind?"

"I'm thinking"—I lean in, voice dropping to a husky whisper—"desperate man gets on his knees for a pretty blonde in a yellow sundress."

Her eyes widen, cheeks flushing. "Oh, I think that's my favorite one." She stands up from the table, holding her hand out for me to take. "We should probably get home, then."

"You didn't finish your muffin."

"Well, I'd let Bentley have it, but I don't think it'd agree with his stomach." She wraps it up in a napkin, stuffing it in her purse without a second thought. "There, all done."

"Eager girl."

"Can you blame me?"

"Not at all."

It doesn't take long for us to make it back to my apartment. Once we're inside, Daisy leads me back to the bedroom, sundress flowing behind her. We leave Bentley alone with a few treats and a rerun of *Dancing with the Birds*.

Now that we're alone, Daisy places her hands on my chest, leaning in close. "Desperate man?"

I groan, wrapping an arm around her waist and pulling her flush against me. "You know I'll do anything for you."

"Prove it."

I grab her hips, pressing her against the wall as I lower my mouth to hers. She still tastes like iced tea and strawberries, her lips soft and pliant under mine. She moans into the kiss, her hands sliding up to grip my hair.

I break away, trailing sloppy kisses down her throat.

"Anything, huh?" she asks, breaths coming in short gasps.

"Anything," I murmur against her skin.

I tug her dress up, revealing the lacy edge of her panties. She shivers, and my cock grows impossibly hard at the sight.

"Mind if I take these off?" I ask, tucking my fingers under the thin elastic waistband.

She shakes her head, eyes overcome with desire. I carefully slide the panties down her legs, my hands smoothing over the soft skin of her thighs. I'm kneeling in front of her now, exactly where I belong.

She bends down, grabs the hem of my shirt, and pulls it over my head, her nails tracing the contours of my abdomen. And once she's had her fill, she wraps her hands around my neck to pull me closer.

Heat radiates from between her legs. I press featherlight kisses up the inside of one thigh as she sinks against my lips. And when she whispers, "I'm so close," I feel like I'm the king of the world.

With her fingers tangled in my hair, another soft moan slips out. I flick my tongue over her clit, moving slowly, alternating between hard suckles and fluttery licks. She's coming already, and I'm desperate to feel her clench around my tongue. But before I can plunge fully inside her, she instructs me to get off my knees.

I look up at her, my face a picture of confusion.

"It's my turn," she whispers. "I want to . . . give you that reward I promised."

"Trust me," I manage to say, my voice husky, "fucking you with my tongue *is* a reward."

She smirks, drawing me up to my feet. "No," she says, her hands deftly working at the buckle of my belt. "I want you in my mouth this time."

A low growl rumbles in my throat, her boldness sending all the blood rushing to my cock. Her hand is already there, skillfully unzipping my pants and pulling them down.

We exchange a long, heated look, the silence filled only with the sound of our heavy breathing. I gasp again when her fingers reach under the waistband, finally freeing me.

She gracefully drops to her knees, hands on my thighs for balance, and takes me fully into her mouth. It's overwhelming, the way her pouty lips suction so perfectly around me. So wet, so warm and tight, that I'm forced to lean against the wall for support.

Her tongue traces circles around the tip when she pulls back, and I whimper, giving her a fresh burst of energy. She's nothing if not enthusiastic about sucking me off. In fact, she works me over like she's fucking starving for it.

The pleasure builds quickly, and I have to fight to keep from coming too soon. But with a final, teasing lick, I let myself shatter. She sucks me dry, and then she stands, a wicked glint in her eye.

"There," she says, pressing a soft kiss to my lips. "That's how much I love it."

I pull her close, still breathless and reeling. "Remind me to get a new tattoo more often."

"Mm, but you're starting to run out of space."

"Just on my arms," I say, holding them out as if to prove myself. "I've got a whole canvas here to work with."

"Well, I've always thought you'd look really sexy with a thigh tattoo."

"Oh, you've *always* thought that, huh? Like on the first day we met when you accosted me on the beach?"

"That's a funny way of saying you fell in love with me at first sight."

She smiles up at me, that big, goofy smile I'd recognize anywhere. "Alright, yeah, I'll let you have this one," I relent. "Even then, I knew you'd be mine."

And when we kiss again, I lose myself in her the way I always do.

My Daisy. My wildflower. My home.

# Acknowledgments

To all of my readers, thank you for sticking around for Elio's story. He's my sunshine hiding behind a storm cloud. And it's been so satisfying to finally give him the happy ending he deserves.

To my husband and my baby girl, thank you for supporting me as I live my dream.

To my lovely group of forever friends, Becka, Erin, and Hannah, thank you for the constant mockery.

To my alpha reader, Megan, for being the first person to read this story. And for being Elio's reluctant cheerleader from the beginning.

To Ellie for inspiring my Daisy girl.

To my editor, Sandra, for sticking with me through publishing my fourth book.

To all the book bloggers and content creators for your constant support and dedication.

# About the Author

Ki Stephens is a romance enthusiast who finds comfort in the happily-ever-after . . . with just a little bit of angst along the way. She has a special interest in works that include neurodivergent characters like herself. When she's not daydreaming about books, Ki enjoys working with kids, creating art in her backyard studio, and spending loads of time with her baby girl, her husband, and their three pets.

She released her debut novel, Spring Tide—Book 1 in the Coastal University Series, in December of 2022.

**www.kistephens.com**